The Kid Who Couldn't Leave The Yard

Here you go Bucko!
Hope you enjoy.
Lee Stanlick

LEE STANLICK

ISBN-13: 978-1547060306

Contents

1

Skunk's Misery

Daniel Samuel Trapper, January 24, 1904

He hadn't planned to hunt. Couldn't say why he'd brought along his rifle. There was nothing he'd hoped to shoot. The old .22 was more like company, something familiar to hold in the crook of his arm as he hiked the Misery.

The Misery. Skunk's Misery...

He opened his eye. The sky had cleared. It was no longer snowing. Trailing clouds from the blizzard that had blown in off Lake Erie now curtained the stars to the east. Above him the snow heavy branches of the black oak twisted across the face of a full winter moon. One final gasp from the passing squall and the upper limbs swayed, sending a skiff of fine powder swirling downwards, illuminating his surroundings like the interior of a festive globe.

What a strange name to have given such a beautiful forest. It certainly didn't do justice...

He wished now that he'd taken the time to discover the reason behind it - an opportunity missed, although he knew at one time it had to have described something. But a skunk could certainly find a less desirable place to live. Maybe it had to do with the legend of the outlaw, who was said to have used these thick woods to escape justice. Perhaps to his pursuers the name came to reflect the same feeling of futility he now felt, as they'd repeatedly looked toward home empty handed.

He closed his eye and yawned. The bite of bitter cold had left him some time ago. He knew that wasn't good. Now he was just tired. Bone tired and incredibly heavy, as though his body were attempting to press itself back into the soil of creation. He smiled inside, wishing for the strength to move and hold it upon his lips - for he knew his mother would receive some comfort suspecting her youngest son's final thoughts had been of a religious bent.

How had his rifle fired?

Bits and pieces of memory flashed, causing lightning bolts of pain to flare behind his brow.

Gloves, barrel against a tree, rough bark, body bent, laces caught, blinding light.

He willed his left forearm to bend, to lift his frozen hand from snow to his damaged eye. Fat fingers bumped against a thick sliver of bark sticking straight out of the socket. It grated against bone. Stuck solid. There was no pain. Slowly, he lowered his fingers to the cold jellied mess of flesh, bone and blood pasted to the side of his face and screamed. A bright wave rose, crashed, and sucked him under.

Warm hands were cupping his head. A lovely upside down face swam inside watery vision. A young girl's voice, tender yet strong. "Do not move. You are safe."

Rhythmic words he didn't understand comforted him as a blanket was spread across his chest. More poetry, hands lifted, brushed away snow and ice then rolled the blanket beneath. Wrapped secure. A horse blew, another nickered and shied at the smell of his blood. He forced his eye open wide.

A group of native men were standing by his side. Five. Their faces shadowed by a moon now hung shoulder height. The young girl placed her warm palm upon his forehead.

"My name is Rose. I heard your cry. These men led me to you." She pointed to a tall man impossibly dressed in moccasins, breech-cloth, tan leggings and breastplate. In his hand was a long-feathered lance. "Sunkwa will lift and carry you to his horse. I will sit behind and hold you. We will take you to the home of your people. Do not be afraid." She leaned forward. "Do you understand my words?"

He pushed his thick tongue through dry lips. A piece of snow was held to his mouth. It tasted sweet. "Understand," he nodded. His eye watered and pressed shut as he winced against sudden pain. He felt her rise.

Strong hands cradled and lifted him as though he were a child. Others steadied him as he was set upon a horse. The mount tensed and quivered between his legs. Rose settled behind him. She wrapped him in her arms. He leaned heavily against her, his head lolled against his chest. Sunkwa mounted, clicked, and they turned towards home.

He woke in the back of the family wagon, which stood hitched near the back door. Rose, the young native girl, was bent over him, tucking the coarse blanket about his shoulders. Light snow began to fall, shimmering about her in a crystal halo backlit by crisp moonlight and the sparkle from a shower of shooting stars. Her eyes were large and dark, her cheekbones high. Around her neck was a choker of bright coloured beads and metal. A similar wristband, wrapped about the sleeve of her left arm, flashed in his vision.

"What is your name?" she whispered.

"Daniel." The weakness in his voice surprised him.

She placed her hand upon his cheek, smiled and was gone.

As the horses pounded across the yard and down the lane a single sharp cry pierced the frigid silence. The back door of the farmhouse flung open. Light spilled to reveal his body. His smile had moved and settled upon his lips. He remained unconscious for almost two weeks.

He never discovered who the natives were or where they came from.

2

A Laying of Hands

Jackson Samuel Trapper, July 6th, 1967

Imagine the year is 1967, you're eight years old, addicted to a powerful drug and you're suffering through withdrawal…

Now imagine you don't know you're going through withdrawal, from the medication you've been given for the past three years to sedate hyperactivity. How could you? It's 1967, you're eight years old and you've never heard those words before. Plus, your parents and doctors have decided it's impossible to explain your situation to you. A decision at least partially influenced by how terrible they all feel for allowing this to happen in the first place.

So, there you are. Every day, you're experiencing uncontrollable periods of shaking. You're having muscle spasms. Convulsions. You're vomiting. You feel anxious and exhausted because you can't sleep - and you're constantly filled with terror that any moment one of the frequent hallucinations that causes you to foul yourself like an infant, is going to drag you kicking and screaming into some new hell your mind has created. And oh yeah, one final thing. Not only do you not understand why any of this is happening - the disease in your legs, the reason why your small-town physician over-prescribed the wrong sedative in the first place, is still ravaging your bones.

But all is not lost...

My name is Jack Trapper and I was still a very lucky boy. My parents remained determined to do everything they could to help me get better. So, they arranged for the pastor and elders of our church to come to our home and perform a 'laying of hands,' - anointing my head with oil and praying for the Lord Jesus to enter my body and rid me of disease.

Is it any wonder, that of the few memories the drug has allowed me to retain from my previous years, this moment I recall in vivid detail?

It's July 6th. Seven pm. A warm summer evening. I'm sitting on a wooden stool in our living room. The windows are open, the curtains pulled back and the occasional breeze wanders in along with the soft rush of a vehicle on the highway. This date and time has been stamped upon my memory as my older brother's birthday was the day before, and a moment ago, my mother told me to turn off Bonanza on our new color television. Hey, Little Joe never let me down. He visited every Thursday at the same time.

Earlier my father rearranged the furniture, pushing the couch, chairs, and end tables against the walls. I'm left on center stage, excited, scared, with no clue as to what's about to happen, but comforted somewhat by the knowledge that everyone present loves me.

Pastor Reg and the elders enter from the kitchen. He clears his throat and everyone takes position. This must have been part of the murmuring I overheard while they were gathered in the other room. Rehearsal. Brother Samuel, a tall man with ears like jug handles and a nose that could chop wood, stands behind me and to my left, alongside Brother Fred, the always smiling leader of our Sunday school. On my right, brothers Bill and Brother Bob take similar station. They're identical twins that for fashion's sake, really should have been placed as bookends on each end of our little row.

The pastor steps forward until the middle button of his shirt is inches from my nose. There are nine of them - four white ones above, four white ones below. Don't ask me why I counted, it seemed important at the time. I look around him for my parents who step forward holding hands.

My best friend Pauly and my older brother Danny appear out of thin air. This has been happening a lot to me lately - objects or people or situations all at once different with no explanation. I've become used to it. It seems a part of life. They're sitting on the floor beside me, looking up wide-eyed and full of excitement. Pauly squeezes my left hand. From his goofy grin, it's obvious he can't wait for things to get underway, while Danny's paying more attention to the order of events, as though he expects to be called upon at some point to take over. Danny's always been this way and I love him for it. Nothing bad ever happens to me when he's near. He's like my walking, talking, personal security blanket.

My eyes return to the pastor's shirt and climb above his collar. I'm not surprised that he's dressed the same as each Sunday. He smiles and what little fear I'm fighting flees as he places his hand upon the side of my face and kisses the top of my head.

"It's going to be okay, Sweetpea," he winks. "I promise. Everything's going to be fine."

Pastor Reg is a pale man, short and thin as a matchstick with flames of red hair licking the wind. He's my father's cousin. They grew up next door to each other on neighboring farms in the thirties. He's also the person who nicknamed me Sweetpea and I'd love him just for that. My reasoning is simple - a proper nickname is a gift, it makes you feel special and he'd given me a good one. So good that everyone starts to use it from the moment they first hear it. At school one day, as we were waiting for the bus, Dickie Moore called him Ronald McDonald. I whacked Dickie across the legs with one of my crutches. After he pushed me to the ground, Danny knocked him flat, explaining the situation perfectly to everyone gathered around.

"I am the only person who pushes or teases my brother."

I was so proud of Danny that day. He's the best older brother a kid ever had. When I was six and developed the disease in my legs, he stayed inside each day with me at school, playing games during recess and lunch. And when I was eight and began suffering through withdrawal, he went to bed early each evening with me, telling me jokes and stories until I fell asleep. Doing his best to calm and help me forget my fears because he knew, I didn't want to close my eyes. Sleep scared the hell out of me. And later, when I'd hallucinate and begin to scream in the dark, he'd take turns with Mom and Dad holding me until I came back. From God knows where - confused, exhausted, shaken, and in tears. Then he'd do it all over again, after Mom tucked us back in for another go around. But here I go, getting ahead of myself and spoiling my story...

Pastor Reg's voice cut through the silence.

"Almighty God, please cleanse the thoughts of our minds and hearts by the inspiration of your Holy Spirit, that we may perfectly love you and worthily magnify your name through Christ our Lord."

"Amen."

I used to always wonder how everyone but me seemed to know the right time to say that.

He continued:

"Lord Jesus, you give of yourself to save us, heal us and to give us strength."

Brother Samuel's hand reached out and I saw the flash from the bottom of a silver bowl. The pastor held it above my head. A spot of warmth began to spread through my hair, down around my ears and the back of my neck. It reminded me of the broken egg joke Danny played on me in the kitchen. For a moment, I wondered if there were an egg in the bowl now, and if this was why I was feeling the same way. The pastor's empty hand lowered and with a finger he drew the letter 'T' upon my forehead. His palm remained flat and the elders placed theirs upon me also.

"In the name of the Father and of the Son and of the Holy Spirit, grace, mercy and peace from God our Father and the Lord Jesus Christ."

"Amen."

I hadn't planned on saying that, but somehow hit the mark.

"Blessed are you sovereign God, gentle and merciful, creator of heaven and earth. Your word brings forth light out of darkness and daily your spirit renews the face of the Earth."

"Amen."

Dang. I was on a roll. Two for two. I glanced at Danny to see if he'd noticed. His eyes were closed so tight that his eyelashes were resting on top of his bunched-up cheeks.

"Your anointed Son brought healing to those in weakness and distress. By the power of your spirit, we ask your blessing upon this child, Jackson Samuel Trapper. May he be made whole once again in body, mind, and spirit, restored in your image, renewed in your love, and serve once again as your son in your kingdom."

"Amen."

Now, I'm not going to lie and tell you that something magnificent happened to mislead or give you false faith, but a tingling feeling swept through my body from my head to the tips of my toes. I felt if anyone were to lift a finger, I might float to the ceiling, separate from my afflicted limbs. I don't know if I was feeling the power of the Lord or the power of suggestion, but without any doubt, I was feeling the power of love. I didn't want it to end.

"Through your anointed Son, Jesus Christ our Lord, to whom with you and the Holy Spirit we lift our voices of thanks and praise. Blessed by God, our strength, our salvation, now and forever, amen."

"Amen."

And just like that it was over. Only it wasn't quite because Pauly began to cry and Danny whispered, "Dad. I saw Jesus. He was smiling at us."

3

Phenobarbital

Have you ever had a conversation with a person who begins to stutter? Everything will be going fine until they come up against a word they have difficulty getting out. And you don't mean to, you try not to, but you find yourself leaning forward, your lips formed around the word you think they're trying to say.

Well, this is the best way I can think of to explain to you, how it feels to me, to be what is called hyperactive.

I've been leaning forward onto the tips of my toes every minute of my life. Not only is it impossible for me not to, it's also impossible for me to do anything without trying to move it along at a quicker pace.

Unfortunately though, all most people see are the outer manifestations of hyperactivity. They witness a child's boundless energy, the inability to sit still, the constant foot and finger tapping and believe this to be the condition.

"Cut back on his sugar," they wisely advise, when they couldn't be further from the truth.

No, what everyone incorrectly pays attention to are the end results, when hyperactivity begins inside the mind.

It took my mom some time to figure it out but she finally got it. She'd tell people, "Jack's a minute ahead of us. While we're trying to decide how to answer him, he's already working on his next question."

Now I don't know how true that is because I've never been inside your mind, but I'm trying to allow you a peek inside mine.

My problem has always been time, not energy, or perhaps more precisely, time and ideas. I have so many wonderful ideas constantly popping into my head, butting in front of others vying for attention, I couldn't possibly have time for them all, but my body still tries. And it doesn't slow when I sleep. In fact, sleeping has always been the most difficult time for me - for it's when my body gives itself over to rest that my mind has complete and unchecked reign. This is just who I am and likely always will be.

So, hopefully you can now understand when I was six, and diagnosed with Legg Perthes, a degenerative bone disease in my hips, how this was the worse thing that could have happened.

One day I was running non-stop, burning through the ideas I was being fed from my mind and the next I was benched and at its mercy. Suddenly my ideas could no longer be acted upon because of the damage being inflicted upon my joints. This created a problem as often I found myself on my feet without planning. So, something had to be done to slow me down or there was a possibility I might lose the full use of my legs. That something was a sedative.

Phenobarbital was the barbiturate, Dr. Wilkes, our family physician, prescribed, and I've never blamed him for what happened next. How could I? I know the decision was made in what were thought to be my best interests, plus this was fifty years ago and he's dead.

Unfortunately, phenobarbital is not a well-tolerated drug and in the sixties few physicians were aware of its dangers and possible side effects in children. These include addiction and paradoxical hyperactivity. In other words, the drug he prescribed to slow me down, sped me up. And as my tolerance grew, he kept increasing the dosage, which caused my addiction.

Believe it or not, I remember the first dose I was given. Partially because it was a suppository and I never dreamed that hole could be used for anything but out, and also because shortly afterward I felt as though I'd been dressed in my snow suit and winter boots. For the next couple of weeks, the drug had its desired effect, but soon I became acclimatized and then all it did was keep me warm and ready to roll.

So, he increased the dosage until I was on the, 'medieval knight in full armour plan.' The added weight became undeniable. Moving required thought and effort. A trapdoor in the rear would have been appreciated. You see, I could drop my armor but I couldn't pull it back up. But soon once again I overcame the drug's desired effect and was capable of mounting and dismounting the porcelain steed.

So, he increased the milligrams again and again, until I reached the 'Houdini, suspended in midair, wrapped in chains and wearing a straightjacket dosage'. However, I didn't have an escape artist's key secreted on my body or the strength to overcome my bonds. My mind felt encased in jello, still producing the same volume of thoughts but the signals were being lost long before they could influence my limbs. Finally, he had me moving at the pace of a diseased boy. But I shouldn't have been. I wasn't sedated. I wasn't healthy. I wasn't me. I was stoned.

Two years later, in the summer of 1967, I began to suffer hallucinations. Specialists diagnosed me with a brain tumour. Fortunately, my mother found another who instantly recognized addiction. But he cut me off and shouldn't have. Phenobarbital has a long life and I'd been taking it for almost three years. I should have been weaned from the drug as is the recognized procedure today. Instead, over the next number of months, I experienced every withdrawal symptom imaginable. I also came to recognize the onset of an hallucination by a putrid wet clay smell that would invade my entire being. This smell continues to haunt me today, fifty years later, when I still experience the occasional flashback. And I'm also not too embarrassed to admit that I'm still frightened to close my eyes, and hallucinate whenever I have the slightest fever.

So, let me tell you what is known about phenobarbital today.

Doctor's rarely prescribe it to children anymore. It affects their cognitive ability, resulting in poor concentration, reduced memory, lower IQ, and poor school performance.

The drug works by reducing brain function. Electroencephalograms indicate a massive decrease in brainwave activity - one of the main reasons why, in it's purest form, phenobarbital is still used in the cocktail of drugs administered during lethal injection.

In 1939, a five-month-old boy born with disabilities was given a lethal dose after being examined by Adolf Hitler's personal physician. Shortly afterwards, psychiatrists summoned to the Chancellery began a Nazi-endorsed policy of eugenics, using phenobarbital to kill children born with disease or deformities. In 1940, at a clinic in Ansbach, approximately 50 disabled children were injected and killed. A plaque remains there today in their memory.

Also in 1940, Winthrop Chemical was producing antibacterial tablets in the same room as phenobarbital. The tablets became contaminated with the barbiturate and hundreds of people died. The Food and Drug Administration investigated, which led to the introduction of Good Manufacturing Practice.

'Hypnosis' is also recognized as one of the primary side effects of the drug - a state of consciousness in which a person loses the power of voluntary action and is responsive to suggestion or direction.

Withdrawal symptoms include vomiting, dizziness, forgetfulness, uncontrollable shaking, muscle spasms, weight loss, convulsions, nightmares, and hallucinations.

And one final thing…

Because phenobarbital was first synthesized in 1904 and is one of the world's first synthetic drugs, it predates the Food and Drug Administration's approval process. It has never been formally cleared for human use.

4

Onion Head

August 17th, 1967

Thursdays are called x-ray day at our house. Every Thursday at 2:00 pm., for the past two years, I've been getting pictures of my legs at Sydenham District hospital in Wallaceburg, followed by an examination by Dr. Wilkes.

Today, as my mother and I sat in his waiting room, we were both in foul moods. Twice during the night I'd hallucinated and now I was tired, my hands were shaking and I kept getting painful muscle spasms in my right thigh. Mom was also exhausted and sat staring out the window at the muddy Sydenham River flowing by. Neither of us willing to make eye contact, as we'd been snapping at each other all morning.

I wasn't blind. I knew that as much as she loved me, she'd begun to tire more easily of me. I didn't blame her. These last few years, she had been forced to give me all of her attention.

When I went outside she kept an eye on me because I wasn't supposed to be on my feet for long. I wasn't allowed to leave her sight. In the neighborhood, I became known as the kid who couldn't leave the yard.

Inside, there were only three TV channels to watch, so we played board games or cards to pass the time. I never napped. I was too scared to close my eyes. So, I read a lot from the children's encyclopedias she'd purchased for me, or Danny and I would play. But Danny was three years older and had friends of his own, so often Pauly came over from next door, but his parents had to keep an eye on him too. That left Saturdays as the only day Mom caught a break. Every Saturday me and Danny went with Dad to visit friends or to help in his shop. But the biggest load always fell on my mom, and I felt terrible for how I'd spoken to her in the car.

Nurse Gibbons opened the office door.

"Colleen, Dr. Wilkes will see you now." She winked at me. "Hey Sweetpea, I think you've grown since the last time I saw you."

She said this every week and when I got home, I'd stand against the pencil mark to see if she was right. I was such a carp. I hadn't grown an inch in the past year, but still fell for it every time.

Dr. Wilkes was standing when we entered. This was odd. Normally he half rose, said hello then sat before we did. His usual cigarette wasn't even burning away in his ashtray.

"Colleen, it's so good to see you," he said. "And Jack, before I examine you, I need you to stand as tall as you can for me." He knelt and pressed my heels to the floor. "Keep your toes pointed ahead and try to put some weight on your heels. I know it hurts, just one more second." He frowned as I shifted to my better leg. "Okay, let's get you up onto the table."

As usual, he began with my reflexes, tapping my knees and the bottoms of my feet. Today I didn't find it funny though when my big toe twitched because my leg muscles tightened at the same time.

"When did your leg begin doing that?" he asked.

"I don't know," I mumbled.

"This morning," Mom said. "While they were taking his x-rays. The nurses massaged it but it didn't help." She sighed. "We had a bad night last night, Wilf. Jack was up twice with his hallucinations. He also soiled himself and was throwing up."

Dr. Wilkes shone a flashlight into my eyes. I blinked and rubbed them.

"Should the light bother him that much?"

Dr. Wilkes turned to face her. I could barely hear him.

"Jack's response to bright light is to be expected, as are his muscle spasms, although I'd hoped by now he'd have progressed through this stage." He crossed his arms and sighed. "Colleen, I wish I could tell you that soon he'll be symptom free but I can't. I've consulted specialists and the consensus is that he should be through the most difficult phase. But we're dealing with a child who's been on medication for an extended period. Personally, I believe we're looking at another couple of months, then things *should* return to normal."

Mom's expression never changed. Dr. Wilkes picked me up and set me in the chair next to her.

"Now, I do have some good news that I know is going to brighten your day. Give me one moment."

He scribbled on some papers, picked up the x-rays then sat on the corner of his desk. On his face was the same smug smile that Little Joe always gets when he's pulled one over on Hoss.

"Colleen, your son's legs are continuing to show tremendous improvement."

Mom began to cry as only the mother of a sick child can. I'd become used to this sound during our many visits to the hospital over the years - mother's crying quietly as they held their sick child, or waited for news from the operating room. I began to cry too because she was my mom and I was Sweetpea.

"Blood flow to the balls of both femurs has returned. Re-ossification of dead bone material is almost complete.

Deformity and collapse of both joints has stabilized." He leaned forward and shook his head. "Colleen, I'm not one to believe in miracles, but I have no explanation for such a dramatic improvement."

He picked up the pictures again. I wanted to tell him that nothing had changed. They were the same ones he'd looked at a moment ago.

"I do believe we need to temper our enthusiasm though," he said. "Jack has a long road ahead of him, and this last month has been the first improvement we've seen. There's still a slight possibility of relapse."

"No. There'll be no relapse," Mom said.

She pulled me from my chair and hugged me. The side of my face became wet from both our tears. I stood stiff as a board because boys don't like to be squeezed by their mothers in front of anybody.

"It's okay, Mom," I said, as I shifted to my better leg. "They don't hurt much, anymore."

Dr. Wilkes smiled. "Jack, most of the pain you're feeling is from the inside muscles of your legs. They haven't had much of a chance to stretch and grow. I think it's time you told your father to pick up that bicycle you've been wanting. Riding will help with your mobility."

I quit paying attention. In my mind, I was on the gold Mustang with the banana seat and high rise handlebars we'd looked at in Canadian Tire. It was a three-speed, with the shifter on the crossbar. Although I hadn't ridden in three years, I didn't expect any problems. It's always amazed me how much easier it is to do most things inside your head. I was pulling a wheelie when I heard something that I didn't like.

"The only thing I can suggest, Colleen, is a brush cut. If he can't grab his hair, he can't pull it."

What? A brush cut? I wasn't getting a brush cut. I didn't even know I'd been pulling my hair.

"We thought of that," Mom said. "Last night, Gus could barely pull his hands free."

"I'm not getting a brush cut, Mom."

"Honey, it's still summertime. It will grow back in no time."

Honey? How come whenever she called me that it was followed by something I didn't like?

"I don't care. I promise, I won't pull it no more." School was starting in a couple of weeks. Didn't she understand that kids with short hair either had cooties or weren't allowed to listen to The Beatles.

"Jack, it will grow back within a month," Dr. Wilkes said.

"I don't care. I'm not getting one." As far as I was concerned, this conversation was over.

A half hour later we pulled out of the barbershop parking lot and onto the highway to head for home. I was livid. I'd cried, pleaded, even attempted to stamp my feet and nothing had made a difference.

"Onion head! That's what Danny's gonna call me. Onion head, onion head, onion head. It's not fair. Why do I have to get a stupid brush cut and he don't?" I kicked the back of her seat.

Mom twisted behind the wheel. "Jack, I'm not going to tell you again. Either sit still and be quiet or I'm going to pull over and paddle your bare butt on the side of the road. Is that what you want?"

I dropped my chin and crossed my arms, creating a table for my dangling lower lip.

"I asked you a question. Is that what you want?"

I snorted and swung my heels into the bottom of the seat. Did she really expect me to say yes?

"And quit kicking your feet."

I continued just loud enough for her to hear.

"Jack." Her foot lifted from the gas.

I kicked three more times then stopped. Her foot returned to the pedal. Now I felt a little better. If there was one sure thing I'd mastered, it was how to take her to the edge. I glanced into the rear-view mirror. Good, she wasn't watching me. I pulled in my bottom lip and tried to stare a hole through the side window.

The small factory town of Wallaceburg slid slowly in behind us and soon row after row of tall green corn began tugging at my eyes. In the sky above, a line of crows sagged down the telephone wire, their beady eyes and beaks pointed at the cobs.

"Yep," Radio Ray excitedly announced over the radio. "It's another hot, beautiful August afternoon in sunny south-western Ontario."

Or, as the barber had agreed earlier with my mom, "Yes ma'am, brush cut weather, that's for darn sure." At the same time sticking out his hand for his fifty cents. I grit my teeth. Some friend Slugger turned out to be. I promised myself that the next time I had to go in there, I was peeing on his toilet seat and tearing pages from his comic books.

What the heck had happened? Just a few minutes ago, Dr. Wilkes said that my legs were getting better, I could ride a bike and soon I wouldn't be having nightmares. And now here I was heading home with my head shaved like I had cooties. Danny was going to be merciless. His hair was touching his ears. My only hope was going to be Dad and Pauly. Dad to tell Danny to leave me alone and Pauly to make him when he didn't. I knew Pauly was the only kid Danny wouldn't fight.

Pauly Cook has been my best friend since before I was born. At least that's how he likes to tell it. He says the two of us met in a dream he had while I was still in my mom's stomach. He says that after we played, I told him we were going to be best friends. I've never questioned him about this because it sounds neat and makes me feel good. Plus, Mom agrees, Pauly told her that I was going to be a boy and what I would look like. But she also says if Pauly believes he's telling the truth, that's all that matters. Mom doesn't believe he's capable of telling a lie. More than once I've heard her tell someone, *'Pauly's one of God's special children, placed on Earth for a reason.'*

Pauly shares all his dreams with me about things that he says are going to come true. He calls them true dreams.

"True dreams are better than regular ones, Jack. Because you remember everything that happened and someday you know they're going to come true."

I told him I'll never have one then, because the only dream I remember is the one I had last week where I could fly. And I doubt I'm going to grow wings. It seems all I've ever had are nightmares that disappear like smoke the moment I awake. Even the ones I've been having lately in the middle of the day, while I'm still wide awake.

Pauly's favorite dream is the one about the house he says the people of Wallaceburg fix up for him.

"They're going to make the porches have no steps, it's going to have extra wide doors and the cupboards will all be the right height. Plus, they're going to put handles on all the walls so I won't fall down."

That's the part I like best because Pauly's always falling. Mom says it's because of his cerebral palsy. She says that when Pauly was born something bad happened and he couldn't breathe right. That's why some people have a hard time understanding him and why he doesn't walk well. To be honest, I've never thought nothing of it, other than to wonder why he got his disease named after him and I didn't. To me, Pauly's just always been Pauly, the same as I've got bad legs, Grandpa's chin shakes, and Mr. Green stutters.

Pauly's one year older than Danny and four years older than me, but he's more than a foot taller than my brother. Dad says Pauly's the biggest, strongest kid he's ever seen. They're great friends. Pauly calls him Fatboy and Dad carries a hanky to wipe away the snot and blood from Pauly's face after a bad fall. Never any tears though. Pauly doesn't cry when he gets hurt. He just gets back up and keeps going. I think that's the only advantage to being handicapped or sick when you're a kid - after a while it just seems normal, so you carry on.

Our car began to slow as we approached the plaza where Dad had his shop. After each doctor's visit, we always stopped in to tell him how I was doing. Today I planned to ask if I could ride home later with him. I didn't want to face Danny alone. I gripped the armrest and searched the parking lot for his truck. It wasn't there. We wouldn't be stopping. I pictured Danny running alongside the car hollering, "Onion head! Onion head!"

I began counting lane-ways as we came upon the first in a row of cookie cutter war homes built close to the highway. Eleven, twelve, thirteen. Up ahead was the Big Chief Drive-in restaurant and across from it my brother, playing catch in our front yard with a friend.

"I'm not getting out and you can't make me!" I screamed. "I'm staying in the car because you don't like me. You like Danny better." I threw myself across the seat as Mom pulled into the driveway.

She parked in front of the garage, lowered the windows and shut off the engine.

"Maybe you should stay in the car, until your father gets home." Mom turned and looked at me curled on the backseat. "And Jack, your hair looks perfectly fine." She slid out, closed the door and seconds later the back screen.

I lay quiet, trying to stifle the sobs in my chest. How could she be so mean? Moments before she dragged me into Slugger's, she'd been telling Nurse Gibbons how proud of me she was.

After a couple of minutes, I couldn't take it anymore. This wasn't where I'd planned this tantrum to lead. Usually I managed much better. I peeked out the rear window. Danny and his friend were nowhere in sight. I pulled on the door handle, expecting them to leap from their hiding spots. Nothing happened. I slid out, turned and there was Danny, sitting on the ground with his back against the front wheel, his long legs crossed and his hair touching his ears. I started towards the house, my back stiffening in anticipation of his incoming shots.

He stood. "Hey, Jack, wait up. Mom told me you were in there hiding, so I grabbed your glove. I figured if you ever decided to come out, we could play catch."

I began to cry, this time with tears I had no control over. I leaned against the house and his gloved hand landed on my shoulder.

"It's okay, Onion head."

5

The Smell of Wet Clay

Danny and me were playing catch in the backyard when Pauly came over. And the first thing he said was, "Hey, Sweetpea, what happened to your hair?"

"Nothin'," I lied, as Danny began to giggle. "Do you want to play Frisbee?"

Pauly couldn't catch well but he could throw better than me. Plus, I wanted to change the subject. And of course, this was one of those times he wasn't going to let me.

"Sweetpea, what happened to your hair?"

I hated it when Pauly did this. Sometimes he'd ask you a question with such an obvious answer, or one that you didn't know, and he wouldn't let go until you gave him something. But you had to be careful. Pauly wasn't stupid. If you decided to make something up, it better make sense or he'd keep asking until it did. More than once I'd seen him make my dad laugh so hard that tears ran from his eyes when he asked how something worked. Funny thing, almost every time, I learned something too.

"Nothin'," I said again. I picked the Frisbee from the picnic table. "Stand by the garage, I'll throw it to you and you throw it to Danny."

"Sweetpea, what happened to your hair?"

Danny laughed out loud. I wanted to punch him. Pauly had me and he knew it.

"I got a haircut," I mumbled.

"What?"

"I got a haircut."

"Oh. How did you get it cut?"

I smiled. I couldn't help it. "Mom took me to the barbershop and Slugger cut it."

"Hmm," he said. "I like it. It makes you look happy."

Happy? For that split second before Danny fell to the ground, I realized Pauly was right. For the first time today I was smiling, then Danny's laughter filled my ears.

"Do you want to play or not?" I snapped.

"Yes." Pauly smiled. "But first Danny has to stand up or he won't be able to catch."

I began to laugh so hard that I had to sit down. And the entire time Pauly kept looking back and forth at us like we were a couple of nuts.

Finally, we formed a triangle. I tossed Pauly the Frisbee and he whipped it over Danny's head onto our roof. We looked up, waiting for it to roll down, but it must have landed flat.

"I'll climb the antennae," Danny said.

At that moment, Dad pulled into the driveway.

"What are you boys up to?" he called, from his open window. "Howdy, Pauly. How are you today?"

"Hey, Fatboy." Pauly grinned.

Seriously, his entire face split from ear to ear. This was the smile Danny and I called his goofy grin. Pauly's the only person I know who can smile so completely. You can't help but smile right back.

My father chuckled as he rolled up his window and stepped out of the truck. "Jack, I see you got a haircut. It looks good. How did your visit go today at the doctors?"

I talked so fast that the entire sentence come out as one long word.

"Dr.WilkessaidtotellyoutobuymethegoldMustangbicycle."

"He did?" Dad leaned against his truck. "Well, I'd have to hear those words from your mother."

"He did and he said my legs are getting better and pretty soon I won't be having nightmares."

"Danny," Dad said. "Ask your mother to come outside."

"I'm already here," Mom said, through the screen door. "What's going on? I can hear you boys all through the house."

"Jack said Wilf told him that I'm supposed to buy him a new bicycle. Did you hear him say that?"

"He did say it would help, but he didn't say we needed to pick one up today."

"And it's supposed to be gold?" Dad reached into the bed of his truck, lifted out a blue one and set it on its kickstand. "Then I'd better take this one back."

I'll admit I was happy. I might have even smiled, but my heart was set on a gold one. I wanted to look like Evel Knievel when he jumped over the cars on TV.

"Oh, wait a second. What's this?" He pulled out a gold one too.

"Two of them?" I was so excited, I ran over without feeling any pain in my legs.

He laughed. "No, they're not both for you. Danny's been such a big help, your mother and I figured he deserved one also." He gave me a hug. "I know it's a day early but happy birthday."

"Thanks Mom, thanks Dad," we yelled, as we grabbed the one we wanted.

Danny sat on his and I tried to swing my leg over mine. It hurt and the sissy bar was in the way.

"No. You have to get on like your brother did," Dad said. He held the handlebars and leaned the bike towards me. "Here, lift your leg over the middle."

I sat on the front of the seat. My legs were killing me but I didn't want to say anything. I figured he'd tell me to get off. That it was too soon.

"How does that feel? Can your feet touch the ground?"

I showed him that they could. He let go and I held it up by myself.

"It's beautiful," Pauly said.

For a moment, I felt terrible because he couldn't ride.

"I'm only going to ride it when we're not playing, Pauly, or if Mom needs me to go to the store." I didn't know how true that was but sometimes you say the nicest things without thinking.

"Can I ride it now?" I still had that picture in my mind of how easy it was going to be.

"I'll help you," Dad said. "Leave the shifter alone. We'll go to the end of the driveway."

When I tried to get moving the handlebars shook. Danny zoomed by. This wasn't working. Whenever Dad let go, he had to catch me or I'd fall. Finally, we made it to the end of the driveway. He picked up the bike with me still on it and turned it around.

"I can't do it," I whined.

"Of course you can. You haven't ridden in three years and these high handlebars will take some getting used to."

"No. I don't want to try anymore. My legs hurt."

Dad helped me off and I limped back to Pauly and Mom. I was embarrassed.

"You did well," Mom said, as she put her arm around my shoulder.

"Yeah," Pauly agreed. The look of wonder on his face proved that he meant it.

That only made me feel worse. I shook off Mom's arm. "I'm going inside. I don't want to ride a stupid bike."

Mom opened the door. "Well, supper's almost ready, you can try again later." She turned to Pauly. "We're going in now. Your mother's going to be looking for you. You can come back over later and play with Jack."

Pauly turned to go home and we went inside.

At the supper table, all Danny wanted to talk about was how well he could stop using both brakes. I wanted to throw him and his bike into the river. He kept trying to get me interested but I wasn't feeling it. My stomach was upset, my legs hurt and my hands had started to shake again. I asked if I could be excused and sat outside on the picnic table. I ran my fingers through my hair. It felt like a bristle brush.

When Pauly came over, we watched Danny and Dad play catch then we went inside to watch TV.

Mom was putting the supper dishes back into the cupboards. She wiped her hands on a towel.

"You boys coming in for a glass of water?"

"No," I whined. "My stomach feels bad and my legs are sore, and Pauly and me don't wanna play anymore." I smiled inside when I realized I'd rhymed.

She knelt in front of me and put her hands on my shoulders. I could feel her eyes searching through mine.

"Are you feeling okay?"

"Yeah, we just want to watch TV."

She gave me a hug then looked at the clock. "Truth or Consequences will be on shortly. You boys turn on the television, I'll fold my laundry, then we'll watch it together."

Mom knew Bob Barker was our favorite. We loved watching Barker's Box and the contestants do funny things for prizes.

"Dad told me to tell you that him and Danny will be in soon. They're still playing."

Mom stood. "Then I'd better hurry. Turn on the TV and I'll be right in."

Our color television dominated the living room. I picked up the Space Command remote control and sat on the couch. Holding it made me feel powerful, like Captain Kirk about to wipe out an army of Klingons. I zapped the screen and a tiny dot appeared in the center. It grew and replaced the emptiness with news. I fired through the other channels but there was nothing else on. We settled on channel three and were watching Sunny Elliott fry an egg on the roof of a car, when I realized the odor I'd smelled outside had followed me in. I jumped to my feet, intending to run to my mom because I knew what was about to happen, and that's the last thing that I remember.

6

Green Eyes

Colleen took the clothes from the dryer. She couldn't shake the feeling that something was wrong with Jack. It wasn't like him to come in while his father and brother were still outside. Usually he was the last one in. And his eyes, although his pupils looked normal, something wasn't right. Even his whining felt different, as though he were warning her to get ready, all hell's breaking loose. Colleen chastised herself. Lately, it seemed that everything he did, she tried to read too much into. She'd become so frightened for him.

All Colleen wanted was her little Jack back. She never thought she'd wish for it but she'd give anything for him to return to being the little fireball that used to wear her out each day. The child no one had been able to keep up with.

"That damn drug," she whispered. And damn her for allowing his addiction. She closed her eyes and balled her hands into fists.

The sound of breaking glass and Jack's screams poured down the hallway. She dropped the shirt she was holding and ran.

Inside the living room, the table lamp lay shattered on the floor, and standing next to it, in a puddle of urine was Jack, his eyes fixed out the front window.

"Jack, wha...?"

At the sound of her voice, his head jerked around. His eyes and mouth wide holes in his terrified features.

"Help me!" he screamed. "The green eyes are coming. They're trying to get me."

He fell to the floor, pulling at his hair.

Colleen dropped to his side. Warm pee soaked through the knees of her slacks as she tried to restrain him. Unable to catch his arms, she collapsed across him, joining him in tears as they clutched at each other on the warm wet floor.

7

A Giant Light Switch

Returning always felt as though a giant light switch had been thrown. One moment I was nowhere, with no sense of being, and the next I was alive, thrown back into the light and brightness of life scared absolutely witless.

"Sweetpea," Dad said. "Can you hear me?"

I nodded and forced my eyes open wide. I refused to blink. I was so scared that everything and everyone would disappear.

"Do you know where you are?"

I nodded again, trying my hardest not to cry. He slid his hands under my arms and lifted me from Mom. The suck of cold wet pants released then returned against my body. I wasn't embarrassed. I couldn't care less.

"Come here."

He held me in his lap with my head against his chest and his arms wrapped around me. I've never felt so almost safe in my life.

"Your mother has to go into the washroom to clean up. She'll only be a moment, then she'll be right back."

"No," I screamed, my body tensed with fear. "I don't want anyone to go anywhere. I want everyone to stay here with me."

"It's okay," Mom assured me. "Sit with your father and I promise I'll be right back."

Dad squeezed me. "And I'll tell you what. After she returns, we'll fill the tub and you can have a warm bath then watch some TV with a popsicle. How does that sound?"

I gulped for air. A hand landed on my shoulder. It was Danny. He was standing beside me. His eyes were wide and he was trying hard to smile but it wasn't happening.

"Are you okay, Jack? I took Pauly home. Do you need anything? Do you want me to get you a glass of water?"

I shook my head and stared at him. Seeing Danny made me feel one hundred percent better. I stuck out my hand, he took it and sat beside me.

Later, when I was getting out of the tub, Mom said I could watch Rawhide. I asked her if I could wear my cowboy pyjamas, because that's what I wanted to be when I grew up - a cowboy like Rowdy Yates. I had this picture in my mind of me riding herd on a black stallion with white stockings. That's what I was going to call him too. Socks. I couldn't care less if the other cowpokes made fun of me around the campfire. They'd all be jealous, riding their swaybacked nags.

Mom said that I could wear whatever I wanted, then she helped me dry. I put on my cowboy pyjamas, cowboy hat, cowboy boots, gun belt, and six-shooters, then returned to the living room for my popsicle and to watch TV. It's always amazed me how horrible experiences often have such good endings.

8

Fatty and Skinny

Danny rose to his elbow in his bed and looked at Jack. He'd been saving up a special rhyme and decided it was time to use it.

"Fatty and Skinny went to bed, Skinny let a stinker and Fatty was dead."

He watched a smile spread on his little brother's face. Jack always liked it best when one of his Fatty and Skinny rhymes included the word stinker. And the thought of one of them killing Fatty, was icing on the cake.

"Come on, it's your turn," he said, when Jack stopped laughing.

Danny waited for a sign that Jack was thinking one up. Sure enough, a tiny wrinkle appeared between his eyes.

"Fatty and Skinny went to France. Fatty let a stinker and ripped his pants."

Danny laughed with him. There was Jack's favorite word again. He was so relieved to hear him laugh and see him smile. They'd been in bed for almost half an hour and everything he'd tried to take Jack's mind off sleep, had failed miserably. He knew Jack was more terrified than usual to close his eyes and didn't blame him. He too was still frightened when he thought of what had taken place earlier in the living room. Danny had another one saved and ready to go.

"Fatty and Skinny went to the lake. Skinny let a stinker and caused an earthquake."

Jack curled his knees against his chest, wrapped his arms around them and laughed.

Danny was ecstatic. From experience, he knew if he could just keep Jack smiling, the greater the chance he'd sleep through the night.

"Your turn," he said, as Jack's laughter began to slow.

Jack flattened on his back and stared at the ceiling. "Hmm. Fatty and Skinny..."

Danny waited. Jack's eyes turned towards the window. His pupils shone, reflecting a sliver of light from between the curtains.

"Come on, it's your turn. Where'd they go?" Instinctively though, Danny knew it was too late. He studied Jack, wondering if he was remembering what had happened earlier. He sat up. "Jack, what's the matter? What are you thinking about?" His brother's face remained blank. Danny pulled back his covers. "Jack?"

Jack turned to face him, his smile gone, his lower lip threatening to cover his chin.

"Danny, where do I go and why doesn't anyone ever come to help me?"

"What do you mean where do you go?"

Tears filled the corners of Jack's eyes, threatening to spill out. Danny could tell he was trying hard not to let them.

"I don't know where I go and I'm all by myself and no one ever comes to help." He rolled onto his stomach and buried his face in his pillow.

Danny got up and sat next to him. His own tears laid a trail down his cheeks. He sniffed and ran his sleeve across them, remembering Jack's screams and the wild fear in his eyes.

"You don't go anywhere and you're never by yourself. Mom and Pauly stayed with you and Dad and I came to help as fast as we could." He sniffed again. "We'd never leave you. We always hold you until you wake up."

"But I wasn't sleeping," Jack cried. "I was watching TV and then I smelled something bad."

"But you must have fallen asleep. You just don't remember."

Jack lifted his head and looked at him.

"Right?"

Jack didn't answer.

Danny rubbed his back. A thought came to him. "Pauly said that you told him about a dream you had where you could fly. He said you just laid down and flew above the houses and the water and you weren't scared."

Jack shook his head. "I didn't just lay down, Danny. I leaned forward."

"Well why don't you try to have another dream like that? One that doesn't scare you." Danny returned to his bed and pulled his covers up. "Jack, why don't you try to have another flying dream?"

Jack crinkled his nose and looked at him like he was crazy.

"I don't know how to have a flying dream. I don't even know how to go to sleep right."

Danny fought back a smile. Sometimes his little brother could be such a smart aleck. "That doesn't mean you can't try." He thought about it for a moment. "Tonight, when you start to fall asleep, think about floating and flying above the houses. Pretend you're doing it. Pretend you can see down like when Dad took us for the plane ride, and I'll keep talking to you about it the whole time. Okay?"

Jack didn't answer him.

9

Rabbit Ears

I didn't understand why I had to dream. It seemed to me to be the only thing my body did that didn't make sense. I mean, at night I knew I had to breathe or I'd die. I learned that from Rawhide, when Pete, one of Rowdy's friends, was trampled to death in a stampede caused by lightning. My eyes stayed closed because there was nothing to see. Only Grandpa's left one remained open and that was because it was a marble. I even breathed through my nose so bugs couldn't crawl into my mouth and my pillow wouldn't get wet. And I never peed. Because if you pee in your pajamas while you're sleeping, you have to take a bath in the morning and your older brother teases you for days. Okay, maybe I peed a couple of times. But why did I dream? Why did my body do something that frightened the heck out of me and that I could never remember when I awoke?

At school, our grade three teacher, Mrs. Killbreath, told us that everyone sleeps for approximately eight hours each night. So, if we lived to be one hundred years old, we'd sleep and dream for over thirty years. Thirty years? Why would our bodies do something for so long if it didn't matter? There was nothing else I could think of that it did for no reason. Except sometimes make my little fellow stick through the button-holes in my pyjamas. And I figured that was to keep me from lying on my stomach too long.

As Mr. Spock would have said to Dr. McCoy, "Dreaming is illogical."

The only way I could figure it - every night Dad turned off the TV and in the morning, it was still off, until Danny or I turned it back on. But when we did, there was always something already running, like Mighty Mouse or the Three Stooges or a movie or the news. That meant even though it was off, there were still pictures inside it. It just needed to be turned back on for us to see them. Well, it seemed to me that my dreams were like TV, only when I went to sleep, my brain wasn't turning off.

I asked Ms. Killbreath if this could be true. She said yes, you can't turn off your brain, although sometimes she wondered if my classmate Stewie Boothe found a way. He liked to pick his nose and eat it along with the flies he caught during recess.

I asked Danny the following Saturday, as we were watching cartoons, if he thought our dreams were like TV. He took the rabbit ears off the TV, set them on my head and twisted my nose.

"Nope," he answered, as I ran crying into our parent's bedroom.

Dad got up to give Danny heck. Moments later I heard them both laugh. For years, I figured a Roadrunner cartoon must have came on at the same moment that he began to chew Danny out. That Wile E. Coyote, he could always make Dad laugh.

10

Flying

My mind was spiralling around and around. Sticky tentacles of sleep relentlessly reaching up, trying to pull me under, like an octopus wrapping itself around me, drawing me closer to its chewy center.

Tonight, I was fighting harder than usual to stay awake. The smell of wet clay was still in my nose and I was terrified of what I knew for certain was waiting. My eyelids sprung open, my eyesight watery and vague, then slowly they fluttered closed despite my commands. Over and over and over again, and behind it all, Danny's voice cutting through like a mosquito buzzing around my head.

"Fly, Jack. Lean forward and fly. Remember how neat it was to look down on our house and the river and the school. How happy you were. I know you can do it. Fly."

I wanted to jump out of bed, swat him and tell him to buzz off. He didn't understand. I wasn't there yet. I didn't need to be reminded how peaceful it felt, how natural, how free. Because I wasn't there yet and never would be if all I could hear was his dang voice.

"Fly, Jack."

I leaned forward. Fighting to stay awake. Fighting to fall asleep. On my terms.

"Fly, Jack."

Despite my efforts, I found myself listening for his voice, wanting to be drawn along. Finally, I let go and gave myself over.

"Fly."

I leaned forward. My feet left the ground. A light breeze pressed my pajamas against my body. I raised my head, opened my eyes and lifted into the sky. My face stretched. My smile was so wide. I laughed as I rose. I'd escaped. Danny was right. I was doing it. I was flying again.

Brilliant silver stars glued to black paper shone between cotton-ball clouds. It was night yet everything was bathed in the glow of a moonlight with little shadow. I floated above our house and looked down - Danny's bicycle was in the backyard, leaning against the garage - the driver's door window was open in Dad's truck - my ball glove was on the picnic table and our old yellow Frisbee was leaning against the chimney. I circled high above the garage, the cornfield behind our home now far below. Higher and higher I rose into the warm air.

Without thought, I lowered my head and levelled in a line toward our school. There wasn't a soul about. I had the world to myself. Not a car on the highway. Not a light in a window. No dogs barking conversations across fenced yards.

I followed the dotted line past Baldoon School, high above the playground and ball diamond, toward the Snye River. The smell of rotting vegetation in the swampy water smacked me in the face. I savoured it. Welcomed it. Comforted by its familiarity - for I'd fished here often from the bow of our wooden boat and knew the odor was misleading; somehow the stench of decay was much stronger than the smell of life, which inhabited and filled it each day.

I turned my head and my body followed suit as I crossed the narrow channel, heading for Walpole Island and the lighthouse on the other side. I soared above treetops and my friend Joseph's house, slowing as I passed, wishing I could shout out and make him aware of my presence above.

I cut toward the St. Clair River, passing over Horse's Ass, searching below for the wild horses that Danny said still roamed free. Dropping lower I skimmed branches, hoping to catch sight of them when I popped out the west side above the black river. Turning sharply to follow the waterway that bordered the United States, I went into a steep climb, gathering speed as I rolled onto my back. I marvelled at the depth of the sky and the thousands of shooting stars crossing above, their long tails glittering in their wake. I traced the Little Dipper with my eyes then flipped onto my stomach, amazed at how quickly I could move and how high I'd risen. With my eyes closed, I revelled in my freedom, allowing the fresh smell of the mighty river to lead me along its path. Any path.

Levelling off, I flew faster and faster then turned inland, my mind wonderfully clear. No destination in mind. Observing a silent and peaceful world from a lofty height. I felt weightless, like a feather carried upon the crest of a breeze. I felt as if I'd flown forever. Found a place where distance, time and my fears were irrelevant, restrained only by the boundaries of my own pleasant thoughts.

I swooped above small towns and farms, cropland and thick forest. Followed streams and valleys, skimmed hilltops and silos when from the corner of my eye, I detected movement ahead on a grassy plain. Curious, believing it to be a trick of the night, I turned, intrigued at the possibility of an interruption. There was nothing. No trail through the grass, no sound rose to greet me.

Then there they were. Climbing the slope of a hill to my right, a line of five horses, racing towards a town nestled along the bank of a river. I dipped low to pursue them, drawing nearer despite their lengthening strides. My eyes widened at the sight of figures bent over their backs. Riders. Native men moving as one on their hard charging mounts. I maneuvered closer, shocked as the lead rider turned to face me. He whooped and pointed ahead with a long-feathered spear.

That's the moment I heard the first echo of a terrified cry, fading as it travelled into the night. My body tensed as I responded with a burst of lightning speed, leaving the riders behind.

11

The Rescue

A white clapboard church with a cross set high upon its steeple dominated the skyline. It was the centerpiece of the small village, placed midway along the only paved street that cut through its heart. Surrounded by wood frame homes and majestic maples lining the backyards and laneways between. It was centralized, situated carefully, as though a beacon lighting the path toward the townspeople's salvation.

I came in a blur across the river and over low square brick buildings lining the water's edge. Flying in a panic and much too fast, I overshot the cries that were now behind me. I banked and retraced my path, drawing nearer as I searched through the limbs of the trees. Dipping beneath and below branches to scan a side street, I spotted them. Two figures - one imposing and threatening, chasing the smaller down a narrow path. I turned to intercept them, my heart pounding in anticipation and dread.

As I swept near, the smaller figure cried out and began to rise from the ground, beating their arms as wings in an effort to escape. Faint lights sparkled beneath their feet. I could see it was a child, about the same size as me but lifting too little, too late. Whoever it was would remain within arms length of the other figure racing forward. Without thought I shot down, grasped beneath the outstretched arms and lifted back into the sky, but not before a tight grip closed below my right knee, slid down and caught fast around my ankle.

I panicked as our ascent was halted. I kicked furiously to escape and glanced down at teeth visible between lips drawn tight around an angry sneer. My heel crashed against outstretched fingers. A curse, the grip loosened then broke.

We shot up out of control, crashing through the limbs of the closely spaced trees. Small branches, twigs and leaves beat against us before we popped free above the crown. To my left, I spotted the cross on the church and soared to its protection, dropping us onto the flat at the base of the steeple. I was in shock. Shaking, I dropped to my hands and knees, gasping for air. My heart was beating wildly. A roaring sound filled my ears. I closed my eyes, attempting to remain calm and regain strength. My companion stood silently beside me. Without the strength to look up, I crossed my arms as pillows to cushion my head and lay. My new friend sat. Minutes passed, although it seemed an eternity before I drew to my knees.

"Are you my guardian spirit?"

Startled, I looked into the face of the person I'd spirited away. She was beautiful. The prettiest girl I'd ever seen. She waited for my response, her hands clasped together in her lap, her head tilted slightly to the left as though in wonder of my silence. I couldn't find my voice. We stared at each other.

She was taller than I'd taken her to be on the ground. I could see now that she was probably the same age and height as myself, perhaps a few months older at most. She was dressed as a tomboy, with jeans rolled below her knees and a long sleeve, red-checked shirt tucked into the waist. Her left foot was bare. The right in a light blue flip-flop. The kind with the piece that jams between your toes. I hated those things. To me they felt like a sock with a hole in the end that let your big toe poke free.

Her long dark hair was tied in a ponytail that she'd draped over her left shoulder and let lie across her chest. Around her neck was a choker of bright coloured beads and metal. A similar wrist band was wrapped over the sleeve of her left arm. But it was her eyes that caught and held my attention. They were large and dark, accentuated by high cheekbones. They seemed to change shape, depending upon the angle from which they were viewed. And did I say she was beautiful? She reminded me of the Ojibwe dancers I'd watched with Grandpa at the Powwow on Walpole Island. Her skin the same color as the deerskin dresses they wore as they danced in the light of the bonfires.

"Are you my guardian spirit?"

I had no idea what she meant. "I don't know," I replied. "What's that?" I pointed to her wristband, trying to hide my nervous fear.

"It's a birthday gift from my grandmother." She slid it off and offered it to me.

I accepted it gently. I'd never seen anything like it before. "What's it made of?"

"Bone and copper and beads. It's very old."

I turned it in my hand and studied the shape of a magnificent bird created by the beads strung together.

"It's the eagle. It gives me strength and carries my prayers."

I handed it back and watched as she slipped it back on. She looked me in the eye. "Where do you come from? Are you here because you heard my prayers?"

I didn't know what to say about that. I didn't remember hearing any prayers tonight, other than my own. "I was flying above the horses and heard you cry. The leader pointed me towards town, so I came to see if I could help." I stood and peered over the edge of the roof. "They should be here soon."

"Who?"

"The men on the horses."

She rose and stood beside me. There was no one in sight. Not on the road or in the fields beyond.

"How do you fly? Are you the eagle? Can you turn into other animals too?"

I shrugged my shoulders. "I'm just me. I can only fly in a dream." I continued to search for the riders.

"Am I dreaming?"

I turned to look at her. "I don't know." I was confused. She was asking too many questions. I wasn't getting a chance to think or ask any of my own. "Why was that man chasing you?"

"He's our neighbor. He tried to make me do bad things," She moved closer and took hold of my arm. "Are you here to protect me from him?"

I didn't know how to answer that. She seemed to have handled our escape much better than me. Besides, he was so much larger than either of us, I wondered who was designated to protect me.

"He can't hurt you," I assured her. After all we were on the roof of the tallest building in town. I glanced down and said a silent prayer for him to be gone. It seemed we were both being heard as he was nowhere in sight. But it would have been nice to see the riders.

"Where do you come from?"

I pointed in the direction from which I'd flown. Her eyes followed my arm across the distance.

"That's the direction where you live?"

"Yes, but very far away."

Her grip tightened. "Do you have to go soon?"

"I don't think so. I don't know."

I hoped not. I didn't want to. Not yet. I was utterly confused. I'd never felt this way around a girl before. We stood quiet. I could feel her eyes upon me. I glanced at her. She was so pretty, I had to look away as my face began to warm.

"Has that man chased you before?" I stammered.

"Yes," she replied, lowering her head. "When I was in the woods he tried to catch me but I hit him with a stick and ran away."

"Why does he want to catch you?" I didn't understand. I'd never been chased by a grownup before. I couldn't imagine why any would bother.

"He says he wants to play with me, to be my friend. But he scares me and when I ran away, he said if I told anyone, he'd hurt my grandmother."

I thought about that for a second. "Then you have to tell your mom and dad, or someday he might catch you."

"Do you know when I'll see my mother?" she whispered.

"She's probably sleeping. I'm sure you'll see her in the morning."

"She's coming tonight?" Her fingers dug into my arm.

"She isn't home now?" Her excitement confused me. I looked into her face.

She tilted her head the same as before then lowered her eyes and voice. "No. She doesn't live with us. I haven't seen her in a long time. I live with my Grandmother Rose and Uncle Bud."

"Oh." I couldn't imagine your mother not living with you. "Then you have to tell your grandmother."

She let go of my arm and sat with her back against the steeple. Tears shone as they trickled down her cheeks. I sat next to her, rubbing her shoulder like Danny did for me, trying my best to make her feel better. I didn't know what else to do.

"I thought you would know where she is," she said softly, as her shoulders shook.

"I don't," I admitted, wondering why she would think that I did. "But I'm sure you'll see her soon."

She began to cry so I put my arm around her, trying hard to fight back my own tears. We sat together in the stillness. I'd never felt so guilty and weak and yet so fine and strong at the same time. She wiped her face with the sleeve of my pajamas and together we gazed into the sky.

For the first time, I paid attention to the stars that were shooting by. I'd never seen anything like them before. There were so many. Sometimes they fell in a blaze all the way to the ground, other times they shot back into the sky to mix among the thousands of others passing by. It was spectacular. It felt like the heavens were mixing with the Earth. For some reason, it made me think of my grandmother and home.

"I think I have to go soon."

She nodded, keeping her eyes turned away. "Do you think someday you might come back?" Her hand reached up and held mine where it lay upon her shoulder. She turned to face me. She was so lovely. My skin tingled wherever her eyes touched. I couldn't believe how she made me feel. I was so glad that Danny wasn't around to make fun of me.

"I don't know," I said, truthfully. "I'd like to." It would be wonderful to visit but I could certainly never stay. I was still trying to understand how a person could live without their mother. "Where do you live?"

She pointed to a roof visible above the trees, the second to last in a long row. The houses themselves impossible to see through the trees lining the lanes.

"Where does the badman live?" I wanted to make sure that I didn't have to go near that one. In fact, I wasn't too crazy about leaving the safety of the roof.

She pointed next door, to the house at the end of the row, closest to the river, next to a stand of trees. My heart sank. All the bravery I'd felt a moment ago, when my arm had been around her shoulders, vanished. I made a decision right then, that if I'd had to make solely for myself, I know I couldn't have.

"I'll fly over the houses and make sure that he's gone."

I closed my eyes, said a silent prayer then stood, leaned forward and left the roof. The breeze pushed me toward where she'd pointed. I couldn't believe how terrified I felt.

From above the trees it was impossible to look into all the corners where a person might hide. After circling and peering from a safe distance, I dropped beneath the branches and searched the laneways, hovering as I peered down each one. The silence was horrible. This was the worse game of hide and seek that I'd ever played. In the past, all I'd ever had to worry about was someone jumping out and yelling boo. Finally, satisfied that it seemed safe, I breathed a sigh of relief and began to climb back into the sky. That's the moment I saw the riders again.

Four of them were sitting on their horses by the river. The leader was standing, looking up at me with his spear tip resting upon the ground. He smiled and held up his hand. I was amazed. This was the first time I could see how he was dressed. He looked just like the pictures of the warriors I'd seen in encyclopedias and in movies. He was tall and slender and had one feather tied in his hair. He waved again then raised his spear and pointed toward the church. I nodded and flew back. She was waiting for me. I floated next to her and she held out her hands.

"The men and their horses are at the river. The leader pointed with his spear to tell me it's safe. I didn't see the man who was chasing you."

I took her fingers in mine and lifted her from the roof. She was as light as a feather. I wondered if this was how my father felt when he picked me up when I was afraid. We floated over the edge, settled upon the road and walked without saying a word. Her hand warm in mine as she led the way. Only the sound of our footsteps, interrupted by the irregular slap of her lone flip flop, breaking the silence.

She led us down a series of lanes and up a cement path to the front door of a green home. She turned and hugged me. Her face was wet. Mine was burning. Although I didn't want to leave, it seemed time.

"Why do you wear those guns?" she asked, pointing at the pistols on my hips.

I looked down and shut my eyes. I could have died. I'd never noticed that I still had them on. I shrugged my shoulders and remained silent. It always worked for Rowdy Yates.

"Will you always protect me when I need you?"

I lifted my eyes to hers and tried to hold them there. "I can only fly in a dream, but I promise if I hear you cry, I'll try to come."

I leaned forward and left the ground, hovering as I crossed the yard, keeping my eyes upon her as I waited for her to go inside. Although I didn't want to leave, it seemed time. I craned my neck to keep her in sight and glanced to where the riders had been. They were no longer there.

"Wait," she cried. "I don't know your name."

I spun back and floated in front of her. It hit me that I didn't know hers either, and for the life of me, I don't know why I chose to answer as I did, but I did.

"My name is Sweetpea."

She smiled, reached up and held me by my shoulders. "Sweetpea," she said, as she canted her head. "My name is Tika." She pulled me down, kissed my cheek, then slipped inside her door.

My face burst into flames, totally illuminating the night. My heart crackled. I shot into the sky as high as the shooting stars, then rolled onto my stomach and hugged my pillow.

12

The Morning After

The moment I woke, I knew something was different. I didn't even need to open my eyes. Something big had changed. For the first time that I could remember, I didn't feel afraid. My first waking thought wasn't about the disease in my legs or the smell that gave me nightmares. I didn't need to reach down to see if my pajama bottoms were wet, or look to see if Danny was on his side, watching me. Instead, I felt rested and excited. I wondered if this was how everyone felt after sleeping and dreaming all night because that's all I could think of - my dream, and I seemed to remember everything that had happened.

I could still picture Tika's ponytail lying across her shoulder, see her bracelet, feel her kiss on my cheek, the badman's grip, the natives, their horses and the long feathered spear the leader used to point me toward town. I could even recall the feel of warm air flattening my pajamas as I flew.

My hands dropped beneath the sheets, feeling for my guns. The grips fell naturally into my palms. Dang. I really did still have them on. My face warmed. I don't know why. It had only been a dream. I had to get up. I couldn't lie still any longer. My mind was running too fast to be kept cushioned on a pillow.

For some reason, I decided to put on what used to be my favorite outfit. I dug through my drawers and pulled out a white t-shirt and the blue bib overalls I hadn't wore in at least a year. As I clipped the shoulder straps together, a familiar lump formed in the chest pocket. I pulled out my Groucho Marx glasses with fake nose, bushy eyebrows and mustache. Perfect. I put them on, snuck through the house and sat on the front porch with my legs and arms poking through the rungs of the wrought iron railing.

I'd never been outside this early before by myself. The sun was just beginning to rise and where its light touched the grass the dew sparkled like diamonds. There was no breeze and except for a crow squawking in a tree across the highway, it was silent. A car passed by, its tires singing on the pavement. A neighborhood mutt, bouncing along the sidewalk, stopped at the edge of our yard. He stood still watching me then tucked tail and scurried back the way he'd came, slowing to peer over his shoulder after reaching a safe distance. I paid him no further attention. My mind was wonderfully clear.

Today was my birthday.

I was swinging my feet and admiring new blond wispy hairs on my forearms when the door opened behind me.

"Jack, what are doing out here?" Mom whispered. "Are you feeling okay? You should be in bed."

"A girl kissed me."

"What?"

Mom came out, sat sideways beside me on the top step and put her arm around my shoulders. I looked up and she tried not to laugh but it didn't work. For the first time, I began to understand where Danny got it.

She squeezed me. "I haven't seen you wearing those glasses and pants in a long time. And what do mean a girl kissed you?"

"Her name was Tika, Mom. A badman was chasing her so I picked her up and flew her to the top of a church, and when the Indian warrior told me it was safe to take her home, I flew her to her house and she gave me a kiss."

(Try saying that as fast as you can.)

"Wow, that's quite a story."

"It's not a story. It was a dream." I told her everything that happened, from Danny helping me fly, to waking and not feeling afraid anymore. When I finished, her eyes were wet and she squeezed me.

"Mom, I want to try to ride my new bike."

She pulled the corner of my t-shirt free and used it to wipe her eyes. What is it with girls crying and getting other people wet? Don't they know how that makes a boy feel?

"I know, Sweetpea. After breakfast, your father will help you, and I'll bet by the end of the day, you'll be riding as well as your brother."

"No, Mom. I want you to help me. Now."

"Jack, I'm not strong enough, I still have curlers in my hair and my pajamas on. Your father will be up soon. Just wait a bit."

"No, Mom. All you have to do is help me get going. Just one time. Please? I don't want Danny to laugh at me." She got that look on her face that told me I had a good chance of winning. I gave her a final push. "Please. If Danny's outside, he'll laugh and I don't want him to." That should do it.

She sighed. "One time. Go get your bike and I'll put on my slippers."

I extracted my limbs and went to the garage. The big door was down and I didn't know how to open it, so I went in the side door. Danny's bike was parked inside and I had to move it to roll mine out.

Mom was just coming out of the house. She'd put on her green housecoat, pink slippers and was carrying my running shoes. I slid them on and she tied them for me.

"Okay, just once," she said. She held my bike as I lifted my leg and sat on the edge of the seat. My legs didn't hurt at all.

"Hold on and walk beside me," I directed. "And don't let go."

"I got you. Are you ready?"

I pushed on the pedals. The handlebars shook like the day before and the front wheel wobbled. She stopped and straightened the bars.

"Jack, you have to hold tight to keep the wheel straight. Don't worry about falling, I've got you."

We started again and this time I made it to the end of the driveway with no problem.

"Once more, Mom. To the backyard."

"Okay, but that's it. You're doing a lot better. Just remember to keep the wheel straight." She helped me turn. "Are you ready?"

I put my feet on the pedals and pushed. The driveway was uphill now so I had to push extra hard. When we reached the end, she helped me turn onto the grass and there was Dad, with his instant camera pointed at us.

He started to laugh. "Smile, honey. I can't believe it. I woke up this morning and found Groucho Marx and Lucille Ball riding a bicycle down my driveway." The camera whirred as the picture came out the bottom.

"Gus," Mom shrieked. "Put that thing away. What do you think you're doing?"

He took another picture.

"I said put that down. Oh, for heaven's sake." She began to laugh. "I never realized what the two of us must look like. Come here and help your son, so I can get in the house."

"Shhh, Lucy. You're waking the neighborhood."

Mom wagged her finger at him. "Are you finished? Have you got it all out of your system? You're just a big kid. Now help your son and give me those pictures."

"Oh, no. You're not getting these." He pulled the second picture free and handed her the camera.

Mom ran into the house. I sat on my bike while Dad shook the pictures and waited for the images to appear.

"Dad, we went all the way to the end of the driveway. It was easy. Hold on and I'll show you."

"Just a minute. I want to see how these turn out." He chuckled. "Oh, yeah." He opened his truck door and set the pictures inside, then picked up my bike with me still on it and spun it around.

We went down the driveway twice and the handlebars never shook once. Dad even let go for a couple of feet. When we returned to the garage, he helped me off.

"After breakfast, I'll lower the seat. It'll make it easier for you to put your feet on the ground." He set the kickstand then opened the truck door and picked up his pictures. "So, Jack, what are you doing up so early? Were you having trouble sleeping?"

"No. I just wanted to sit on the porch."

"Did you wake your mom?"

"No." I had a question I wanted to ask but I was embarrassed. Grandpa said that's when a person needs to just jump in, so I did. "Dad, if a girl kisses you, does that mean she's your sweetie?"

He smiled. "Jack, little boys get kissed by their mother's all the time. You just remember she's my sweetie and you can't have her."

"Yuck." I shook my head. Was he crazy? "I don't mean Mom, she's really old. I mean a girl my age. If she kisses me, does that mean she's my sweetie?"

Dad rubbed my head. "I was kidding. Who kissed you? Cheryl?"

Cheryl was the girl I gave all my valentines to. Cindy, another girl who lived down the road, got mad and her mother came over and told my mom. Now Danny and Dad tease me about it all the time.

"Nobody kissed me in real life, only in a dream. But now I don't know if that means she's my sweetie."

"Oh, a dream girl. I've never been kissed by a dream girl before. What's her name? Is she one of the girls from school?"

"No. She was just in a dream. Her name is Tika." I told him everything that had happened.

He asked me about flying and the riders and how scared I was when the badman grabbed me.

"Gus, Jack, breakfast," Mom called.

"Jack," Dad said. "I think you're going to have to ask your mother about this one. I don't think if you're kissed by a girl while you're dreaming, that means she's your sweetie. She's not real."

Honestly, I hadn't learned a thing.

My mother made bacon and eggs and my father showed us his pictures. They were funny. Mom didn't want to give them back but finally she did and then she called Danny again, and told him his breakfast was ready. He didn't sit until we were almost finished.

Dad set his coffee down. "So, Jack told you about his dream?"

"Yes," Mom said. "Wasn't it unusual? I don't think I've ever heard anything so extraordinary. Flying people and horses and Indians and bad men and little girls. It sounds like a Walt Disney movie."

"Mom." I raised my eyebrows toward Danny.

"Oops, sorry," she said.

"Flying dream? You had another flying dream? I wondered when you fell asleep so fast. I didn't even hear you get up. Who's the little girl Mom's talking about? Cheryl?"

If there was ever a hint of anything to tease me about, Danny's ears lifted like a rabbit's.

"Nothin'," I said. I had to change the subject. What had she been thinking? I should have made her promise not to say anything. "What time's Grandpa coming for my birthday? I want to practice riding my bike and show him how good I am."

Mom caught on. "He said he'll be here after lunch. Around two. That will give you plenty of time. Danny and your father are going to mow the lawn while I clean the house and bake a cake." She stood and pointed at my brother's plate. "And you, stop talking and get eating."

I slid out of my chair, opened the door and reminded Dad that he was going to adjust my seat. We left Danny at the table.

Mrs. Cook came over as were working on my bike. "Good morning, Gus. Is Colleen in the house?" She noticed me sitting on the floor. "Hey, Sweetpea, how are you feeling? Pauly was worried about you last night. I hope you slept well."

I liked Mrs. Cook a lot. As Grandpa would say, *'The apple doesn't fall far from the tree.'* She was as nice as Pauly and her smile reminded me of his. It was beautiful and made me feel special.

"Good morning, Hazel. Colleen's inside. We just finished breakfast."

"Good morning, Mrs. Cook. I feel a lot better now. I've been riding my new bike. Is Pauly coming over?"

"He has to run into town with his father for an appointment. Don't worry, he'll be back in time for your birthday. That's what I came to talk to your mother about."

"She's in the kitchen."

"Well, you two have a good morning and Sweetpea, I'm happy to see that you're feeling better. Be careful on that new bike." She went into the house and I heard my mom say hi.

"Come on, Jack," said Dad. "Let's see how this works."

I sat and put my feet on the pedals. They stayed on all the way around. I had a good feeling. I slid back on the seat and pedaled to the end of the drive. Dad helped me turn onto the sidewalk then gave me a push.

"I'm going to let go. You're doing great. Just keep the front wheel pointed straight."

I was doing it. I rode past the Cook's and the Harrison's then turned into the paved circle drive of the next house. An old man lived there. He was nice. He'd just moved in just a couple of months ago. A younger man was kneeling inside the entrance, behind the shrubs. He was holding a handful of weeds that he'd pulled from the flower bed. He had long brown hair and was wearing blue jeans, a t-shirt and black running shoes.

I almost ran him over. I put my feet on the ground and slid to a stop. He grabbed the handlebars when I started to fall. I wondered if I was in trouble. I hoped my dad was coming.

"Sorry," I said. "I was just gonna turn around. This is my new bike and I don't know how to stop very well."

"Don't worry about it, kid. You're lucky I was here." He tossed the weeds he was holding into the bushes, lit a cigarette and stepped back to admire my bike. "Hey, that's a beauty. I've never seen one with a shifter and sissy bar before."

"It's my birthday present. Today's my birthday. It's called a Mustang. My brother got a blue one." I was happy that he seemed nice.

"Well, happy birthday. What's your name?"

"Sweetpea."

"Sweetpea?" He looked at me like he thought that was funny. "How old are you?"

"Nine. My grandpa's coming over and we're going to have a birthday party. How do you blow smoke circles?"

He flicked the ashes off the end of his cigarette. "Maybe I'll show you someday, when you're older. In the meantime, I'll tell you what. I just came by to check on my father's house, but until you learn how to ride, you can keep using his driveway to turn around in." He looked over my shoulder then knelt back over the flowers. "I think your father's coming."

I got off my bike and looked. Dad was waving for me to return. "Thanks."

"No problem. Have a good birthday."

I pushed my bike back.

Dad looked past me when I reached him. "I thought you'd fallen. Who was that you were talking to? I thought Cecil was up at his cottage."

"It's his son and he's real nice. He kept me from falling and he blows smoke circles with his cigarette. He said I can use his driveway to turn around in, for as long as I want."

"Huh. Cecil never told me that he had a boy. Well, it sounds like you made a friend. It will sure make things easier. Just make sure you don't ride on his grass or make black marks on the pavement." He patted my shoulder. "You did well there, but why didn't you ride your bike back?"

"I don't think I can get going by myself."

"Well, you won't know until you try. Come on, I'll make sure you don't fall."

I used my feet to get rolling then pushed on the pedals. I picked up speed and stopped when I got to our driveway. Dad ran up and kept me from falling.

"Way to go. After you've ridden a bit more, you'll get the hang of stopping. I'll watch for a couple more minutes then I have to get the mower out."

He helped me turn around. I took off down the sidewalk and turned in the circle drive. The long-haired man was sitting behind the wheel of a green truck. I waved and he smiled as he started the engine.

13

True Dream

Tika lay in her bed with her eyes closed. Though she was right on the edge of awake, knew exactly where she was, a piece of her remained in that in-between place, where sometimes you can hold onto a fragment of a dream and direct its conclusion. She was focusing hard on the pictures flashing in her mind when the memory of Sweetpea burst through.

Tika rolled onto her back, her heart pounding, her face warmed by a single blade of morning light that slashed between her curtains. She lifted her arm, opened her eyes, and staring back from her wrist was the eagle. Her heart swelled as she clasped it against her chest.

For the first time in weeks, she didn't feel that she wasn't facing her fears alone. Her first waking thought hadn't been about the neighbor who'd attacked her or the threat he'd made against her grandmother. She didn't need to slip from her bed to peek between the curtains, praying for his truck to be gone, or wonder how she was going to make it through the day. Instead, she felt hope and encouragement.

Had it simply been a dream? Or had she really been visited by someone who cared?

Tika could still picture the view of the town from the top of the church, feel the leaves and branches beating against her as she was lifted to safety and her astonishment to find her rescuer a young boy. She remembered asking if he was her guardian spirit.

'I can only fly in a dream.'

Wasn't that exactly what her grandmother said a vision was? A dream where your spirit guide speaks to you? Had he really come because the eagle had delivered her prayers?

'I was flying above the horses and heard you cry. The leader pointed me towards town, so I came to see if I could help.'

Yes. He had come to help her, but when she'd told him about the neighbor, he'd told her to tell her mother. If Sweetpea really was her guardian spirit, shouldn't he have known that she didn't live with them?

Tika's mind raced as she tried to penetrate his riddle. It was all so confusing. Perhaps it had only been a dream. After all, whoever ever heard of a spirit guide named Sweetpea, wearing cowboy pajamas and six guns, who promised to appear whenever you cried? Tika smiled. It was impossible for her to lie still any longer. She needed to figure out what to do next.

Tika decided not to change as she didn't want to wake anyone. Besides, she'd slept in her clothes. She searched for her flip-flops. One was on the floor, the other between her sheets. She slipped them on, crept through the house and sat on the front porch.

The sky was clear and the air fresh with the smell of the heavy morning dew. There was just the slightest breeze whispering through the tops of the trees and tiny birds were flitting about in a rush, greeting each other with their morning chatter.

Today was her tenth birthday.

Tika was looking up at the steeple, its cross reaching high into the sky, when the door behind her opened and her grandmother whispered, "Tika, what are you doing outside so early? Did you not sleep well last night?"

Tika turned and smiled. “I slept very well, Grandmother. I just wanted to sit outside and think.” She stood and glanced at her bracelet and felt for the choker around her neck, the birthday presents her grandmother had given her just before she’d went to bed. “Thank you for my presents. They’re the most beautiful things I’ve ever seen.”

“You’re welcome and happy birthday.” Her grandmother hugged her and kissed her cheek. “Bud’s just getting up. I know he’s planned a special breakfast and surprise for you. It will be ready shortly. Wash your hands before you come in and sit at the table.”

“Yes, Grandmother.”

The door closed and Tika sat back down. A wave of guilt rolled over her. She didn’t deserve their attention and gifts. They were only giving presents to her because of her nightmares, and because she hadn’t been telling them the truth.

Tika looked at her uncle’s truck. It sat in the same spot where her mother had parked when she’d been left to live with them, in January, almost nine months earlier.

After the accident that took Tika’s father’s life, her mother hadn’t been the same. Helene had been driving and blamed herself for his death, despite witnesses who’d seen the truck that forced them from the road. Her mother’s injuries also had caused the loss of their unborn child, an unexpected gift of a brother for Tika. And with the loss of her baby and her husband’s death, so went Helene’s will to live. She became depressed, leaving Tika to fend for herself each day. Until finally, after a nasty argument with Bud, she agreed to allow Tika to live with them, while she began treatment from a friend of her mother’s in Springfield.

Tika looked back to the steeple, her mind awhirl. It didn’t matter if Sweetpea had been a dream. He was still right. She needed to tell them this morning about the neighbor. She shouldn’t have made them worry.

Tika glanced at the house next door. It was quiet. She wondered what they were going to say. Would they believe her or blame her? Would her uncle yell? Would the neighbor call her a liar? Would they want her to leave?

She was so scared. Her uncle drove to work each day with the man. His name was Orv. Tika didn't know his last name. He was younger than Bud. A dark wiry man with greasy hair and pockmarked cheeks. He dressed as a cowboy, in long sleeved shirts and jeans with a chrome belt-buckle hanging over his dust coloured boots.

Orv used to wave to her, often with a bottle of beer in his hand, as she walked between their homes to the path that led to the river. Then one day, three weeks ago, when she was returning, he stepped from behind the trees and blocked her from continuing up the bank.

"I just want to play with you, Tika. To be your friend." He moved sideways, keeping her in front of him. "You're so beautiful. I just want to make you happy."

Orv said those words so easily, his smile so plain, that every whisper of breath was driven from her. Tika almost fainted, her mind frantic with fear as she realized the danger an arm's length away. He reached towards her. Instinctively she drew back - their eyes locked together in the dance of predator-prey.

"I promise I won't hurt you," he said. His smile remained in place, the tip of his tongue visible between his lips. His eyes were lifeless, flat and hard. "I just want to make you happy. I'd never hurt you."

Despite her instincts, Tika's eyes darted left, searching for escape. That's exactly what he'd been waiting for. Orv rushed forward, his smile flattened to a slash beneath his feral eyes. Tika stepped back, ducking and twisting beneath his arms. Her laces caught on a fallen branch reaching from the forest floor. She cried out and fell to her knees. Off balance, reaching across and down, Orv's feet slid on the shaded grass. He landed on his side, grasping and clawing at her feet. Tika's fingers dug into the soil for purchase to pull herself away and closed around a knotted limb, the length and girth of her arm. In one smooth motion she rose, spun, and swung it across his face. Orv cursed, raising his hands in defense. He needn't have. Tika was already gliding through the undergrowth, up the embankment.

Orv cursed through torn and bloodied lips. His words an arrow that pierced her heart. "I'll hurt the old woman. You say one damn word to anyone and I'll kill her."

Tika raised her palms to her face. She'd been crying. Her grandmother and uncle had been so kind and this is how she'd repaid them? With lies? She should have told them right away but Bud hadn't been home, so she'd waited. But when he'd returned, she'd been even more frightened. She thought they might not believe her, so she'd tried to forget. But each time she saw Orv, and every night when she lay down, Tika remembered his threat. And now, because they loved her and were worried about her, they were giving her gifts and a birthday surprise. Tika wished she could run away. She stood, her decision made. She had to do what Sweetpea said.

When she entered the kitchen, her uncle was waiting. Bud was a tall, handsome man, dark and slender, with his long hair pulled and tied behind his back.

"There she is. There's my birthday girl." He swept her from her feet and spun her around, giving her a huge hug. "Happy birthday, Tika. Ten years old today." He set her down and held her hands. "Let me have a good look at you. I want to remember this day forever. Pretty soon you're not going to want old Uncle Bud picking you up." His eyes widened when he noticed her choker and the bracelet around her wrist. Bud looked at his mother. "Son of a gun." He smiled. "You must have the most wonderful grandmother in the whole world." Bud shook his head. "Those gifts are going to be tough to match, but let me see if I might have something that surprises you." He opened the door, stepped outside and came back in, wheeling a new bicycle.

"For me?" Tika was shocked. She'd ridden before but never one of her own.

"It's from your grandmother and I. Come take a look. It has a basket and a bell so everyone will know that you're coming." Bud rang the bell and laughed.

Tika burst into tears, something she'd allowed them to witness only once before, on the day she'd been left to live with them. She couldn't hold back.

"Whoa, there's nothing to cry about," Bud began, stopped by his mother's raised hand. He looked questioningly to her.

"Come here, child," her grandmother said.

Tika ran across the room and buried her face in her grandmother's arms.

"I'm so sorry. I didn't mean to lie to you."

"It's all right. Take your time and calm down. Let your tears clean your spirit, then tell me what's wrong." Her grandmother stroked her hair. When Tika's tears began to slow, she wiped them away with her thumbs. "Now, what has been troubling you. What are you so afraid of?"

"Last night I prayed like you showed me and the eagle sent a spirit to me. I was having a nightmare and running away. He picked me up and carried me to the top of the church. He was a young boy. He said his name was Sweetpea. When I told him who was chasing me, he told me I had to tell you or someday he might hurt me." Tika began to cry again. "I was going to tell you, I promise. But I didn't want him to hurt you. That's why I got up early today. I was trying to think about what to say. I'm so sorry," she wailed. "You and Uncle Bud don't need to give me any presents. You can have them all back, so I won't cost you any money." Tika pressed her head against her grandmother's chest and bawled.

"It's alright, child. Bud and I didn't give you your presents because you made us worry. It's your birthday and we love you." Her grandmother continued to stroke her hair. "Now, tell me, who is this person who frightened you? Was it Orv?"

"Yes," Tika sobbed. "He tried to catch me in the woods. He wanted to touch me, but I was afraid. He said he wanted to play with me and make me happy, but when I ran away, he said if I told anyone he'd kill you."

"That son of a..." Bud spun on his heels and opened the back door.

"Bud, stop," her grandmother said. "Please, don't go outside. Tika and I need you. You'll end up in jail. Call the sheriff's office. Ask Carter to come. He can be here in twenty minutes."

Bud turned, his face dark and his hands clenched into fists. "Mom, he tried to hurt Tika and he threatened you. If you want to call the police that's fine. While you're at it, you'd best call for an ambulance as well. When I finish with..."

"No. We have to do this right. If you harm Orv, there will be two stories to tell, and Tika's will be more difficult to believe. Call Carter. He'll know what to do." Rose nodded at the phone on the wall. "Please. For Tika's sake and mine."

Bud stood in the doorway. His shoulders dropped as he accepted his mother's decision. He picked up the receiver, dialed and asked for Carter. He explained what happened and Carter said he was on his way. Bud hung up and stared out the window at Orv's home.

Tika stayed in her grandmother's arms. She was spent, her tears had drained all her energy. Her grandmother lay her head back against the chair and whispered a prayer in her native tongue. Tika loved how it sounded like poetry. It calmed her.

She'd just closed her eyes and began a prayer of her own when her uncle yelled.

"He's leaving!" Bud ran outside, calling out as he crossed the yard. "Orv!"

Tika and her grandmother ran to the door. Orv was carrying a rifle in one hand, his duffle bag and a beer in the other. He opened the driver's door, tossed the bag onto the seat, and hung his rifle in the rack above the rear window. He turned to Bud with a grin, a cigarette between his lips.

"You changed your mind, Bud. I'm glad. Grab your rifle." Orv looked into the sky. "It's going to be a perfect morning for some target shooting. There's hardly a breeze."

"You're not going anywhere," Bud snarled.

"What?" Orv looked confused. He took a pull from his bottle. "What are you talking about? Are you still mad about that fifty dollars? I told you I'd get it." Tika saw him glance over Bud's shoulder at her and her grandmother. "Or is that what you're sore about?" He pointed at her. "Has that little girl been telling you stories?"

"I called Carter, Orv. He'll be here in a couple of minutes. You're not going anywhere."

"Now why would you do that, old son?" Orv's face changed. His smile thinned and his tongue poked between his lips. He tossed his cigarette to the ground and kicked the gravel with the toe of his boot. He looked sideways at Bud. His eyes were expressionless. He tipped his head. "Bud, if she's been telling you stories about me chasing her in the woods, that's a damn lie."

Bud spread his feet and clenched his hands at his sides. "How did you know it was about the woods? You're not going anywhere. You're waiting right here until Carter arrives and then you can tell him your damn lies, including how you tried to keep Tika quiet by threatening my mother."

Orv tossed his empty bottle into the bed of his truck and lifted his hand. The blade of a knife shone in it. "Well, Bud, I hate to tell you this but when Carter shows, I won't be here. I'm going shooting. Perhaps you can give him my apologies for having run out here for no reason." He smiled and began to turn towards his truck. "Unless of course you're thinking you'd like to stop me? That wouldn't be a smart thing to do."

"You're not leaving," Bud said. "I wouldn't care if you were still carrying your rifle. You're not going anywhere."

Orv took a step towards his truck.

Bud grabbed his shoulder. Orv spun around. The blade sliced through the air where Bud had been but he was ready and had stepped to the side. He hit Orv in the face as his momentum carried him through. Orv stumbled back and slammed closed the door of his truck. He wiped his mouth. There was blood on his hand. He smiled and smeared it on the leg of his jeans. He crouched low, knife hand up, his other loose as he stepped forward. The blade flicked back and forth. He lunged and Bud sidestepped. Tika's heart jumped into her throat as her uncle's feet slipped on the gravel and he almost went down.

Orv smiled. "Almost got you there, old son. Now why don't you turn around and let me get out of your hair? I've got no reason to hurt you. Unless you're just mad I tried to get to that little thing before you." His laugh was a short bark. "Is that what it is, Bud? Is that's what's bothering you? You jealous?" He laughed and lunged again.

Bud stepped forward, blocked his arm and hit him in the face. Orv fell back and caught himself with his hand on the truck mirror. Blood gushed from his nose. He shook his head and crouched low.

"Now you're going to pay. Now I'm gonna make sure you get your fifty dollars worth."

Orv circled left with the knife between them, feigning back and forth. When Bud made the mistake of moving towards his truck, Orv faked left again until Bud had the truck behind him. Then he struck. He feigned right, ducking beneath Bud's arms when he stepped forward and swung. Orv stood and plunged the knife into Bud's chest. Bud's mouth opened in surprise at the force of the blow. His arms dropped and Orv pulled the blade free. Bud's hands rose to cover the stain spreading on the front of his shirt as Orv raised the knife again.

"No!" Tika's grandmother cried.

Orv smiled over his shoulder and then looked back to Bud. "How you feeling now, partner? Was it worth getting yourself killed? He turned, pointed at Tika and winked. "I'll be coming back for you." He pushed Bud aside, opened the door and slid behind the wheel of his truck. The engine roared as he spun on the lawn and turned down the lane. Tika and her grandmother ran to Bud, who'd fallen to his knees.

"Oh, son," his mother moaned.

Bud tried to smile. A froth of pink appeared in the corner of his mouth.

Tika's grandmother ripped open the front of his shirt. "He's nicked your lung. We need to stop the bleeding and keep you up, so it won't fill." She turned to Tika. "I need you to press your hand right here." She took Tika's hand and placed it firmly against the bloody wound. "Push hard." She looked at her son. "Bud, we've got to get you up against that tree." She pointed to the stump at the end of the drive. "I'm not strong enough to do it by myself. You're going to have to help." She moved behind him and put her arms under his and lifted, while Bud pushed back with his heels. Slowly, they made it.

"Tika, keep your hand pressed tight. I'm going to call for an ambulance and get bandages." Her grandmother ran into the house.

Tika looked into her uncle's eyes. She wanted to cry but couldn't. No nightmare she'd ever had could measure to the fear pounding in her chest.

Bud smiled. "Don't worry, it's just a nick. Your grandmother's the best doctor within a thousand miles." He coughed again and more blood ran down his chin.

Tears rolled from Tika's eyes. "I'm so sorry, Uncle Bud. I should have told you, but he said he'd kill her."

Bud reached up and held her arm. "There's nothing to be sorry about. I'm the one who didn't notice how evil Orv is." He squeezed her arm. "Your grandmother's going to need you to be strong, to help her around the house. It will make me feel a lot better knowing you're here and that I can count on you." He coughed again and dropped his hand.

Tika's grandmother returned and knelt beside Bud. She was holding a piece of a plastic bag, a cloth, a blanket and a roll of tape.

"Tika, when I put this over the wound, I need you to press tight while I tape around it."

Tika nodded.

"Okay, take away your hand."

Tika removed it then put it back quickly, after her grandmother placed the cloth and bag over the hole.

"Press tight while I tape it." Her grandmother looked at her son. "Bud, how are you feeling?"

"I'm okay. I've got the two best doctors in town." He coughed. "My chest does hurt a bit though and I'm cold. I could use a blanket."

"I've brought one." His mother finished taping around the wound. "Tika, help me spread this."

They were covering him when a police car pulled into the drive.

Carter slammed the door and ran over. "Bud, Rose, what's going on? Where's Orv? Is this his doing?" He put his hand on his pistol and looked towards Orv's home. "Is he still around?"

"Carter, Orv's gone," Rose said. "Bud tried to stop him. I've called for an ambulance but it won't be here for at least fifteen minutes. He needs to get to the hospital now. Orv stabbed him and punctured his lung. With your car, we can get him there quicker."

Carter knelt next to Bud. "Do you think you can make it if I help?"

Bud groaned. "I think so." He coughed and tried to smile. "Besides, if that's what mother thinks is best, you'd better listen."

For the first time, Tika noticed tears running down her grandmother's face.

"We have to hurry," her grandmother said. "He's going into shock."

Tika helped Carter and her grandmother load Bud into the back seat of the police car. She sat up front. Carter turned on the siren and lights and they raced out of town. Tika didn't realize until they were speeding down the highway, toward Jefferson City, that she'd been holding onto her necklace and praying to Sweetpea.

14

A Sound Plan

Orv made up his mind before Medicine Falls disappeared in his rear-view mirror - he wasn't running far. He had cash, a handgun and papers in his home that he needed to retrieve. Sneaking back shouldn't be a problem. He knew the sheriff wouldn't have the manpower to keep an eye on it for long. And they certainly wouldn't be expecting him to return.

He pulled off the highway, onto the service trail that led into the backcountry, towards the run-down shack he'd found a couple of years ago while scouting wild turkey. The place where he'd met the fellow that he'd purchased his game rifle from.

This wasn't Orv's first time on the run and he knew it likely wouldn't be his last. Trouble always seemed to be just one step behind him, so he'd learned a long time ago the value of making and sticking to a sound plan. Radio travelled quicker than his truck, or blind luck. He figured to lie low until the police were sure he'd left the area, then return. Orv knew most men gave themselves away, running fast and popping up for gas, money, or food. Not him. His knew his best bet would be to hole up quick, maybe sneak back tomorrow night, grab whatever he could, then hole back up again for a couple more days.

Orv was a survivor and he took great satisfaction in knowing that. It seemed whenever a situation arose, he was likely to come out on top. This despite being born into a family of drunkards and thieves and a father who'd beat him from the day he could talk. Somehow, Orv always found a way to win. Did the authorities think it had been luck, that by the time they realized his father's skull had been busted *before* his house burned around his ears, that Orv was long gone? Working under a new name as a farmhand two states away. Yes, if there was one thing Orv prided himself on, it was recognizing the value of a good plan and sticking to it. After all, it had kept him out of prison and the law's hands for almost twenty years.

Orv slammed his hand against the steering wheel. "Damn you, Bud. Why'd you have to go and make such a fuss over that little girl anyways?"

He felt his damaged face. His nose was broke. He'd set it later. Already it had swollen shut and there was a steady headache drumming behind his eyes. He ran his tongue over his lips. They were ripped open again too, in the exact same spot where Tika had struck him with the limb.

"You're going to pay this time, little girl," he muttered.

Maybe that's what he'd do when he returned for his money? Visit next door and pay her and the old lady back for his troubles. He took a long pull on the bottle he'd taken from his bag and emptied it. That just might be an idea.

"What would you think of that, old Bud? How would you like me to bust the two of them up, the same way you done me?"

Orv took satisfaction in the thought. He knew a man was hard to kill and there was a good chance Bud would live. It would all depend on how quickly they were able to get him into the hospital, in Jefferson City.

"And maybe while I'm at it, I'll pick up that rifle collection of yours."

That was another good idea. A person could never be too sure when they might need another gun, and some of the ones in Bud's collection were worth hundreds of dollars. They'd be easy to sell as he made his way across country. And he was going to need the money. Yep, that would be another part of his new plan. After grabbing what he could from home, he'd visit next door. After all, it was just an old woman and a child. What trouble could they give him?

Orv pulled off the narrow track and began to travel across country, the old truck bouncing as he dodged between trees and exposed roots. Shortly he came upon the dry creek that led to the back of the battered shack. He dropped his wheels carefully over the bank and followed the rocky bed until he came up behind it. Orv shut off the engine and carried his rifle and rucksack inside. An old rocker sat outside on the porch. He pulled it onto the hardpan, out from under the eaves, lit a cigarette and opened another beer.

Orv smiled and barked a short laugh. There was little chance the authorities would guess that he'd travelled just a half dozen miles.

15

Wakanda

Rose checked Bud's wound. The tape was holding. The plastic remained tight against his chest. She pulled the blanket back up and tucked it around his shoulders.

"How do you feel, son?"

"It hurts to breathe," Bud gasped. His voice was powerless and rattled in his chest. A tear had formed in the corner of his eye. He turned his head. "I'm sorry, Mom. I never considered that Orv had bothered Tika. I've let the two of you down."

"Hush. There's no need to talk. We'll be at the hospital soon." Rose brushed his hair from his forehead. "And son, you've never let me down."

Bud moaned as he inhaled. "I'm also sorry about Helene." The tear ran down his cheek. "It was never my intention to run her off." He closed his eyes and lay his head back against the seat.

"Oh, Bud. I told you. Helene agreed that she needed help, and I wanted Tika safe with us."

Bud coughed again and she wiped his lips.

"Helene will find her way, I'm sure of it. We just need to make sure when she returns, that you're here for her."

"I'm trying," he wheezed.

Rose glanced out the front windshield. They'd just entered the city limits and would soon be at the hospital. The car in front of them, after noticing the cruiser's lights and siren, pulled to the shoulder to let them pass.

"Hold on," Carter said, over his shoulder. "We're almost there. Only a couple more minutes.

Bud opened his eyes. Tika had turned to look at him.

"We're almost there, Uncle Bud," she said, biting her lower lip to keep it from trembling.

Bud smiled weakly. "Tika, I want to hold your hand."

Tika leaned over the seat and reached back as far as she could. They wrapped their fingers together.

"I want you to know how proud I am of you. I love you as though you were my own daughter." Bud coughed and winced.

Tears streamed down Tika's face. "I love you too, Uncle Bud. You've got to get better."

"I will," he promised.

"They're waiting for us," Carter said.

He pulled under the canopy at the hospital entrance. Two nurses ran to the car. Carter opened the back door and Rose helped Bud lean forward so the deputy could get his arm under Bud's shoulder. Carter helped his friend to the stretcher and with the nurse's assistance they lay him upon it. Rose took Tika's hand and they followed everyone inside. A nurse stopped them before they reached the counter. Rose watched as her son was wheeled through a set of double doors, a little further down the hall.

"We've been waiting for you," the nurse comforted. "Dr. Westshot has been called. He's here. Your son's in good hands." She pointed to a door across the hall. "We have a private waiting room that you can use. Please, follow me." She held the door open to a small room with a row of windows facing the parking lot.

Rose could see Carter's car. He'd left the flashing lights on. She sat with Tika on the couch and the deputy took the chair opposite.

"Is there anything I can get for you?" the nurse asked.

"No, thank you," Rose replied.

Tika slid next to her and Rose put her arm around her shoulder.

"Nothing for me," Carter added.

The nurse closed the door.

"Carter, I can't thank you enough for everything you've done," Rose said. "I don't know where we'd be without you. You've given Bud a fighting chance."

"You're welcome," Carter replied. "Bud looked good when they took him in. He's a tough man. I'm sure he'll pull through." He reached into his shirt pocket and pulled out his notepad. "In the meantime, I'm sorry, I hate to have to do this. I know we went over a lot on the way in, but I have a couple more questions." He flipped open the book and looked up apologetically.

"I understand," Rose said.

Carter bit the end of his pencil then pulled it from his teeth. "Tika, I need to ask you a question and I want to make sure that you understand that no one is going to be angry with you." He glanced at Rose then continued. "Had Orv ever tried this before? Has he ever touched you?"

"No." Tika began to cry. "He wasn't going to be nice to me. He didn't want to be my friend. He was going to make me do bad things."

Rose pulled her granddaughter tight to her and pressed her head against her shoulder. "It's okay. We believe you." She stroked Tika's hair. "Carter doesn't wish to ask you these questions, but he must."

The deputy waited for Tika to calm. He nodded at Rose. "When Bud confronted Orv this morning, you said he put a rifle in his truck. Do you know if he has any other weapons?"

"I believe he has one other rifle and a shotgun. The one he put in the rack he uses for target practice and small game.

Yesterday he asked Bud to go shooting with him this morning but Bud told him no. Today is Tika's birthday. He wanted to spend it with her."

"So, the rifle in the truck is the smaller one? Do you know what calibre it is?"

Rose shook her head. "No. I have no interest in weapons." She thought for a moment. "Bud was with him when he bought it, I'm sure he knows what it is."

"So, there were no other weapons in the truck? The other rifles should be in his house?"

"There was no other rifle in the rack, that's all I can tell you. Whether the others are in the house, I can't say."

"He's got a little pistol too," Tika said. "He fired it behind his house and showed it to Uncle Bud."

"Do you remember what it looked like?" Carter asked. "Did he say anything about it?"

"No, but Uncle Bud knew what it was. He told Orv that it was old and he shouldn't be shooting it."

"One last thing," Carter said. "Orv moved next door about two years ago. Do you know where he lived before then? Do you have any idea where he might run?"

"No," Rose said. "He moved in right after he began working where Bud does. In November. I have no idea where he came from. I never had the desire to speak with him. I found him to be a braggart." She looked down. "I also don't believe Bud would have had anything to do with him, other than their shared interest in hunting."

"Okay. That should be it." Carter stood and put his notepad in his pocket. "I need to radio this information to the sheriff." He turned towards the door, stopped and put his hand on Tika's shoulder. "Thank you, for answering my questions. I know it wasn't easy." He smiled. "Now I know why Bud thinks the world of you. You're an extraordinary young lady. If you think of anything else, let me know. Okay?"

Yes," Tika said, as she stood and wrapped her arms around his waist. "Thank you for helping Uncle Bud."

Carter patted her shoulder and left the room.

Rose sat silent for a moment, thinking.

"Tika, I need to use a phone. Will you be okay, until I return?"

"Yes."

"When Carter comes back, tell him I'll only be a minute." Rose stood and left the room.

When Rose returned, Carter was sitting in the chair and Tika was standing at the window. Rose sat on the couch. "Any word, Carter?"

"No. The doctor hasn't spoke to the nurse."

"I'm sorry. I meant about Orv. I spoke with the nurse too."

"Oh, sorry," he said. "The sheriff is searching the house right now. They've found his other rifles. I told them about the handgun. They'll find it if they have to rip the place apart. In the meantime, they've sent out a statewide bulletin. Orv won't get far." He took his hat off and ran his fingers through his hair. "It's a wait and see game now. I told Sheriff Neall that I'm staying here today, until Bud comes out of surgery. I also told him that I'd like to drive you and Tika back to Medicine Falls and patrol the town tonight, in case Orv returns. He's agreeable with that."

"Thank you."

"Right now," Carter said, "I'm going to run out and grab a bite to eat. Can I bring back anything for you and Tika?"

Rose opened her handbag and pulled out her wallet. "A couple of sandwiches would be fine."

Carter raised his hands. "No, please allow me. It will give me a chance to pay you back for some of those meals I've enjoyed." He picked up his hat. "I'll be a half an hour. Is there anything else you'd like?"

"No, thank you."

Carter left.

Rose lay her head back, closed her eyes, and said a quick prayer. When she looked up, Tika was still at the window.

"Tika, I'd like to speak with you."

Tika turned. Her eyes were dry and she seemed composed. Carter was right, she really was an extraordinary young girl. She was also very pretty, a younger copy of her mother.

"I wish to speak with you about your vision."

A mature expression flit across Tika's face. "Grandmother, how did you know that I was just thinking about that?"

"Tika, after today, I'm going to start looking at you quite differently." Rose patted the cushion next to her. "Please, sit." Tika sat and Rose took her hand. "Before we talk, I'd like to tell you about the bracelet and necklace I gave you last night for your birthday."

Tika looked up expectantly.

"Many years ago, your great, great, great grandmother, Wakanda, was a wise woman in her village. She was very respected and shared many of her visions with the people."

She squeezed Tika's hand.

"One fall, the people waited for the buffalo but the great herds did not come. Scouts were sent from each village to find them, but they returned after having no luck. The winter storms came early and the people began to starve. They were cold and weak and many became sick. Council was held and it was decided that the villages needed to come together, to determine what must be done. Differences were to be forgotten, enemies to become friends, as every family grieved the loss of loved ones. When the day came, many chiefs, warriors, medicine men and wise woman sat together.

When Wakanda spoke, she told of repeated visions she'd had of where the herd was to be found. She said that a great blizzard had stopped their winter march. Because of her wisdom, many people wished to move camp and follow her, but many others did not. They were weak and scared. If Wakanda was wrong, it was feared that many more would die. Finally, it was decided that those who were strong enough would follow her. Either the herd would be found, or they would perish."

Rose closed her eyes and reflected upon the courage of the small group.

"For three days, they travelled through deep snow and freezing temperatures. On the morning of the fourth day, Wakanda sent five men ahead, led by Sunkwa, the people's greatest warrior. She told him that he must ride his white horse, while the others were to ride horses of different colors, a roan, black, buckskin and bay. Late the next day, the men returned." Rose smiled and squeezed her granddaughter's hand. "The herd had been found. Great Grandmother had been right.

Scouts were sent back to the villages and many braves returned. The buffalo were harvested and meat was loaded onto travois and taken back to the villages. Much was dried, pounded and mixed with melted fat to make pemmican, to last the winter. Hides were made into winter clothing and shelter. The people were saved.

In the spring, a great ceremony was called to celebrate - to give thanks for the hunt and for the visions received by Wakanda. Your Great Grandmother was presented with her choker and two bracelets, made by the wise women from the other villages." Rose smiled at her granddaughter.

"Tika, I have passed the remaining bracelet and choker to you. Someday you will pass them to your child or granddaughter and tell them the story of Wakanda. In this way, our circle will remain unbroken." She turned the bracelet on her granddaughter's wrist, until the eagle faced them. "Now, I wish you to tell me of your vision."

Tika smiled shyly. "I don't know if it was a vision, Grandmother. I've been thinking about it and I think it might have been just a dream."

Rose waited for her to continue.

"I prayed like you showed me and asked the eagle to carry my fears to Wakan Tanka, so I wouldn't have nightmares anymore. But as soon as I fell asleep, Orv began to chase me again. I was so scared." Tika clenched her hands together and Rose held them within hers.

"This time he was going to catch me. I couldn't hide or run away fast enough. Just as he was about to grab me, I was picked up from above and carried to the roof of the church." Tika looked up, embarrassed. "At first, I thought it was the eagle, or my guardian spirit, but now I believe it was just a dream. It was a boy, Grandmother. He was about the same age as me but he could fly. He said his name was Sweetpea. At first, I thought maybe my guardian spirit only chose to look like a boy, so that he wouldn't frighten me." Tika smiled at the memory. "But he was wearing pajamas and a holster with play guns. So now I'm pretty sure it was just a dream."

"Did the boy tell you where he came from, or why he appeared?"

"He said he lived far away. He said he was flying above the men on the horses and when he heard me cry, the leader pointed him toward town."

"Did you see the horsemen?"

"No, but before he carried me from the roof to bring me home, he flew above our house and said he saw them again, by the river. He said that the leader pointed with his long spear, to tell him it was safe."

"Did you tell the boy about Orv?"

"Yes. He asked me why he was chasing me. I told him that Orv tried to hurt me and that he'd threatened to hurt you if I told anyone." Tika looked up at her. "When he told me that I had to tell my mother and father, that's when I started to wonder how he could be my guardian spirit. A spirit would know that my father is dead, and that my mother doesn't live with us."

"One last question. Did you see the boy fly away?"

Tika looked up at her in wonder. "Yes. After he brought me home and I went into the house, I ran back outside and saw him shoot into the sky. He turned into a ball of light and flew so high and far away, I couldn't see him anymore."

Rose closed her eyes and smiled.

"Grandmother?"

"Yes?"

"Do you think Sweetpea was just a dream?"

Rose opened her eyes. "Give me a hug." Tika squeezed her and Rose kissed her forehead. "Tika, only the person who has the dream can say what it is. Our people believe that dreams are the connection between the physical and spiritual world. We believe that everything and everyone, having come from the creator, is connected. The animals, trees, water, wind, and plants. Everything." Rose paused in thought. "Do you know that your grandfather, my husband, was the pastor of the church that you and Sweetpea sat upon? And that our home was given to us by the church?"

"No."

"Tika, your grandfather was a missionary. I met him when I was a young woman, when he came to speak with us on the reservation. After we married, he was sent to Medicine Falls. That was many years ago, when there were only a few homes." Rose smiled at the memory. "Your grandfather and the people built the church in the center of town. They wanted everyone to be able to see the cross from their homes, to know that they are a part of something much bigger than Medicine Falls. To know that they belong in the circle of life."

There was a knock on the door, it opened and Carter peeked in. "Okay if I come in?"

"Yes," Rose said. "I was just telling Tika about her grandfather."

"Pastor Flowers." Carter smiled. "I think of him often." He set a brown paper bag on the table in front of her. "On my way in, the nurse told me that the doctor will be in shortly to speak with you. Oh, and I almost forgot." He reached into his pocket and pulled out his notepad. "They found Orv's pistol and something else. It seems he's been living under a false name." Carter flipped through a couple of pages. "His last name is Brooks not Shaw. They found papers along with his gun and some cash under loose boards in his home. They're running his name right now to see if he's wanted." He looked up. "I'm betting he is. Why else would he bother to change it?" Carter gestured towards the bag. "Please, don't let me hold you up, your sandwiches are inside. I'm going back out to the radio, to see if they've learned any more. I'll be back shortly."

When Carter returned, he had the doctor with him. Carter was grinning from ear to ear as he held the door open and introduced Dr. Westshot - a short, elderly man with thick glasses, magnifying kind blue eyes.

Rose stood and the doctor took her hands.

"Your son is going to be fine. He's resting comfortably."

Rose's heart fluttered and her legs shook. She wobbled and sat on the couch.

Without letting go, the doctor sat on the edge of the table. He patted and rubbed her hand. "I took quite a bit of fluid from his lung and air from his chest cavity." He shook his head and smiled. "I don't know how you knew to sit him up and cover the wound as well as you did, but you saved his life." He reached over and patted Tika's knee.

"And you. You must be Tika." He chuckled. "Right now, your uncle is more concerned about you than himself." Dr. Westshot turned back to Rose. "I'm going to remain here the rest of the day, to keep an eye on your son and see how well his lung inflates. I don't believe he'll require surgery. The knife, although it penetrated deep, had a narrow blade. I'd like to give the wound a chance to close on its own." He smiled at both of them. "In the meantime, you're welcome to visit him for a couple of minutes, but then we must allow him to rest. I don't want him talking or getting excited for the next few days."

Dr. Westshot studied her face. "Mrs. Flowers, by any chance was your husband the late Pastor Thomas Flowers, from Medicine Falls?"

"Yes, and please, call me Rose."

He nodded. "Your doctoring skills makes sense now. I must admit, your reputation does you justice. Do you have any questions you'd like to ask?"

Rose squeezed his hand. "Thank you, doctor, from Tika and I and my son. Do you foresee any complications?"

"Well, with a puncture wound there's always a risk of internal bleeding or respiratory distress, although I don't expect those problems to arise. The wound was clean and your son is in very good shape." He winked. "So, if that's it, let's go visit him." He stood and turned to Carter. "And deputy, please remember, no questions today."

"No problem, sir. I can wait until Bud's well enough. Come on Tika, let's go see Bud."

The moment they entered Bud's room, Tika ran over and grabbed his hand. Bud smiled and his oxygen mask steamed over. He looked up at Rose and winked as Carter slapped his leg. Rose bent and hugged him. Bud reached up and squeezed her arm.

"Son," she said, kissing his forehead and patting his face. "Dr. Westshot says that we can only stay for a moment, so don't try to talk. Carter's going to take us home. He's staying in Medicine Falls tonight to patrol the town, in case Orv returns." She moved to the side so Tika could give him a hug. "When we return tomorrow, I'll bring clean clothes and your shaving kit." She kissed him again. "I love you. If there's anything else you need, have the nurse call."

"I love you too, Uncle Bud," Tika said.

Carter squeezed his arm. "I'm not going to tell you I love you, but it's sure good to see you doing okay. Don't worry about anything. We've got roadblocks set up all the way to Illinois. I've got your family, and for the next couple of nights I'll be staying in town. If you need anything, let me know. Okay?"

Bud nodded and patted Carter's hand.

"I know, pard. Goes double for me."

"Okay folks. Let's allow him to rest," Dr. Westshot said. He held the door open. "I promise, he's in good hands."

16

Genuine One Hundred Percent Character

At two o'clock, me, Danny and Pauly were sitting on our front porch waiting for Grandpa. We were all excited because he was the most fun person in the entire world. Dad said Grandpa was what people used to call, 'a genuine, one hundred percent character.'

Daniel Trapper was a tall bony man who'd farmed his entire life, and whose belief in hard work, boiled cabbage and the church, kept him skinny, gassy, and pious.

We loved visiting him on his farm. In the summer, he'd give us a warm bottle of Coke, then we'd sit under a willow and listen to a Tiger's ballgame on his radio. Games we seldom paid attention to. You see, Grandpa had a glass eye to replace one shot out when he was a kid and nerve damage that caused his chin to flop up and down, repeatedly opening and closing his mouth. This made wearing his false teeth so uncomfortable, if we weren't eating corn on the cob, he didn't have them in. So, the combination of watching his chin flap, listening to his gums slap and staring at his painted eyeball, entertained us far more than any ballgame. Grandpa knew it too, from our snorts and giggles and the way he'd smile after acknowledging a homer with a gum smacking round of applause. He was something else.

Grandpa was also the only grandparent Danny and I had left. Our mom's parents had been killed in a car accident before we were born and Grandma Trapper died the winter before I turned seven. She was the nicest person I ever knew. Her name was Honor. I think that's the neatest name. Kind of like Justice or Comfort or Charity. Only better. We had pictures of her all around our home. In each one she was round with yellow hair, smiling and wearing a thin cotton dress with flowers on it. She always smelled like baby powder. That's the only other odor that reminds me of anything, and since it's a good one, it far outweighs the other.

Honor Trapper was a religious woman who told Danny and me that everyone in the world is connected. She said life's just one big circle, so you have to treat others the way you want to be treated, because sooner than later it all comes back. She also liked to tell us about visions she had of the fight between good and evil. The one I remember best is the one she told us when I was about six. Danny and me were sitting in her kitchen and we must have done something bad, because she was worried about our future and decided to tell us about a fight she'd witnessed between the Lord and the devil. And to prove she wasn't perfect, she used herself in her example.

"I was sitting right here, right in this chair, praying to the Lord to forgive me, when two red hands came shooting from the sky and grabbed me by the wrists." She held her hands out upside down to show us the marks. Of course, there weren't any, but that didn't make a difference.

"I wrestled and tried to pull free, but the devil's grip is much too strong. Finally, I relaxed, closed my eyes and prayed to the Lord Jesus to save me. And do you know what happened?" She closed her eyes and smiled angelically, "The two most beautiful hands you'll ever see appeared out of thin air. They swooped down, grabbed the devil's and pulled them away with no problem." Grandma opened her eyes and looked us over. "And that's what you boys need to remember - when the devil has his hands on you, only Jesus can set you free."

I'll never forget that story because it still gives me goose bumps.

"Here comes Grandpa," Danny said, pointing down the highway.

"Are you sure, Danny?" All I could see was a black spot about a mile away.

"Yep, that's Grandpa," Pauly confirmed.

We waited at the end of the driveway. Grandpa's car got bigger and bigger. Finally, just before turning in, he honked the horn. It made a loud 'heehaw' that everybody in the neighborhood must have heard. If my overalls didn't have straps, I'd have jumped right out of them. Pauly and me laughed and yelled, "Grandpa's here, Grandpa's here," as we walked alongside his car. You could have hooked the corners of all our smiles over our ears. Grandpa's included.

"There's my boys," he said, from his open window. He turned off the engine and set the brake. "Now you lad's step back. I don't want to knock you down with this here door."

Danny and I looked at each other and laughed, at the same time inching back and pulling Pauly with us. Unfortunately, Grandpa wasn't kidding. At one time or another, we'd both received goose eggs in our eagerness to greet him.

Grandpa cranked up his window, pulled a handkerchief from his shirt pocket, and began to wipe clean the steering wheel and dash. We waited like a pack of hungry dogs hearing a can of Dr. Ballard's being opened. All of us aware that nothing would speed him up. Grandpa never left his car until the interior was spotless. And what a car it was. It was the largest, shiniest vehicle most people had ever seen - a gigantic two-tone maroon and tan, 1930 Willys Knight, four door, which, he liked to inform curious onlookers, he'd purchased brand spanking new.

Finally, he opened his door and stepped onto the running board that ran between the wheels. With one hand on the spoked side-mounted spare, he climbed down. We sprang forward and clamped ourselves around his bony waist before he could turn and wipe the handle. I can't speak for anybody else, but there was nobody I liked to hug as much as my grandpa.

He laughed. "Whoa now. You boys wouldn't be trying to butter up an old man, would you?" He lifted us off our feet and squeezed us.

"Good morning, Dad," our father greeted from the garage, where he stood wiping his hands on an oily rag. "Old Rosie sounds like she might need a tune-up. When I'm finished in here, we'll roll her inside and take a look under her hood."

Grandpa shook his head. "Just you never mind. Old Rosie's fine and dandy, thank you." He patted the chrome headlight perched atop its sweeping fender then polished it with his cloth. "I'll have you know that in thirty-six years, she's never once failed to bring me home or get me where I needed to be." He winked and rubbed the tops of our heads. "Gus, these boys are growing like weeds. You putting manure in their slippers at night? They're squeezing me so tight, I can't feel my feet."

Dad laughed. "Okay boys, let Grandpa be. You've got all day to play with him."

We let go and Danny and I rose onto our toes, trying to catch a glimpse of any presents hidden inside his car. Unfortunately, we weren't tall enough. Grandpa followed our line of sight and teased us by turning and looking inside too - his chin flapping like a helicopter coming in to land.

"Gus," he said, rubbing his belly. "I'm sure hungry. You don't suppose Colleen's got supper on the table?"

Dad smiled, as I tugged on Grandpa's arm. "No, Grandpa, you're just trying to make me wait for my birthday present."

"Birthday present?" He slapped his leg and shook his head. "Son of a gun. I knew there was something I was supposed to remember. I thought we made plans to go fishing. Last night I packed my pole and caught us some worms. Big night-crawlers." He stretched his arms wide. "Couldn't pull them out of the ground. Had to tie them around the trees and get the tractor to yank em out."

"No, Grandpa. After you got out, you looked inside. You're just trying to trick me."

"Yeah," Danny jumped in. "You looked inside when you saw us trying to."

Grandpa cackled and smiled. "Sweetpea, you're getting too smart for your britches." He tried to change the subject. "Did I ever tell you boys about the catfish I caught using one of my giant worms? Had to use the anchor for a hook. Darn fish was bigger than my boat."

Danny and I rolled our eyes.

"Give it up, Dad. They're onto you," our father said. "An anchor for a fishhook?" He chuckled.

"Well if I'd known you fellas wouldn't believe me, I'd have taken a photograph." Grandpa sighed. "Well, let's get this over with. Where's that wife of yours? I learned a long time ago not to hand out presents without approval from the head of the house."

Dad laughed. "Danny, go get your mother. She must not have heard your grandfather pull in."

Danny went inside and came right back out with Mom. She gave Grandpa a hug and kiss.

"I'm sorry, Daniel. I tried to come out when I heard you pull in but I had a cake in the oven. And you know how slow the minute's pass when you're watching the timer. It's good to see you. How have you been?"

"Never better, Colleen. Never better." Grandpa stood back and smiled. "Dang, you're more beautiful every time I see you. Why don't you come and live on the farm and leave these savages behind?"

"Don't tempt me." She winked. "I just might take you up on it."

"When I show him those pictures of you and Jack riding the bike this morning, he'll change his mind," Dad said.

"Don't you dare." Mom turned back to Grandpa. "What do you need me for?"

"Well, I've got birthday presents inside the car and I'd like your approval before I hand them out." He and Mom peered into the back seat. "What do you think? Is he old enough, or should I take it back?" He winked.

"Well," Mom said, playing along. "It is his ninth birthday. How be, I leave it up to you?"

"I saw him wink at you, Mom," I said.

They both laughed and Grandpa opened the door. He pulled out three fishing poles.

"I told you boys we we're going fishing. I got worms in the back, Cokes in the cooler and I'll bet your mother already has our sandwiches put together."

"They're inside on the table. I'll go get them." She went into the house.

Grandpa let me pick the pole I wanted and gave the others to Danny and Pauly. They were all the same, just different colours. This was his tradition. On our birthdays, he always gave us all the same thing, including Pauly.

"We're going fishing?" Pauly asked, his eyes as wide and round as saucers.

Mom returned and handed a couple of paper bags to our dad. "Your mother and I talked it about it this morning, Pauly. When you boys get back, we're going to have a barbeque and a birthday cake. Reg and Ida will be here too." She turned to Dad. "Are you leaving now, Gus?"

"Just as soon as I can get in the car," he said. "Everybody ready? I haven't had a ride in old Rosie in longer than I can remember."

Danny, Pauly, and I piled into the back after Grandpa put our fishing poles inside, then we backed onto the highway.

All we ended up catching were a couple of small perch and a sunfish. Nothing big enough to keep. We fished off the ferry dock in Port Lambton. There were a lot of boats running around and people swimming. Dad said that's why the fish weren't biting, they'd been scared off. Of course, Grandpa pretended he had a whale on the hook and yanked and played with it until his line broke, but I'd seen the current wrap it around one of the pilings.

When we got home, Pastor Reg and Ida were sitting in the backyard, talking with Mom and Hazel and Glenn Cook. There was food on the picnic table and Mom lit the barbeque. Danny and I showed everyone our new bikes. We rode them up and down the driveway a couple of times. Reg was especially happy. Afterwards he gave thanks for the opportunity of friends and family to get together and for Jesus healing my legs. Everyone agreed and said it was a miracle.

After supper, Danny looked for our Frisbee so we could play catch. He asked if I knew where it was.

"It's on the roof. Remember when Pauly threw it over your head? We didn't get it down because Dad came home." As soon as I said it, I knew I'd made a mistake. Danny had just got in trouble last week for climbing the antennae and promised not to do it again.

"What? You better not have been going up there," Dad said. "I told you boys, if you need something down, you come and get me. One of these days you're going to fall and break your neck." He shook his head and went into the garage for the ladder. He brought it out and leaned it against the eavestrough. "Whereabouts did it go up?"

"Right over the door," Danny said. "We waited for it to roll down, but it must have landed flat."

Another thought hit me and I spoke again without thinking. "Our old yellow Frisbee's up there too, leaning against the front of the chimney. I saw it."

Dad stopped and looked at me.

Uh oh.

"You saw it? Okay, which one of you is going to start telling me the truth? Now I find out you've both been up there?"

"I just saw it against the chimney, is all," I muttered.

Dad gave Danny a sharp look. "Didn't I tell you to leave the ladder in the garage and stay off the roof?"

"I did, Dad, honest. I don't know what he's talking about. I never touched the ladder or the antennae. Not after you told me. And I never saw him go up there either."

Dad turned to me. "Jack, when did you see the Frisbee on the roof?"

I felt so stupid. I'd seen it in my flying dream but I couldn't say that. Even I didn't really believe it was up there. The dream had just seemed so real, the words had popped from my mouth.

"I'm waiting. When were you on the roof?"

"I wasn't on the roof," I said to my feet.

"Then how do you know it's up there?"

I couldn't think of any way out, other than to tell the truth.

"Jack?"

"I just saw it, that's all." I hated to look foolish in front of Reg and Grandpa.

"I'm not asking you again."

I kicked the grass and looked to my mom. I needed someone to believe me. "I saw it when I was sleeping, Mom. Really. I only saw it in my flying dream and I wasn't thinking and just said it's up there. I swear, I never climbed on the roof." Mom could usually tell when I was telling the truth. I hoped this was one of those times.

She reached out and took my hand. "Gus, Jack couldn't get the ladder out by himself. It's too heavy. And he certainly couldn't climb onto the roof. He's just mixed up and thinking about his dream. Come here, Sweetpea. There's no need to get upset. The silly thing isn't up there anyways."

I let her put her arm around me and didn't look at anyone. "But Mom," I whispered, "What if it's really there? I saw Danny's bike in the backyard too, and the window open in Dad's truck."

"What's that?" Dad asked.

I hung my head. I didn't think he could hear me. "I said I saw Danny's bike outside and the window open in your truck."

Everyone sat silent.

"Well, there's only one way to get to the bottom of this," Grandpa said. "Gus, I'll hold the ladder. You go on up and take a look." He straightened it and Dad disappeared. A moment later Dad came back, holding both Frisbees. He climbed down, handed me the yellow one and then walked around the side of the house. Grandpa followed him. No one said a word. A couple of minutes later, they came back and sat.

"Jack," said Dad. "When did you see the window open in my truck?"

Dang. He wasn't going to let this go. I looked at Grandpa. He was watching me with a funny smile on his face.

"I only saw it in my flying dream," I whined. "Really, Dad. And I saw Danny's bicycle in the backyard too. But this morning when I got up, it was inside next to mine."

Dad looked at Mom. "Colleen, when I went to the store last night, I forgot I'd put the window down. I didn't remember until after we went to bed. I had to get up to close it." He paused. "Jack couldn't know that. I went to the store after he went to sleep. I also put Danny's bike inside." He shook his head. "The Frisbee was right where he said it was. And Dad and I checked, you couldn't see it from the ground."

"He saw it in his flying dream," Danny stated, matter of factly. "Pauly told me about the one he had last week and last night I helped him have another one."

"Sweetpea," Reg said, "I'd like to hear about this flying dream."

I'd already told Mom and Dad about it. I didn't want Danny to hear about it too. He'd tease me about Tika.

"I'd also like to hear about it," Grandpa said.

I could see I wasn't going to win this one either, so I started at the beginning and told them everything. About Danny helping me, how I flew over Walpole Island and the school and the farms and soared with the stars. I described seeing the horses race through the grass and how the leader pointed me towards town when Tika cried. I told them how I picked her up and saved her from the badman, landing on the roof of the church, her eagle bracelet, and taking her home after the man with the spear had said it was safe.

Everyone sat quietly and listened without interrupting. I looked into each of their faces. They knew it was just a dream. An amazing one, but a dream nonetheless. And I knew it didn't explain how the Frisbee was where I saw it. I wish it hadn't been. I wished I'd been wrong.

Grandpa was the first to speak. "Sweetpea, tell us more about these men on horseback. How many did you say there were?" He leaned forward in his chair, his head turned with his good eye focused upon me. His chin had stopped flapping.

"There were five, Grandpa. And even though it was a little bit dark, I could see that their horses were different colors. The leader's was white, and it was bigger and faster."

"And how were they dressed? You said like on TV?"

"Yes, like in a movie. The leader's shirt was made from rows of sticks with little feathers on it." I tried to remember more. I pictured him standing next to his horse. "And he was wearing moccasins, and even though he had on pants, he also wore a little dress."

Danny snickered.

"I believe what Jack is describing, Danny," Grandpa said, "is what the native people call a breechcloth. It was used to cover the front and back of their leggings. The legs weren't sewn together like we do today. His shirt sounds like a breastplate. The sticks are bones, but from a distance it would be difficult to tell. It was a garment worn by a warrior."

Geez. I didn't know Grandpa knew so many things.

"Daniel," Mom said, "I didn't know you were so knowledgeable about native culture. This must be an interest of yours."

He smiled. "You forget my age, Colleen. When I was a boy, there were still natives living on the plains in Manitoba and Saskatchewan. Their culture and spirituality were always of great interest to Honor and I." He looked at me. "Sweetpea, you said he was carrying a spear?"

"Yes, it was long and had feathers on it." I was starting to feel important.

"That would be a lance, more of an ornamental weapon." Grandpa leaned back in his chair. "Well, I think you've had yourself a wonderful dream." He paused. "This little girl that lived with her grandmother, what did you say her bracelet looked like?"

"She let me hold it, Grandpa. It was beautiful. It was made of bones and copper and beads and looked like an eagle. Her necklace was made the same way."

"If I showed you a picture, would you recognize one like it?

"I think so." I remembered something else. "She said it was a gift from her grandmother Rose. She lived with her and her uncle." I chuckled and shook my head. "She asked me if I was her garden spirit."

"I believe she said guardian spirit, Sweetpea."

"Jack," Pauly said.

"Yes?"

"You have to stay away from the badman. If he catches you, he will hurt you real bad."

I smiled. "No, he won't." Between him and Danny and Mom and Dad and Grandpa and Reg, I couldn't see how anyone could hurt me. Or why they'd want to. "When he tried to grab me, I flew away, and he isn't real. He was just in a dream."

"But it was a true dream."

"Pauly," his mother said, "Don't be trying to scare Jack. I don't want to hear any more of that talk. There's no such thing as a true dream." She turned to my mom. "I'm sorry, Colleen. You know he doesn't mean any harm."

Pauly started to hiccup and Mom patted his hand.

"Hazel, you don't need to apologize, and Pauly, neither do you. I know you just worry about Jack because he's your friend. But it was a dream and it's over now and he's sitting right next to us. There's no need to worry."

"Well, if you folks don't mind," Grandpa said, "I've got to skedaddle. Old Rosie don't like being out after dark." He folded his chair and leaned it against the garage. "Colleen, that was a terrific meal. I believe I put on five pounds." He gave her a hug and turned to Reg. "It's too bad you didn't arrive earlier. You could have come fishing with us. But I'll be sure to tell your father I ran into you. We spoke last week at the granary. He's got a fine-looking crop this year."

Reg stood. "It was wonderful seeing you too, Daniel. Next time Ida and I visit Dad, we'll stop in for one of your Cokes."

"Please do," Grandpa said. He shook Reg's hand and gave Ida a hug. He looked at me. "Well birthday boy, you sure gave me something to think about on the drive home." He rubbed the top of my head. "Give me a hug." I squeezed him as hard as I could. He hadn't put on five pounds. It was still like hugging a bag of nails. Grandpa held onto me longer than usual. "You be careful on that new bike, you hear."

"I will, Grandpa. Thank you for my fishing pole."

He gave Danny and Pauly a hug too. "You're a good friend, Pauly. It makes me happy knowing that you're around to keep an eye on Sweetpea. And Danny, you stay off that roof or I'll be chasing you with a willow switch." He laughed and rubbed his head. "Good night, Mr. and Mrs. Cook. That's a fine boy you have there." He turned to Dad. "Gus, before I forget. What's the chance of you and the family coming out to the farm tomorrow? I've got a couple things I need a hand with and I'd like to have a talk with you."

"Sounds good. Colleen, do we have any other plans?"

"No. We'd love to visit. How be we drive up after lunch?"

"It's a date."

We walked Grandpa to his car and waved goodbye as he backed onto the road. Reg and Ida left shortly afterwards, as did the Cook's. Pauly didn't want to leave though. I could tell that he was still worried about the badman. I didn't think until later that I should have told him it couldn't have been a true dream, because I still didn't know how to fly.

Danny and I went to bed early so we wouldn't have long to wait before going to Grandpa's. I didn't smell anything bad and slept without any nightmares or dreams - for the first time that I could remember.

17

A Good Boy

Pauly wasn't happy. He hadn't slept well and this morning didn't feel like playing with his toys. He pushed them under his bed and straightened the sheets so they couldn't be seen. In his world, everything had to be kept in its proper place. It was far too easy for him to trip over or lose something that was right under his nose. He leaned back against his dresser and frowned.

All he ever wanted, besides going to school with the other children, was to be a good boy. With his parent's assistance, he'd even developed a list of five rules to help him. They were simple. All he had to do was never lie, say bad words, hurt anyone, take anything that didn't belong to him, and always be happy. But lately Pauly found it impossible to be happy. How could he be, when no one would listen when he tried to tell them that Jack was in danger?

Ever since the night they'd poured oil over Jack's head and prayed for his legs to get better, Pauly had been scared. He'd even cried and couldn't say why. All he knew was that a terrible feeling came over him that something bad was going to happen, and he needed to protect his friend. And then, after learning last night about Jack's flying dream and the badman grabbing him, his fears only grew worse.

Pauly didn't know what to do. When he tried to tell everyone the badman was real and wanted to hurt Jack, they wouldn't listen. And now his mother said he couldn't talk about it anymore. Pauly could never do what he was told not to. So, now he had six things on his good boy list and this last one didn't make things any easier.

Why was he the only person who believed in true dreams? Pauly didn't understand it. Didn't plenty of other people have them too? And even if they didn't, when one of his came true and they'd been in it, why didn't they remember? Especially Jack? He was the one who'd visited him in his sleep before he was born and told him they were going to be best friends. Heck, he'd even told Jack's mom that she had a baby in her belly before he knew that's where they came from.

Dang, now he felt even worse. Inside his head, he'd just said the 'h' word. He bit his lower lip to fight back tears. Why wouldn't anyone listen to him? Pauly hated feeling this way. Now his head was going to get all jumbled up and he'd never be able to figure out what to do. If only they'd let him go to school.

Everyone who met Pauly learned quickly that he was not stupid. Unfortunately, children born with cerebral palsy were considered mentally handicapped and there were no public facilities to educate them. Instead, they were all lumped together, despite their varying levels of disability, leaving their families with one of two choices. They could either commit their child to an institution or keep them home and do their best to meet their special needs. Fortunately for Pauly, Hazel and Glenn Cook were as exceptional as he.

They knew their son wasn't mentally challenged. In fact, quite the opposite. Sure, he had difficulty reading and writing was out of the question, due to the spastic nature of his hands, but he was smart. His manner of retaining and processing information just happened to be different. The fact he couldn't walk and talk as well as others, only made them more determined to teach him to use his other assets to the best of his abilities.

They practiced for hours teaching him how to ask simple questions and demand simple answers. Then they taught him how to use his extraordinary memory to retain what he'd learned, through visualization and association tricks, which helped with more difficult words and concepts.

One funny side effect was the nickname he'd given Gus. For whatever reason, Pauly always had difficulty saying, 'Mr. Trapper', and then one day he blurted out the picture of him that he'd created in his mind. He called Gus 'Fatboy.' Gus had laughed. He knew Pauly would never say anything to hurt anyone, and he had to agree, he'd put on a few extra pounds. He responded by calling Pauly, Wolly, as in, 'Polly, Wolly doodle all the day.' With the end result that Pauly learned a new song and the two became even closer friends.

Pauly also learned that he needed to pay more attention to what was going on around him, not only with his eyes and ears, but also with his intuition. He spent hours watching workmen repair the road, restring telephone wires, construct homes and perform other activities, all the while learning that there were steps necessary to completing difficult tasks. In the meantime, he also became the eyes and ears of the neighborhood, at times drawing the attention of children whose parents were as misinformed as they. More than once he'd endured taunts and name calling, but only twice did he experience physical bullying. Pauly was as big and strong as his father. He found that all he needed to do was wrap his arms around a couple of the bigger boys and the others left him alone. Which was all he'd been after. Pauly would never hurt anyone. He really was a good boy.

His mom called from downstairs. "Pauly, let's go next door and visit Jack and Colleen."

"Okay."

He found her waiting at the back door.

"You're not going to bring any of your toys?"

"No."

Hazel straightened his dark curly hair with her fingers, brushing it back from his eyes. "What's the matter, Pauly? You've been so unhappy lately. It's not like you. Is there something you'd like to talk about? Or would you rather just stay indoors?"

"No." He'd already tried everything he could think of to get her to listen. Until she was willing to believe in true dreams, there was nothing more for him to say. Of course, he wanted to visit his friend.

Hazel opened the door.

Outside it was hot and sticky with no breeze. The kind of weather Pauly hated most. It made his shirt and pants stick to him and he didn't like the feel of material clinging to his body. It also restricted his movements, making it easier for him to fall. By the time they reached next door, he was drenched with sweat. They stepped onto the porch. Colleen was visible inside, through the screen door.

"Good morning," Hazel greeted.

Colleen turned and smiled. "Good morning, you two. Come on in. I was just going to pour myself a glass of ice tea. Would you like one?"

"I'd love one," Hazel replied.

"Good morning, Pauly," Colleen said, over her shoulder. "Jack's in his room."

Pauly tried to smile because he liked Mrs. Trapper, but it was too hard. He stood with his eyes lowered.

"What's the matter, Pauly? I hope you don't think I'm upset with you?" Colleen glanced at Hazel, who raised her eyebrows and shrugged.

"Is Jack happy today?" Pauly mumbled.

"I think so," Colleen replied. "He slept well last night." She turned and faced him. "I'll tell you what though. Sometimes he won't tell me how he's feeling, but I know you can always tell. Could you do me a favor? Could you tell me what you think, after you've finished playing?

A spark of happiness lit inside his chest. Despite himself he looked up and smiled. He knew what she was doing. She was treating him like a big boy.

"Okay," he said, as he turned towards the hall, his chest a little thicker.

"Thanks, Pauly. You're a good friend."

"You're welcome. I'm going to play with Jack now."

Pauly found his friend in his bedroom, sitting on the floor between the beds. Jack was wearing his overalls again and the funny glasses with the mustache. In his lap was an open book.

"What are you doing, Sweetpea?"

Jack looked up. "Hi, Pauly. I'm looking at pictures of Indians from a long time ago." He turned the book so he could see.

Pauly's eyes widened. He liked books, although he hadn't learned to read well. He sat next to Jack. "Wow. I've never seen pictures like that before. Why are you looking at them?"

"I just wanted to. That's all."

"Was the book in your room?"

"No."

"Did you have to go get it?

"Yes."

"Are you looking for the person from your dream?" Pauly made extra special sure not to say badman.

"No, I just wanted to find a picture of a man wearing a..." Jack searched for the word he was looking for in the description below the photo. "A breastplate. Grandpa said they were made of bones and warriors wore them when they were fighting, so they wouldn't get hurt. I just wanted to see what one looked like."

"His shirt is made of bones?"

"Yeah."

"What kind of bones?"

"I don't know."

'People bones?"

"I don't think so. They're little bones. It says here they're called pipe bones. I'll ask Grandpa today where they come from. He'll know."

Pauly watched Jack turn the page and look at other pictures.

"Where's Danny?"

Jack didn't look up. "He went for a bike ride to his friends."

"To Billy's house?"

"I don't know. Maybe."

"Is he coming back soon?"

"I think so. He left a little while ago."

"Oh." Pauly wanted to talk with Danny. He created a picture in his mind of him riding his bike and saved it with a big number two.

Jack turned the page. There were pictures of men on horses and people standing in small groups in front of pointy tents. Pauly didn't pay any more attention.

"Do you feel good today? Are you happy?" Pauly asked. He erased a big number one from his memory.

Jack looked up. Pauly could tell that he knew what he meant. His friend seemed to look right through him, at something inside his head.

"I think so. A little bit."

Pauly waited for him to continue. It's funny how sometimes you know a person is going to keep talking. Jack didn't disappoint him.

"Pauly, do you really think that my flying dream was a true dream?"

Uh oh. He hadn't expected that. Pauly sat quiet. He wanted so badly to answer but couldn't figure out how, without breaking rule number six. When he didn't say anything, Jack continued.

"How does it feel when you have a true dream?"

That was easy. Pauly had thought about this lot of times. "True dreams are like right now, when you hear things and smell things and feel things and you know you're not dreaming." He poked Jack in the ribs. Jack giggled. "See? Regular dreams don't feel like that. Regular dreams are like TV." Pauly hoped that he'd explained it right. He remembered something else. "True dreams, you remember everything that happened too. Even after you wake up."

"I remember everything from my flying dream," Jack said. "But how could it be a true dream when I can't fly? People don't fly."

There was rule number six again. Pauly sat quiet.

"Pauly, how do you know you're supposed to call them true dreams?"

"Because that's what my father said they are."

"Your father has true dreams?"

"No." At least Pauly didn't think so. "Before you came from your mom's stomach, when I told him we played together and were going to be best friends, Dad said I only had a dream I *wished* would come true. He said people do that all the time."

Pauly smiled, proud of how he'd figured it out. "So, when my dream came true, I knew it had to be a true dream." How could anyone argue with that?

Jack turned the book over on his lap. They both looked out the bedroom window. A big cloud, square and puffy like a marshmallow, was floating by. Pauly waited.

"Pauly, did you really have a dream about playing with me before I was born?"

"Yes."

"What was I like? Was I little or big like now?"

"Like now," Pauly said. Even though he'd told Jack about it a thousand times, he enjoyed retelling the story. "I was playing outside and all of a sudden you were there. You told me who you were and then we played with my toys. We were best friends right away. When you said, it was time for you to go, you told me you'd be back as soon as you came from your mother's stomach." Pauly smiled at the memory. "I didn't even know that's where babies came from. In the morning, after I got up, I asked your mom if it was true, if there was a baby in her belly. She said yes and I told her about you."

Pauly remembered sitting at the kitchen table with Fatboy and Mrs. Trapper. His mother and father had been there too. At first everyone laughed, but then they decided he must have heard someone say she was pregnant. They didn't understand. He hadn't heard that word before either.

"Pauly," Jack whispered. "Sometimes I'm scared."

Pauly didn't expect to hear that. Jack was the bravest kid he knew. All the things that had been happening to him lately, his shaking and getting sick and having nightmares. Pauly had never considered that Jack was frightened. Sure, sometimes after a nightmare he cried, but who wouldn't? He'd cried too after Jack screamed about the green eyes trying to get him. In fact, it still scared him.

"I think there's something bad inside of me that wants to take me away."

That terrified Pauly. On the spot, he became even more determined to protect him.

"Sometimes my body does things and I don't know why," Jack said. "And sometimes when I go to sleep, I smell something bad. It waits for me to close my eyes and then it grabs me and won't let go. It smells terrible and I don't know if it's ever going to let me come back." Jack paused, as though he were afraid to share a secret. "Pauly, Danny says that sometimes I scream during the night, but when I wake up, I don't remember."

Pauly shuddered. He knew. He'd heard Jack. Their bedroom windows were right across from each other and because it was summer, they were usually open. He'd never told anyone but whenever Jack had a nightmare, it seemed to wake him. A couple of nights ago, he hadn't even closed his eyes when he'd heard Jack scream and seen his light come on.

Jack started to shake and looked up. His eyes were red and wet in the corners. Pauly hiccupped and his bottom lip shook as he gulped for air.

Jack patted his shoulder. "I'm sorry. I didn't mean to scare you."

Pauly sniffed and wiped his face. There was one question he wanted to ask but he'd have to break rule number six. How was he supposed to stay good and protect his friend at the same time? He might never get this chance again. "Jack," he said, without looking up.

"What, Pauly?"

He didn't answer.

Jack shook his shoulder. "What, Pauly?"

Pauly had to know. He whispered as though his mother were sitting on the floor beside them. "When you had your flying dream, did you see lights shooting across the sky?"

"Like shooting stars?"

"Yes."

"They were beautiful," Jack exclaimed. "Sometimes they shot down to the ground and other times they shot into the sky." He bent forward and looked into his eyes. "How do you know about them, Pauly? Have you had a flying dream too?"

No, he'd never had a flying dream. But every true dream he'd ever had, the sky was full of shooting stars. He couldn't let Jack know this. Then Jack would know that his dream was true, that Tika was real and the badman too. Pauly's parents would be really angry with him then. Pauly sniffed and hiccupped again. "No, I've never had a flying dream," he answered, truthfully.

"Then how do you know about the lights and the shooting stars?"

"I just wondered," Pauly said, keeping his head down and his face turned away.

18

Into the Misery

Despite the steady patter of overnight showers thrumming against the metal roof of his farmhouse, Daniel hadn't slept well. His discomfort began before his drive home. A trip he couldn't recall, other than backing down his son's lane and parking Rosie in the barn. The rest was a foggy blur, his grandson's story had so dumbfounded him. In bed, he'd replayed the events of his rescue in the Misery over and over again, matching details that squared against Jack's dream. Or the boy's vision as he'd come to consider it. In his mind, there was no more appropriate description. There were just too many similarities and Daniel didn't believe in happenstance. In his experience, the unexplainable almost always was, after a person boiled off fanciful human desire and faulty memory.

Daniel made toast and coffee then straightened the house. It didn't take him long. He'd lived within these walls his entire life and although housework wasn't something he enjoyed, as a widower it had become a necessary evil. Daniel didn't put much stock in structure other than in the planting and reaping of his fields, which gave him enormous pleasure. To him life consisted of two distinct parts - the necessary and the enjoyable, partaking in the wonders provided by the creator. It just so happened that in his particular situation, the two had always been closely entwined.

He pulled out his books on native culture and sat at the table. Though he hadn't looked through them in years, there was nothing in particular he searched for, other than comfort in familiarity. Before he realized it, the morning had passed. His son and family would be arriving soon. He put his books away and went outside.

A light breeze from the west was taking with it most of the day's humidity. Everything smelled fresh and clean and there wasn't a cloud in the sky when he pulled his old Ferguson tractor from the barn. It was a '46, imported from England after the war. Too small for heavy field work but perfect to harrow his land or to pull the small wagon he'd hitched behind it. Daniel ran it down the lane and around the yard before shutting it off in the shade of the willow, the engine ticking as the block cooled and oil drained from its head. He leaned forward in the seat, his arms loose about the wheel as he scanned the outer edge of the forest bordering his land.

"Skunk's Misery," he whispered.

Daniel smiled and shook his head, amazed at the pull it still had on him. The same yank it exerted when he was a boy. Daniel couldn't remember a time when his mind or thoughts weren't drawn toward it. The thick woods as much a part of him as an arm or a leg. Or an eye, he thought wryly.

Daniel had hunted and trapped the Misery since he was a child, at times spending days crossing its grasslands, wetlands, and watercourses, hunting quail, deer, coon, and even bear. Back then it had covered hundreds of thousands of acres, stretching sixty miles from London to the east, Bothwell to the west and south to the shore of Lake Erie. These were the woods where Tecumseh, the Shawnee Chief, had been killed in the Battle of the Thames. A Carolinian forest, it contained a variety of trees more typical of a southern climate, such as chestnut, tulip, dogwood, and sassafras. Now, seventy years later, after continuous agricultural expansion and forestry, its size had been reduced to one tenth its former glory. A dang shame and the reason why much was now held in public ownership through conservationists. And why Daniel himself had been purchasing tracts as they became available over the years.

Today he planned to take Gus, Colleen and the boys, deep into what once had been its heart. To a spot a little less than twelve miles away, where the Thames River looped around the edge of a newly proposed conservation area. One of two pieces of land containing black oaks, grassland and marsh that he'd offered to donate under the condition of anonymity. An old man's foible but one for which he felt most passionate. Daniel climbed down and arranged the cushions on the bench of the wagon. He wanted Colleen as comfortable as possible.

His son's wife reminded Daniel a great deal of his late wife, Honor, or Great Honor as he'd addressed her when the two of them were alone. Because that's what Daniel always knew had been bestowed upon him when she'd agreed to be his wife. They'd married late, in their early thirties, through no fault of hers after being sweethearts since first meeting at the Cairo schoolhouse. After his accident and disfigurement, he'd withdrawn, ashamed to hold her to any conceptions they'd made. Fortunately, Great Honor had been wiser. She'd waited almost seventeen years for him to return to his senses. Daniel smiled as he remembered the day he approached her after spring services in Newbury. Honor had always made a point of smiling and waving to him whenever she'd seen him in town, while he'd look away and pretend not to notice. But on this day, after a rousing sermon about everyone being responsible for their own happiness, he'd smiled back and sought her out afterwards at the picnic in the yard.

"Well now, look who's decided to grace us with his presence," she needled, as he cut behind her in the serving line.

Daniel's face warmed as he shifted so his scars and counterfeit eye weren't visible.

"Daniel," she said, turning to face him and brushing the hair from his temples. "I can't believe how well your scars have healed. It's certainly given you a most rugged, handsome look." Her smile washed away all his fears. "You know, after all these years, I still find it hard to believe you're the same gangly boy who used to chase me around the schoolyard."

And just like that they were a couple again. They shared a table, eating, talking, and laughing about the years gone by, as though none had passed. Six months later at the fall festival, at the same church, by the same pastor, they married.

Subconsciously Daniel raised his fingers to the hollow next to his left eye, where the corner of his orbital bone had been blown away.

"Oh, Great Honor," he whispered. "I miss you terribly. But every day I feel your presence and today I especially need you near." His eye watered as he lowered his head. "Somehow my love, I may have found an answer to what happened all those years ago, and I'm not sure if I can face it alone. Please darling, strengthen me as you always have."

Daniel wiped his face with his sleeve and started towards the house. He made it halfway when Gus pulled in off the highway, Colleen and the boys waving from their open windows.

"Grandpa," Danny yelled, after he slammed his door and raced across the yard. "Mom says it's okay to ask if we can go for a ride in the forest later, after you and Dad are finished. Can we, please?"

"Yeah," Jack echoed. "We promise we'll be good."

Daniel smiled and rubbed their heads. "Well, isn't that a coincidence. That's exactly what I had in mind. I've already got the wagon hitched and parked out by the willow and I was heading indoors to pack my cooler. Why don't you boys come along and give me a hand."

"Pauly came too," said Jack. "Can he come?"

Daniel laughed. "Of course." He turned and looked for Pauly, who was sliding out the rear door. "Good afternoon, Pauly."

Pauly's face split into a wide smile. "Hi, Grandpa."

Colleen gave Daniel a hug. "I'm sorry, Daniel, I told the boys to ask you later. I know there's something you wanted Gus to give you a hand with."

"There is," he said. "But it's not on the farm, Colleen. I'm sorry if I've misled you, but I was planning on taking everyone for a ride into the Misery. The something I need a hand with is out there."

"What's that?" Gus asked.

"I'm not saying. You're just going to have to wait and find out." Daniel turned and gazed toward the trees. "It's probably something I should have done years ago, but I believe now's as good a time as any."

"Hmm, he won't tell us. I like a mystery." Colleen smiled. "Well boys, let's give Grandpa a hand getting ready. How long will we be, Daniel? Would you like me to pack some sandwiches or a snack?"

He smiled. "I've already put supplies together. They're inside, in the fridge. I was just going to throw them into a cooler, along with some water." Daniel looked again at the Misery. "I figure we'll be gone most of the afternoon. We're going to a spot along the Thames, through my favorite part of the woods. I've put extra cushions in the wagon so you'll be comfortable. Gus and the boys can fend for themselves."

Colleen smiled. "You're so wonderful. Why couldn't your son be more like you?"

"Phht." Gus nodded towards the tractor. "Have you fueled it, Dad?"

"I was going to, right after I finished inside. I'll tell you what though. If you wouldn't mind running it out to the pump, you can pick us up at the house afterwards. We'll be waiting."

One of the things Daniel loved most about the Misery, was how it seemed to embrace you the moment you entered. After less than a couple of hundred feet, the temperature under the canopy of leaves dropped to a more comfortable level and then the sounds of the birds and insects took over. The rapid-fire knock of a woodpecker on a hollow tree. The melodious whistle of a warbler, keeping track of where others sat and the constant chorus of katydids and grasshoppers as background music. Daniel drove a few yards further then shut the tractor down.

"Grandpa, why are we stopping?" Jack asked.

"Shhh." Daniel turned and put a finger to his lips. He knew this was likely the only chance he'd have for the boys to remain quiet. "Sit still for a minute, Sweetpea. It's quiet now but in a moment, you're going to hear one bird call and then another, and then the whole forest is going to come to life. Sit still, listen, and enjoy."

Everyone remained quiet.

The sharp chirp of a flycatcher came first, followed by another and then the hesitant rattle of an oriole, checking to make sure everything was safe. There was a quick answer from behind and the forest burst into sound. It lasted forty-five seconds before Jack yelled, "Hey, Danny, look at that big moth."

Gus and Daniel chuckled and Colleen squeezed his arm. "Thanks, Daniel, that was beautiful, as long as it lasted."

"You're welcome, Colleen," Daniel said. "You know, the Misery's a whole different world when a person's on foot. I dislike bringing the tractor in here, but these paths have been used for logging and getting about for a hundred years. I still like to make as little dent as possible though." He started the engine. "Well, we've got a nice ride ahead of us. Sweetpea, you try counting how many different birds, butterflies and moths you see. I'll bet you run out of numbers." He chuckled, threw the tractor in gear and they continued down the path.

Twenty minutes later they came out of the forest onto a gravel road. Daniel followed it for half a mile before turning through an opening in a fence row, then back onto the path through the trees.

He spoke over his shoulder. "In a couple of minutes, we'll cross Highway 2. I'll pull over and show you where the Battle of the Thames was fought by Tecumseh and Proctor in 1813. Although there's no evidence of the fight today, it'll give us a chance to stretch our legs and have a drink. Then in less than fifteen minutes, we'll reach our destination."

Daniel was right. Nothing marked where the battle had been fought, although as a boy, he told them he'd dug many arrowheads and musket balls from the trees. Daniel thought it a shame that no monument or memorial had been erected in memory of the great chief. His exploits so disregarded in Canada, while his concern for his people, leadership, and battlefield expertise, were revered by the Americans, who honored him with a statue at the Naval Academy in Annapolis.

After a short break, they climbed back into the wagon.

"We're going back onto gravel as there's no access from the north. We've another four, four and a half miles. Then we'll circle in from the east, with the last mile down a lane Honor and I created over the years."

"You came here often enough to make a lane?" Colleen asked.

Daniel smiled wistfully. "Yes. We made this trip a couple of dozen times each summer. The last, just a week before she passed. It was something we both wanted to enjoy one last time."

After turning off the gravel and down a narrow lane, it was obvious this was the path the little tractor had created. Tall grass and thick bush grew tight to its sides and scraped against the bottom of the wagon. The vegetation quite different from what they'd been travelling through. At times grassland along the bank of the Thames, at others scrub brush and scattered trees.

Daniel read their thoughts. "Here along the river are more open sections than just about anyplace else in the Misery. I'm not exactly sure why, though I assume it has to do with snowmelt and runoff. Just ahead we're going back into the trees, into my favorite part. One of the few areas that still has old growth hardwood."

A few minutes later they were back in the shade. Daniel shut the engine off and climbed down.

"We'll walk the rest of the way. It's only about three hundred yards." He picked up his cooler from the wagon. "Gus, I threw a couple of lawn chairs under the bench." He pointed. "Right there, under the corner. Would you mind bringing them along?"

"I'll carry one, Grandpa," Danny offered.

"Me too," Jack said.

"No, Jack," Gus said. "You walk with Pauly and your mother. Danny and I will carry the chairs."

Daniel led the way. The path was shaded and cool, running close to the water of the Thames. The insects and birds quite a bit more raucous here, due to the proximity of the water. Colleen also thought she could smell the scent of wildflowers.

Daniel stopped where the trail turned right and followed the waterway. "If you don't mind, I'd like you folks to go ahead by yourselves," he said, as he sat on his cooler. "Just follow the river and you'll come upon a stand of black oaks. Carry through and you'll know where we're stopping when you get there. I'll be along in a few minutes"

"I'll stay with you, Daniel. Gus and the boys can go ahead," Colleen said.

"No, Colleen, if you don't mind, I'd like a few minutes to myself. I haven't made this trip without Honor in over forty years. I'd like to have a couple of words with her beforehand."

Colleen squeezed his shoulder. "You take as long as you'd like then. We'll be waiting for you. Are you sure we'll know when we get there?"

"Oh, I'm sure you'll know."

Gus, Colleen and the boys continued on.

"Remember, follow the river all the way into the tall oaks."

"Okay," Gus said. "We'll see you in a bit."

Daniel watched them turn and follow the waterway. He'd never considered bringing anyone here other than his wife. That had been difficult enough. He looked at the trees surrounding him and closed his eye. Sixty-three years. How could that be possible? When he wanted to, he could still bring the pictures to mind as though it were yesterday. And wasn't that exactly what he'd done last night in bed? Daniel prayed that he was doing the right thing. He'd already promised himself that he'd take his cues from his son and his wife. They'd talk openly and Daniel would accept whatever decision they made. He said a short prayer, asking for guidance and strength. He could feel Honor by his side.

"Well, Great Honor. There isn't much more to say. Please watch over me and help me do the right thing. I love you." Daniel rose, picked up his cooler and followed the others.

Colleen was sitting in the middle of the large clearing when he stepped around the oak with the scar on its trunk. Gus was standing on the bank with one eye on the boys, the other on the meadow. Pauly sat on shore while Danny and Jack were ankle deep in the water, splashing each other. Daniel set his cooler down and his daughter-in-law turned to face him.

"Oh, my Lord," Colleen said. "I've never seen anything like this. It's so beautiful." She gazed about in a circle, her eyes wide and her mouth open as she raised both arms to envelop the view. "Daniel, who did all of this? Who takes care of everything? What's it all for? Was this Honor's creation?"

Daniel smiled with his lips pursed as he enjoyed her awe at the thousands of wildflowers in bloom within the dale. There were Bur Marigolds, Bell Flower, Bellwort, Black-eyed Susan, Blazing Stars, Buttercups, Canada Lilies, Chicory, Daisies, Dogbane, Dogtooth Violets, and those were just some of the b's, c's and d's. He couldn't remember all their names, but he knew there were over two hundred different types, surrounded by a half dozen varieties of roses, their pink, white and red petals spread wide in the afternoon sun. And they looked as spectacular as he'd suspected they might, after last night's showers and today's brilliant sunshine.

"It is breathtaking, isn't it?" Daniel sat on his cooler and gazed in admiration. "Those roses to the left of that oak with the scar on it, were the first flowers Honor planted here. That would be in '22. They're prairie wild roses. To the right of the tree are Virginia wild roses and behind and around you are meadow, pasture, wood, prickly and shining roses. My favorites are these here, the climbing prairie rose." He pointed to a bush containing a burst of red and white flowers to his right.

"Why, Daniel? Whatever gave Honor this wonderful idea? Was it something she envisioned, or did it just keep expanding? I can't imagine how much work this must have been."

"Actually, Colleen, it was very little work. Finding the different flowers was the hardest part. All these plants are wild, chosen by Honor over the years. Some blossomed while others were unsuited to the conditions." Daniel swept his arm across their vision. "What you see now are the ones that through her trial and error, continue to thrive each year. They require no feeding or weeding. Though I must admit, Honor did like to baby them." He smiled at the memory of his wife clearing weeds and aphids from among the leaves. "As for the why..." He pointed to the oak with the scar three feet up its trunk. "That's the tree my rifle fired into, that cost me my eye."

"I thought this had something to do with your accident," Gus said. "But, Dad, why have you waited so long to show us this?"

Daniel lowered his head. "Well son, to be honest, it's not something I'm inclined to talk about, for my own selfish reasons. But something came up yesterday that seems to have changed all of that. Something I need to speak with you and Colleen about. I need your advice and opinion, and I've already promised myself that I'll abide by whatever you decide." He pointed to a spot next to Colleen. "Set your chair up here and let me get started before I change my mind. You're going to want to keep the boys from the river and I'd also prefer if they didn't hear what I'm about to say."

"Danny, Jack," Gus called. "Come on up and put your shoes on. There's plenty up here for you to explore."

The boys sat on the bank and slipped on their shoes. Danny tied Jack's, as he was still unable to bend over far enough to reach them.

"Can we go down the lane, to where the tractor is?' Danny asked. "I promise I'll keep an eye on them."

"No. Stick around here. You can play along the bank and a ways down the lane, but don't wander out of sight."

"Okay. Come on, Pauly. Let's go look for frogs and snakes." The three of them turned down the path they'd come in on.

"Okay," Daniel said, clearing his throat. "Honor began planting roses here right after she asked me to show her this place, so I'm going to start there, at the beginning, and tell you exactly what I told her. But first, I need a drink of water." He stood, opened his cooler and poured a cup from his thermos.

"Colleen? Gus?"

"No, thank you," they answered.

Daniel closed the lid and sat back down, taking a long sip as he gazed about the clearing.

"In January of 1904, I was fourteen years old." He looked up at the tops of the trees. "Mother said I spent more time in these woods than I did around the farm and she was right. I hunted, trapped and hiked out here so often, I knew every inch between London and Bothwell." He paused to choose his words.

"One day at school, a couple of boys were talking about an old cabin out here that was said to have been used by an outlaw before we were born. Well, like I said, it was the middle of January, a mild winter with hardly a trace of snow, so I decided to take a look. For whatever reason, I carried the .22 my father gave me for squirrels and rabbits, though I had no intention of using it." He shifted on the cooler.

"Anyhow, I found the cabin but it wasn't nearly old enough." He pointed in the direction from which they'd entered. "It's still down the trail just a bit. My hike had turned out to be a wild goose chase, so I turned and head for home. About this time, it started to snow and the temperature dropped. It was obvious we were in for one of those gales that blow in off Lake Erie. I wasn't worried though, like I said, I knew these woods better than the back of my hand and the worst that could happen was I'd have to make shelter and spend the night. I'd done that plenty of times, running my trap lines. Although I knew my mother would be worried. It being winter and all." He stopped, took another sip then gazed at the scarred oak.

"By the time I hit this clearing it was coming down so hard I could barely see, so I changed my mind and figured it best to stay west. I'd follow the river to Wardsville and then turn north towards home. It would cost me a bit of time but I knew some church folk out this way, in case I ran into trouble. Anyways, my bootlaces had become loose so I stopped next to that tree to tie them. When I bent to lean my rifle, I tripped on a branch buried in the snow. I fell forward, slammed the barrel into the tree and it fired, tearing off a chunk of bark where that scar is and depositing most of it in my eye and out the side of my face." Daniel shook his head. "By all rights, I should have died, but obviously, I didn't." He smiled. "I fell backwards, out cold. When I came to a couple of hours had passed. The snow had slowed and I was frozen near solid. I couldn't get up. My head was ringing and sorer than I thought possible. And I was tired. More tired than I've ever been, but I knew that was because of the cold. I didn't even have the energy left in me to shiver. I passed out again, thinking that was it."

He stood, walked to the river and stared at the water. A squadron of dragonflies were buzzing the surface in search of insects to eat. Daniel wiped his eye and returned to the cooler, his face turned to the ground.

"I feel like a fool."

"Daniel, of course you're going to feel emotional. I'd be amazed if you didn't," Colleen said.

"It's not that, Colleen. I cry like all of God's creatures. I just still cannot believe I shot myself in my own dang face, with my own dang gun, and then dang near froze to death."

Colleen laughed along with Gus. "Men. For the life of me, I'll never understand why you're all so stubborn and proud."

Daniel looked at his daughter in law and smiled. "That's exactly what Honor said when I sat next to her at the church picnic after seventeen years of hiding." He nodded at Gus. "You got yourself a keeper, son. I'm glad you realized it a hell of a lot quicker than I." He turned to make sure the boys were in sight. "Well, here's where things get interesting and where I need your help." He studied them both, determining whether to continue. He arrived at his decision.

"When I came around again there was a native girl, no older than myself, kneeling above me, holding my head. I was sure I was seeing things. She told me her name, said she'd heard my cry and was there to take me home." He sniffed and rubbed his eyes. "Like I said, I thought I was dreaming. She wasn't dressed for the cold. She didn't have on a coat, boots or gloves. Just when I was starting to believe that somehow she might be real, and was wondering how she planned to do that, I heard voices. I was rolled onto my side and a blanket was wrapped around me. Then she told me I was going to ride home on the back of a horse with her sitting behind me and that her friend would pick me up and set me on it."

Daniel stood and pointed to the right of the tree. "As God is my witness, there were five native men standing there, right beside me, and each of their horses a different colour." He shook his head. "And the men, they weren't dressed for winter either. They had on summer gear, in the middle of a dang blizzard. The leader wearing moccasins, leggings, a breastplate, and breechcloth." He paused and looked at them. "What Danny last night called a dress. And in his right hand, he held a long-feathered lance."

"What..." Colleen began.

"Please, Colleen, let me finish. I promise I'll answer all of your questions. But I know if I don't continue, I won't be able to. Other than Honor, you and Gus are the only people I've told this to in over sixty years."

He sat back down. "The next thing I know, I've been picked up and I'm sitting on a horse, being held from behind by this little girl. Then I believe I must have blacked out again because I don't remember anything until waking in our backyard, lying in our wagon. I don't know if I directed them home or told them where I lived. I have no idea how they knew that was the right place. When I opened my eye, she was tucking a blanket around me. She asked me my name and I believe I may have told her." He stood up abruptly. "I need another drink."

He filled his cup and remained standing.

"They left me in the wagon and as they rode off there was a yell. At first, I thought it might have been me, calling for help, but in the house my brother's and father said it sounded more like a whoop the natives might use. They opened the door and found me unconscious. I stayed that way for almost two weeks, which was a blessing, because it gave the doc time to take out what was left of my eye and the pieces of bone that had been blown from my skull." He raised his hand to the side of his face.

"The next morning, my brother Wymon went out to look for tracks, but the wind had come up during the night and filled them. Garnet, he rode into the Misery. He had a rough idea where I'd been headed and thought he might have better luck where the wind couldn't kick up as strong. Somehow, he found my rifle and one short stretch with just one set of footprints. Mine. There was no horse sign. When he came home, mother wouldn't allow my rifle in the house, so he took it into town and sold it. While he was there he asked questions and also at the farms on the way home. Nobody saw or heard a thing. We never found out who the natives were. In fact, other than my family, I don't think anyone believed me. Though how they figured I walked out on my own, half-blind, froze solid and with the side of my face blown off, I'll never understand."

He looked at Colleen. "Two months later, Garnet and I rode out here to look for sign. We searched and postulated and came up empty. After we returned and were putting our horses in the barn, we searched the wagon, which hadn't been used."

Daniel sat and reached into his shirt pocket, took out a leather bag that was tied at the top and handed it to Colleen.

"Garnet found what you're holding, underneath the seat, at the front. I figure she must have dropped it when she was tucking the blanket." He looked into Colleen's eyes. "One last thing before you look inside. Do you remember that I told you when the young girl found me, she said her name?"

Colleen nodded.

"The first flowers Honor planted are next to the tree. Now go ahead."

Colleen's fingers trembled as she untied the leather string.

Gus leaned forward, his eyes glued to the pouch. His wife's fingers slipped inside and she gasped as she pulled out a bracelet, made of copper, bone and colorful beads, intricately arranged in the image of a magnificent eagle.

"Her name was Rose," Gus whispered.

"That's right, son," Daniel said. He stood and faced the river. "Now how do you suppose Jack dreamed about the same horses, men, and the granddaughter of the woman who saved my life, sixty-three years ago?"

19

Smell the Flowers

Gus's mind went blank. He had no answer for his father. Perhaps it was from the emotions of the day, he didn't consider, didn't know and didn't care. He'd never experienced anything like this before. It seemed too many thoughts tried to butt in front of too many others and his mind simply emptied.

He rose and walked among the wildflowers. Unaware he was doing so. Dimly cognizant of the hum of the honey bees, the rush of the river and the birds chattering overhead, but otherwise completely lost. Circles. For some reason the only thought that held in his mind was circles.

Colleen nudged him from his reverie. "Gus, can you think of any other way?"

He didn't respond.

"Gus?"

"I'm sorry?" He glanced over his shoulder.

"I was asking if you thought it possible, Jack might have heard about your father's accident from someone else?"

Gus rubbed his forehead. "I'm sorry, Colleen. You're going to have to start over again. What is it you're asking?"

Daniel interrupted. "Colleen, other than Honor, you and Gus are the only people I've ever told. She would never have discussed it with the boys and my brothers have been gone for a number of years. There's no one left who could have told him."

Gus walked to the edge of the river. "You know Dad, it's funny you mentioning Mom."

"How's that?"

Gus picked up a stone and flipped it into the water. A kaleidoscope of colors glimmered on the waves as they spread and thinned. "Old Rosie." He smiled. "I remember the night Mom named her." He turned. A thin smile was upon his father's lips. "It was a bad storm then too. Remember?"

Daniel nodded. "You would have been about Danny's age."

"No, I was nine, the same age as Jack. It was in '41. You and Uncle Wymon drove to Peterborough to help Doris and Garnet with Rob, after he'd been sent home with injuries he'd received when his tank was hit." He looked at his father. "You know, I still remember counting the rings of the phone praying it was you. One short and one long..." Gus looked at his feet. "Mom was frantic. We'd been expecting you home the day before but on the radio, they said it was worse up north, with eleven, twelve foot drifts and temperatures of minus thirty-five."

"I was lucky," Daniel admitted. "I spent the night in the car on the side of the road. In the morning, I found that I'd stopped in front of a farm. They let me in and said the phones were out but I could try if I wanted." Daniel chuckled. "Your mother answered before the end of the second ring. Even Mr. Bell wouldn't let Honor down."

Gus looked at his wife. "Mom told Dad to stay where he was and ride it out. She told him we'd see him in a couple of days, but he said he could make it. We sat at the windows until midnight, waiting for his lights to appear. And then here he comes, pushing through drifts the tractor couldn't have busted through." Gus smiled and shook his head. "So, that's how the old car got its name. When Dad came through the door, Mom started to cry. She said, Daniel, I'm going to call that old car

Rosie because she's done it again. She's brought you home to me." Gus walked to his chair and sat. "It makes sense now, you're holding onto her all these years."

"I promised your mother I'd keep her, to look after me."

"So," Gus said. "Why can I think of nothing but circles."

"What?" Colleen asked.

"Circles," he replied. "Mom believed everyone in the world is connected. That every action we take comes back to us at a later date. If not before we die, then during judgement." Gus ran his fingers through his hair. "I don't know, maybe I'm just talking but that's what comes to mind. Circles. Maybe because this Rose saved your life, we're now a part of hers. Or maybe she's become a part of ours. Or maybe Jack just had a fantastic dream that seems to be related to your accident." He looked at his father. "I can't think anymore. Dad, you must have given this some thought. What would you like us to do?"

"I'm not one hundred percent sure, son. I do know that I don't want Jack to believe his dream might be anything more than that." Daniel sighed. "Last night Colleen, you were surprised at my interest in native culture and I wasn't entirely honest with you. The reason it took me eighteen years to marry Honor wasn't just because of this." He rubbed the side of his face. "For seventeen years, I searched for the people who saved me. I read everything I could about different tribes and their beliefs. I thought maybe the eagle on the bracelet or the way they dressed might lead me to them. Many nights I even camped in this clearing, hoping they'd return. I told Honor all of these things. She understood. She knew I needed closure. Someone to thank. In time, she too began to express interest."

Daniel looked at Gus. "The circle… Son, every native culture believes in the power of the circle. To them it represents life. The Earth, the moon, a tree trunk, a bird's nest, the seasons, the four directions." Daniel paused. "Black Elk, the famous Sioux chief, said everything tries to be round. Your mother found a great deal of common sense in that." He stood. "The only thing I'm wondering right now is, what if Jack learned more about this girl than he realizes? What if he knows the name of the town where she lives?" Daniel held up his hand. "I know, it was just a dream and I might be a silly old man, but so many other things he said are spot on. I can't help but wonder what else he might be aware of, perhaps without knowing." Daniel paused. "So, I guess what I'm asking is, what are your thoughts about showing Jack the bracelet? To see if it's the same as the one this Tika wore. If it isn't, I believe I could let things go."

Danny's yell from down the trail interrupted him.

"Mom, Dad, come quick. Something's wrong with Jack."

They ran from the clearing.

"Where are you?" Colleen called.

"In the grass by the tractor."

"Gus, he's having a seizure."

Jack was lying on his back shaking violently. Pauly was bent over him, rubbing his shoulder and calling his name.

Gus lifted his son into his arms and pressed him to his chest. He looked into his face. "Sweetpea, can you hear me?" Jack's eyes were open but unfocused. "Colleen, speak to him."

"Jack, it's okay. Your father has you. Try to relax." As Jack's tremors began to subside, Colleen stroked his face and hair. "It's okay, we've got you. Everything's going to be fine."

Jack's eyes turned toward her and he began to cry. Colleen took him and laid his head upon her shoulder.

Gus turned to Danny. "What happened?"

"We were just walking and he said he didn't feel good and then he started to shake."

Daniel put his arm around Danny's shoulders.

Pauly looked like he was about to cry too. Gus lifted him to his feet and squeezed him. "It's okay, Pauly. I'm proud of you. You stayed with Jack and made sure he was safe. You're a good boy. Come on, I'm sure he'd like to see you."

Colleen knelt until Jack's feet touched the ground. Pauly, Danny and Daniel surrounded him. Gus noticed tears on his father's face before he rose, turned and walked down the path. Gus followed him and put a hand on his shoulder.

"He's okay now, Dad. He'll be alright."

"I know," Daniel said. "It's just so hard watching everything that tyke's been going through." He wiped his eyes and looked up apologetically. "You know, I've always had a special place in my heart for Sweetpea."

"I know, and he has a special spot for you too."

They turned and watched the others comfort Jack.

"I think it best we head for home, so he can rest," Daniel said.

"I agree," Gus said. He turned to his wife. "Colleen, we're going back so Jack can lie down and rest. Danny and I will grab the cooler and chairs." He turned to Danny. "Come on, I need you to give me a hand."

When they returned, Pauly and Colleen were sitting in the wagon with Jack, who was smiling. Daniel climbed onto the tractor while Gus stowed their gear.

"I'm going to take a different route home," Daniel said. "It leads back to the county road quicker. We can run faster on gravel and it will have us back at the house in under twenty-five minutes." He started the engine and moments later they were under the shade of the trees.

Five minutes later, after passing a stone and wood cabin set back in the trees, Daniel stopped and climbed down. "Is everyone okay?"

"Yes, you didn't need to stop, Daniel" Colleen said.

"Well, I wanted to check, but I also noticed the door on Clarence's old cabin is open." Daniel nodded down the path. "I'll only be a moment. Kind of an unwritten rule out here is we keep an eye on each other's property. It's likely just been blown open by the wind. I'll be right back."

"I'll go with you," Gus said.

"Me too." Danny jumped out.

Gus looked questioningly at Colleen.

"We'll be fine. Just be quick." She motioned for him to slide the cooler to her. "I could use a drink."

Gus opened it and handed her the thermos and a glass.

Sure enough, the front door of the cabin was open. Daniel stuck his head inside then shut it while he and Danny walked around back. Other than a half dozen beer bottles on the ground beside a fire pit and a mud-covered spade leaning against the wall, nothing seemed out of place.

"Likely just kids," Daniel said, when Gus told him about the bottles. "Clarence has been in poor health for a number of years. I know he hasn't been out here." Daniel glanced at the rustic building, built tight along a natural berm running perpendicular to the trail. "Son, this is the old cabin I found when I was looking for the outlaw hideout. Clarence's boy fixed it up when he was in his teens. He used to stay out here a fair amount, though I doubt it's been used since." He turned and started back towards the wagon. "Come on. Let's get back on the trail."

Jack was sitting in Colleen's lap. She was rocking him back and forth. As Gus neared the wagon, he could hear his wife attempting to comfort him.

"It's okay. I'm with you. I've got you."

"I can still smell the flowers," Jack said. "I can still smell the flowers."

Gus leaned over the side of the wagon. "Is everything okay?"

"I don't know," Colleen said. "We were talking and Jack noticed that sometimes when the wind blows, he could still smell the flowers from the clearing, then he began repeating himself and hasn't stopped." She put her hand to the side of his face. "I know, Sweetpea. I can smell them too."

Jack's eyes widened and he screamed. "Mom, I can still smell them. I can still smell the flowers. Help me. Help me."

"Is he hallucinating, Colleen?"

"I don't know. I don't think so. I'm not sure."

Jack continued to scream.

"It's okay, you don't need to be scared." Colleen looked down at the bench and the front of her slacks. "He's peed himself."

Gus lifted Jack and shook him gently, trying to wake him or bring him back from wherever he'd gone. "It's okay. I've got you." He carried him down the path, rocking and talking to him.

Jack stared into the sky and screamed, "I can still smell the flowers."

Gus's eyes filled as he squeezed his son and comforted him. What the hell is going on? He walked a little further then turned and started back. By the time they reached the wagon, they'd both calmed.

"Colleen, did you bring any extra clothing?"

"No. I'll just take off his underpants." Colleen took Jack to the edge of the trees and pulled off his shorts. "It's okay, I just want to get you out of your wet clothes."

"Fatboy," Pauly whispered. "Jack's afraid of the badman."

"No, Pauly." Gus squeezed his shoulder. "Jack's just been sick, but he's getting better."

Pauly shook his head. "No. He's afraid of the badman. He knows the badman wants to hurt him."

"Shh, Pauly, that was just a dream. I want you to promise me that you won't talk about it again. It will only upset Jack. Can you do that for me?"

Pauly looked down. "But Jack knows."

Gus tussled his hair. "You're a good friend, Pauly. I'm glad you came along with us today."

"We're ready," Colleen said, as she and Jack climbed into the wagon.

"Good to go, son?" Daniel asked.

"Yes. Let's get back to the house."

They let Jack lay for a while before they ate a light meal and left for home. By the time they pulled into the driveway, the sun had set. Gus carried Jack indoors.

"Lay him on his bed and I'll be right in," Colleen said. "I want to give him a bath before he puts on his pajamas." She turned, knelt and gave Pauly a hug. "Goodnight, Pauly, and thank you for your help today." She kissed his forehead. "Jack will see you tomorrow." She turned to Danny. "Walk home with Pauly and tell Hazel I'll see her in the morning."

Gus sat in the living room while Colleen bathed Jack then put the boys to bed. He was spent. Finally, Colleen came down and sat next to him on the couch.

"Well, how is he doing? Has he settled?" Gus asked.

"He's not one hundred percent. His hands are still shaking, but his stomach isn't as upset." Colleen tried to smile. "I think we're in for a long night. We may have overdone things today." She brushed her hair back from her face. "Danny says he's going to try to help Jack keep his mind off what happened, and help him have another flying dream." She gazed towards nothing in particular. "I didn't know what to say about that."

"I don't either," Gus admitted. He sighed. "I should have known better Colleen. When we were walking to the clearing, I began to worry about him. I just had a funny feeling."

"It's not your fault. I did too. But he was so happy and normal, and it was so wonderful seeing the three of them having such a good time."

A smile tugged at the corner of Gus's mouth. "They were. I've dreamed of seeing the three of them play together like that for a long time." He bunched his lips. "Two steps forward and one step back. That's how I'm going to start to view things, and pretty soon, there won't be anymore backward steps." He sat quiet for a moment. "So, would you call what happened today another hallucination?"

"I don't know," Colleen replied. "When you found us the other night on the living room floor, his eyes were open then too. He hadn't fallen asleep. He and Pauly had just come in." She sighed. "I don't know. It's almost like he falls into a trance and begins screaming. Last time it was about green eyes trying to get him. It didn't make any sense."

"Well it didn't make sense today either." Gus paused for a moment. "Have you given any thought to what Dad had to say?"

"I've thought of nothing else," Colleen whispered. "Even while Jack was screaming." She took the small leather bag from her pocket and squeezed it as her shoulders began to shake.

Gus held her. "Everything's going to be fine. We've made it this far."

"I know but I'm scared. I'm scared for Jack, I'm scared for me. I'm scared for you and your father, but I don't know why, or what I'm supposed to do about it."

"Colleen, listen." Gus had never admitted this before, even to himself. "'It's my fault. When you and Wilf wanted to fit Jack for braces to slow him down, I'm the one who said no. I'm the one who insisted on him being given a sedative. I don't know," his voice lowered. "Maybe from seeing how well Dad handled the loss of his eye, I didn't want Jack to get used to a crutch. I was scared that if his legs didn't heal, he might never learn how to fight." He sat quiet for a moment. "I'm the one who told Wilf to give him that damn drug."

20

Orv Returns

Orv finished cleaning his rifle, leaned back in his chair and took stock once again of his situation. It wasn't good. Other than the beer in his hand, he had one can of beans that he'd found in the shack. He needed supplies. And fuel… He slammed his bottle on the table and cursed. He'd almost forgotten that his truck was running on empty.

"Damn you, Bud. I hope you appreciate all the trouble you've caused me."

Orv knew that his neighbor was alive from a news report he'd picked up the previous afternoon on his truck radio. Plus, he'd learned that somehow state authorities had discovered who he really was, and were concentrating their search area hundreds of miles to the west. In the long run, he supposed that worked in his favor. He'd just change his name again and let their information continue to lead them in the wrong direction.

He reached up and felt his nose. It was sore and difficult to breathe through.

"I only wish I could visit next door and bust the two of them up, like you did me," he muttered.

Yesterday, after he'd had a chance to calm down and think, Orv came to the conclusion it would be best to leave the old lady and Tika alone. Calling next door after retrieving his stash would only alert the police that he hadn't left the area. He was also going to have to forget about Bud's rifle collection. With so few places in the area for him to hide, once they learned he hadn't run, it wouldn't take them long to find him. No, it would be best to stick to his original plan, sneak back, grab what he could and then come back to the shack for a couple more days. He emptied his bottle, blew out the candles and carried his rifle outside. He laid it on the floor on the passenger side of his truck.

This was going to have to be a quick in and out job. First, he'd locate some gas, hopefully syphoning it from one of the vehicles parked at the implement dealer on the way into town, then come in from the east, shield his truck under the trees bordering the river, then cross under the base of the falls using the boulders poking out of the water. He'd done it before, most recently on the day he'd confronted Tika.

Orv looked up at the quarter moon filtering through a thin veil of clouds. He was good to go. The meagre light provided was just enough to navigate through the woods with his lights off. He started the truck and pulled out from behind the shack.

"Well, Bud, I can't say I'm happy. I was looking forward to passing along my condolences." His tongue split his broken lips as he leaned over the wheel and drove through the dark.

Orv's luck was holding. With the length of hose he kept behind the seat, he topped up from a stake truck parked next to the office at the implement dealer. He also switched plates with an out of state Chevy.

Ten minutes later, with his lights off, he rolled into the stand of trees above the falls. He removed the bulb from overhead, opened his door and stepped out. The dark green of his truck looked almost black in the dim light. From a few feet away, it was almost impossible to see. Orv made his way down the bank to the river.

There were no lights on in either home and Bud's truck was still parked in the same spot as the day before. Orv crossed the river, using the top of the rocks that shone in the faint moonlight, letting the sound of the waterfall cover his steps. Within a few minutes, he was back in the trees.

He climbed the bank to his back door. There was yellow tape stretched across it. Orv stood still and listened. There was no one about. He pulled one end loose and let it hang. No use advertising that he'd been back. Best to replace it the way he found it. He turned the knob. It was locked and his key didn't fit. The owner had changed it out after the sheriff's men left. Orv swore and refastened the tape.

He'd brought along nothing he could use to jimmy the jam. Now he had no choice but to break in through a window. Orv skirted the left corner of the house where the trees grew tight and stopped at the kitchen. If he were lucky, no one would hear the glass fall inside. He might even be able to push up hard enough to break the wooden clasp on top. Orv pressed evenly on both sides and the window slid up silently. His luck was still holding. No one had bothered to check. He hoisted himself in.

Other than the closet and cupboard doors being open, everything looked the same. He went into his bedroom and emptied the drawers, throwing his clothes into his duffle bag. In the kitchen, he grabbed his canned goods. His toiletries were still on the bathroom counter. Orv threw everything into the bag and knelt before the cupboard. The bottom corner boards had been lifted, his hiding spot emptied of both his handgun and cash.

"Dagnabit."

Now he had no choice but to go next door. He needed the money he could get from selling Bud's rifles. Orv stood and looked at his beaten features in the mirror.

"Just remember, old son, this is all your fault. I was going to let the two of them be and shuck out. Now I've got no choice."

Orv went back into the kitchen. On impulse, he searched an open drawer. It was empty except for an old rusted skinning knife. He took it with him, his tongue poking between his lips as he dropped his bag and then himself through the window. He turned and closed it.

As he came around the back of the house, a knock sounded from next door. His heart jumped as he fought the urge to run. Orv poked his head around the corner. A patrol car sat in the driveway. Somehow, as he'd been coming out through the window, he'd missed the lights and sound of the engine.

Carter was standing on the back porch, holding the screen door open. Orv backed into the trees and watched. First the kitchen light then the outside light came on, then the old woman opened the door.

"Carter, it's you," she said. "I wasn't expecting to see you again this evening."

The deputy took off his hat. "I'm sorry, Rose, but I promised Bud I'd stop by regular, to make sure you and Tika were safe." He peered over her shoulder. "Is everything's fine inside?"

"Yes, Tika's sound asleep. The poor child went to bed right after you brought us home. She still refuses to believe that what happened yesterday wasn't her fault." Rose reached out and grasped Carter's hand. "Thank you again, for running us into the hospital today."

"It was my pleasure, Rose. Bud and I go back a lot of years." Carter looked down with a smile. "I'm afraid Sheriff Neall figured out that I was lying though today, when I told him I needed to speak with the three of you. But I think he understands. Have you heard anything more from the hospital?"

"Bud's doing fine. Dr. Westshot called and said better than expected. He thinks he'll be ready to come home the day after tomorrow." Rose released his hand and held the door open wide. "Come on in. Let me make you a cup of coffee."

"No, but thank you. That's great to hear about Bud." Carter put his hat back on. "The sheriff said I can spend two or three more nights patrolling Medicine Falls, to keep an eye on things, unless of course Orv's caught. I'm going to take a look around his place right now and then drive the town. I'll be by every half hour or so, to make sure things remain quiet. I promise I won't bother you again." Carter stepped from the porch and turned. "Before I forget, I'm off duty tomorrow morning at eight. How about I accompany you and Tika to church, then we can drive into Jefferson to visit Bud again?"

"That would be wonderful. We'll be waiting for you."

"Good. I won't wake you again. I'll park down the street and walk between the houses. Make sure you lock up."

"I will and thank you. I'll sleep better knowing you're about." Rose closed the door and left the outside light on.

Orv slipped deeper into the trees as the deputy checked his back door and walked around his house. He wouldn't be calling on Bud's family after all. Not with the deputy in town. Best to light out now and hit the road while he still had the chance. He cursed under his breath as he thought about his missing money. Oh well, there was nothing he could do about it.

After the deputy left, Orv crossed the river and stood on the bank, searching for the shine of the patrol car's headlights on the side streets. Seeing nothing, he made his way across the rocks and back to his truck.

21

Sweetpea Flies Again

I couldn't keep my eyes closed. The smell of wet clay had returned. It was inside of me, waiting for me to fall asleep - thick, sticky and spinning, slower on the outside, faster towards the middle. At first, if I concentrated hard enough, I could hold myself above it, but as the weight of sleep increased I'd sink lower, nearer its center. Then terror would build and finally erupt and I'd jerk awake just before it could grab me. Gasping. Paralyzed. Not relieved but panic stricken by how close I'd come to being sucked into a nothingness a lot bigger than the size of my head.

My shakes, muscle spasms, the time loss and bright lights that sometimes flashed behind my eyes, these I could handle. They were like the disease in my legs - something physical to wonder about and learn to accept. This other was different. This was the place where I ceased to exist. A place I was terrified to disappear into again but I was exhausted, and so my eyelids began to flutter closed.

My brother was all I had to hold onto. I needed him tonight more than ever.

"Danny, I'm scared."

"It's okay, I'm right here."

He didn't understand. He may as well have been on the moon. It wasn't his presence I needed, it was something more. It was his light.

"I can't close my eyes," I cried. "Something bad's going to happen."

Danny left his bed, sat beside me and rubbed my shoulder. "I'll talk to you."

That couldn't last forever. Sooner or later I was going to fall asleep. How could I explain to him that I didn't think there was anything anyone could do?

"What if I don't come back?" My chest felt like a belt was being tightened around it after every breath.

"What do you mean? You're not going anywhere. Do you want me to tell you some more Fatty and Skinny jokes?

"Fatty and Skinny can bugger off."

Danny laughed. "You better not let Mom and Dad hear you, or you'll get your butt paddled."

I didn't care. I didn't swear. I'd used the words right. Mr. Cook said it all the time when the squirrels got into his bird feeders. Fatty and Skinny couldn't help me. It was that simple. I clenched my hands together as my entire body shook.

"Danny, there's something inside of me that's wants to take me away. I can smell it. It's waiting for me to fall asleep." Tears ran down the sides of my face onto my pillow. "It's going to grab me and I don't know where I'm going to go, or if I'm gonna come back" I rolled onto my side. "I'm too scared to close my eyes."

"What do you want me to do? Do you want me to go get Mom?"

"No! You can't leave." We'd tried that before. I was still going to fall asleep. It would still be inside waiting.

"Then why don't you try to have another flying dream? You slept good the other night and didn't have any nightmares."

I'd thought about that too but it meant I'd have to go to sleep willingly. I wasn't brave enough. It was like when Little

Joe surrendered to the marshal, knowing he might be hung for cattle rustling. What if it didn't work?

"Jack, we'll do it the same way as before. You think about flying and pretend you're doing it and I'll keep talking to you. And I promise, if it doesn't work, I'll get Mom and Dad. Okay?"

I didn't have a choice.

"Here," he said. He lifted my holster and six-guns from my bedpost. "Put these on. You were wearing them last time. Maybe you can shoot whatever comes after you."

I glanced at him. He was smiling but we both knew he wasn't making fun of me.

"Really, put them on. We have to do everything the same as before."

I felt like a fool but did as he said. At this point I was willing to try anything. Even changing my name to Kid Sweetpea, Fastest Crybaby in the West.

"When you close your eyes, and begin to fall asleep, I'll keep talking to you. I know you can do it."

My eyelids were so heavy. They'd close then I'd pull them back up, the lashes blurring my vision like rain streaking down a window. I was spiralling and behind everything, I could hear Danny's voice.

"Fly, Jack. Just like the last time. I know you can do it. Remember how happy you were? How much fun you had looking down at everything? Do it again, Jack. Fly."

I leaned forward, willing my feet to leave the ground. Concentrating. Remembering how wonderful it felt to lift into the sky. How happy I'd been. How free it felt to go wherever I wanted. But another part of me was fighting. The part I was scared of. It kept reaching up, trying to drag me under. I concentrated hard on the sound of his voice, willing it to pull me along. To set me free.

Don't stop, Danny, I wanted to shout.

"Fly, Jack, I know you can do it."

I'm trying but I'm scared. Please don't stop talking. Please don't let me just fall asleep.

"Fly, Jack. Forget about sleeping. When I count to three, do it."

I allowed myself to be drawn along. I loosened my grip on my pillow. My eyelids closed. I waited for the sound of his voice. I began to fall.

"One… Two."

I touched the spinning wetness. The smell was rotten. It overloaded my senses. Terror filled my lungs. I couldn't breathe. Sticky tentacles began to wrap around me.

Help, Danny!

"Get ready, Jack. Fly."

I leaned forward and pulled free with a wet sucking sound. I was doing it. I'd escaped. I was flying again.

Everything was exactly as I remembered - the comforting press of warm summer air rising and rolling beneath me - the horizon in pace dead ahead - familiar landmarks unfolding from long shadows, lifting into view like signposts along an expected path. Nothing had changed. It was as though time had simply been called after my last flight, patiently awaiting my return.

I levelled high above the Snye and banked instinctively toward Walpole Island and the St. Clair River, which embraced its opposite shore. I pushed forward faster, dropping my nose to soar across the wetlands of the Native Reserve, to the lighthouse guarding the shipping channel, then rolled to follow the waterway past Harsens Island before cutting inland again.

I flipped onto my back. The same cotton ball clouds were floating against the same black paper sky. Bright stars winked down while hundreds of others shot past, leaving multi-coloured tails in their wake. I was free. I closed my eyes, relishing in my weightlessness. Up here I felt no sense of fear, only a sense of calm and security. I looked back to see how far I'd flown. The moon was the same distance away, but the river and island had disappeared. I wasn't concerned. I knew I could return whenever I wanted. I rolled onto my stomach and sailed across the forests and farmland, anticipation welling within me. For I knew where I was headed. Where I wanted to go. I was flying back to the town with the white church and the cross set high upon its steeple.

I came in above the trees lining the river's edge and hovered above Tika's home. There were no lights on and everything was silent. A bicycle was leaning by the side door. A red truck was parked in the drive. I circled her house, wondering which window was hers and how I could let her know that I'd returned. I didn't know what to do. I certainly couldn't knock or peek inside.

I let the breeze float me above the trees where the horsemen had been waiting for us to return. There was no one there, although a truck was visible through the leaves, parked above the waterfall at the base of the bridge. I rose and banked towards the church, the cross a welcoming beacon shining in the moonlight, and standing at its base was Tika.

My heart leapt until I heard she was crying. I slowed, unsure of what I should do. I felt guilty. Should I leave and pretend that I didn't know she was there, or was there something I could say to make her feel better? I continued forward and settled in front of her.

"Sweetpea," she cried, as my feet touched the roof. "I knew you'd come back. I knew you'd hear me cry." Tika ran forward and hugged me.

I was embarrassed. This was the first time the same girl had hugged me twice. Plus, I hadn't come because I'd heard her cry. I'd almost left because of it. I had to admit though that it sure felt good. I hugged Tika in return and patted her back. A person could almost get used to this. She didn't let go as her entire body shook with her sobs.

"Tika, what's the matter? Why are you crying?"

"Uncle Bud's in the hospital and it's all my fault. Yesterday, I told him and my grandmother about the neighbor and they got into a fight. The neighbor stabbed him."

What? I was shocked. I didn't know what to say. The neighbor stabbed her uncle? I thought things like that only happened on TV. Why would anybody want to hurt anybody else?

Tika pulled on my shirt sleeve and used it to wipe her eyes. It felt completely different than when my mother did it. I needed to find out more.

"Why did he hurt your uncle? Did he try to hurt you and your grandmother too?"

"No. We were watching from the house and afterwards he jumped in his truck and drove away. He said really mean things and called me bad names. The deputy came and put my uncle in his police car and drove him to the hospital." Tika's voice caught in her throat. "He almost died and it's all my fault. If I hadn't said anything, nothing bad would have happened."

This time I was the one who squeezed her. Hard. I hated that Tika was blaming herself, and I realized what might have happened if she'd kept quiet - Tika could have been the one who'd been hurt.

"Tika, if you didn't tell them, the badman might have hurt you, and that would be a lot worse."

"That's what my grandmother said too. Oh Sweetpea, what's going to happen to me now? Will they make me leave?

Have I caused too much trouble? What if Uncle Bud doesn't get better?"

I kept my arm around her shoulder, trying to figure out what to say, thinking about what Pastor Reg or Danny might come up with. I hoped I got it right. "If your uncle and grandmother didn't love you, they wouldn't have been mad at the neighbor, they would have been mad at you. They don't want you to leave. They want to protect you. Your uncle must love you very much. I promise, he'll be okay." I thought of something else. "Where's the neighbor now? Did the policemen catch him and put him in jail?"

"No." She wiped her eyes again with my sleeve. "He never came back. The deputy said he ran away but he's sure that they'll catch him." Her voice dropped and she whispered so softly that I could barely hear her. "But before he left, he said he was coming back to get me."

Something inside of me shook. It was as terrible as the fear I felt when the bad smell came over me. I shuddered. What if they didn't catch him? I looked over the edge of the roof. Where were the men on the horses? Why weren't they here protecting her?

Tika must have been thinking the same thing. "Sweetpea, what if he comes back?"

I had no idea what to say. I needed time to think. We sat with our backs against the steeple. I held her hand and put my arm around her shoulders. My mind was whirring. What could I do? I was so little.

"Did you tell the policeman that he said he was coming back?"

"Yes. My grandmother told him while we were driving to the hospital. He's a friend of Uncle Bud's. He took us there again today."

"Is he staying with you until your uncle gets better?"

"No. When he dropped us off tonight, he told my grandmother that he'd only be able to stay in town one more day."

"Then Tika, you have to stay in your house. You have to lock all the doors and windows. You have to wait inside until they catch him." I couldn't think of anything else to say.

Tika squeezed my hand. "What about you? Could you stay with me?"

I wished I could but I couldn't. I lived with my mom and dad and Danny. Besides, what could I do? The badman had almost caught me. I was too little to take care of myself.

"I can't," I said, as I glanced at her. Tears were shining on her cheeks and her lips were trembling. I felt useless. "Tika, I'm just a little boy. I can only fly in a dream. I can't stay. I live far away and I'm not big enough to fight a badman."

"But my grandmother said you're my friend and that you already helped me," she cried.

Tika was my friend but that didn't change anything. I still couldn't stay and I couldn't help her, except in a flying dream.

"I am your friend, and I wish I was bigger and I wish I could stay but I can't." I felt horrible. I was letting Tika down. I hoped she understood. "Did you call your mother and tell her what happened? I'm sure she'll come to help."

"I don't know where she is. I haven't talked to her for a long time. I don't know what to do."

"Maybe your grandmother can call her? You have to ask." I was out of suggestions. "Tika, I'll stay as long as I can, but then I have to go. Maybe tonight the policemen will catch him, or maybe tomorrow."

I hoped that sounded better outside of my head than it did inside. Tika didn't answer. How could something like this be happening? I looked over the town. Everything seemed so peaceful here. So quiet and calm and the moon seemed to be shining only upon us.

On the outside of town, a light burst from the ground and shot straight into the sky. I followed its blazing arc until it dropped in a brilliant flash miles away. I'd never seen anything like it before. It reminded me of the firecrackers we'd watched in Wallaceburg on Victoria Day, only these remained lit all the way up and back to the ground.

"That's what you look like when you fly," Tika whispered.

"What?"

"A shooting star. When you fly, you make a streak of light just like they do. I watched you when you left the other night. I ran out the door but you flew straight up and your light flew so far away, I couldn't see where you landed."

I was amazed and confused. When I flew I was like one of the shooting stars? I looked at Tika. He head was tilted slightly to the left, as though she were surprised that I didn't know.

"That's why I was standing up when you came tonight. I saw your light shoot by and I knew you went to my house." She squeezed my hand. "And then I prayed for you to come back and you did." Tika kissed my cheek.

Okay, now I was confused, amazed and embarrassed. My face felt like it was on fire. Maybe that was the light she'd seen the other night - my crimson onion head, after she kissed me on the cheek before I left.

"Sweetpea, how do you fly?"

I had an easy answer for that. "I just think about it and then I do."

"Could you teach me?"

I'd never thought of that. Why not? Hadn't she been flying a little bit when I first saw her running from Orv? A thought struck me. "Tika, how did you get on the roof tonight?"

"I don't know. I went to bed and then I was here." A look of wonder spread on her face. "Do you think that I flew?"

I stood and held out my hands. "There's only one way to find out. Hold on." She put her fingers within mine. "Now think about flying and lean forward like this." My feet left the roof and I hovered. "Don't worry, I'll hold onto you. I won't let you fall."

Tika concentrated and leaned forward. Nothing happened.

"Don't try so hard. Just believe that you can."

She smiled and shut her eyes. Her grip loosened as she leaned towards me. Her feet slowly left the roof.

"You're doing it!"

"Yes, I'm flying," she cried, her eyes so wide and her smile so beautiful. "Sweetpea, I'm flying!"

I laughed. "Now hold on and we'll fly over the edge. Don't think of anything else. Just let yourself be free."

We floated over the edge of the roof.

"I'm not even scared," she said, as she let go of my fingers and floated higher. "I'm doing it. I can't believe I'm doing it."

"Come on, follow me."

We flew across the field of grass where I'd first seen the horsemen, above the farms and forests. Tika skimmed the tops of the trees the same way I had, laughing as the leaves brushed against her. She soared past me and around me in wide circles, flying faster and faster until finally she shot straight into the sky, so high that I couldn't see her, just the trail of lights that she left behind. Tika was right. When we flew, we became just like the shooting stars. I never would have believed such a thing.

I waited until she came back, then we flew to the protection of the church.

I'd never seen Tika so happy. It was as though all her fears had disappeared. That was exactly how flying made me feel. She gave me a hug and squeezed my hands.

"Thank you. I've never felt so wonderful. Will I be able to fly now whenever I want? Could I visit where you live?"

I smiled. That would be wonderful. "I don't know. I don't think you'd be able to find me. I live very far away. Maybe the next time I visit, we'll fly back together and I'll show you. Would that be okay?"

"Oh, yes." She smiled. "And then we can be best friends forever."

"I'd like that." It really would be terrific. Tika was by far the nicest girl I'd ever met, and the only one I wasn't afraid to talk to. Or hug. "Tika, I think it's time for me to go, but first you have to promise me something."

She nodded.

"In the morning, ask your grandmother to call your mother. I know if she tells her what happened, she'll come to protect you. That's what mothers are for."

"I promise," she said.

We flew from the church. I hated this part because I didn't want to leave. When we flew above the river, I looked down for the truck that had been parked among the trees. It wasn't there anymore. I dropped beneath the branches and hovered to take a closer look.

Tika followed me. "Are you looking for the men on the horses?"

"No. When I got here I saw a truck, but now it's gone."

"There was a truck parked here?" Tika's voice was filled with panic.

A terrible chill ran through me as I realized what she was thinking. Why hadn't I considered it? It must have been Orv. Why else would anyone be out here so late?

"It was Orv," Tika cried. She grabbed my hand and pulled me above the trees. "Sweetpea, what am I going to do? He didn't leave! He came back. Just like he said he would."

I couldn't take my eyes off the trees. "You have to tell your grandmother. She has to call the police right away."

Although I was scared for myself, it felt much worse being afraid for my friend. What should I do? Why weren't the horsemen here keeping an eye on her? Tika squeezed my hand so hard that it hurt.

We flew quickly to her house, our heads swivelling about as we made sure that he wasn't around. We landed and walked quickly to her front door. I hugged her and felt her trembling.

"Can you come back tomorrow?"

"I don't know," I answered truthfully. "I'll try to come back whenever I can. Wait for me on the church. If I don't see you there, I'll come here. Which window is yours?"

Tika pointed to the one around the side, facing the neighbor's house.

I nodded. "If I don't find you on the church, I'll come here and tap on it."

"Okay." She hugged me again, kissed my cheek then pointed to my waist. "You still have your guns on."

This time I didn't feel embarrassed, I felt comforted, even though I knew they weren't real. For some reason, Tika made me feel like I wasn't a kid anymore.

"Goodnight, Tika. Remember, lock the doors and tell your grandmother to call your mother. And promise me you'll tell her about Orv, and make sure she calls the police."

"I will."

I hovered until she went inside then I lifted into the warm air. I didn't want to leave. I floated along the river.

Moonlight reflected off the water and the stones at the base of the falls. I crossed to the other side, to take a closer look at where the truck had been. Even though it terrified me, I floated lower. Suddenly the odor of wet clay enveloped me. It filled my throat. I couldn't breath. I tried to climb back into the sky but my body became so heavy, I started to sink to the ground. I landed on my hands and knees and threw up. My head was spinning. I had to get back into the sky and go home.

A shadow moved in front of me. I lifted my head and opened my mouth to scream but nothing came out.

"Got you, you little bugger."

Strong hands grabbed my shoulders. I twisted to escape and was hit on the side of my head. My ears rang and I fell to the ground. An arm reached down and wrapped around my waist. I was carried through the trees to a truck parked along the edge of the field. The man reached into the box. I wiggled and was struck again. Before my head could clear, a wet bag was pulled over me and down around my feet. I was thrown into the back of the truck and the end was tied. I couldn't breathe. I kicked as hard as I could. Another blow, this time to the top of my leg. The pain was unbearable.

"You can fight all you want but you're not going anywhere." He laughed. "I knew I'd catch you sooner or later. Who do you think you are, snooping and poking your nose into places it doesn't belong? And what kind of name for a boy is Sweetpea?" He snorted. "Now I'm going to do to you what my daddy used to do to me. I'm going to throw you in a hole, where no one will find you." He struck me again. "Now keep quiet or I'll hit you over the head with the shovel and bury you right here."

His footsteps went around to the driver's door. He climbed inside and started the engine. The truck pulled ahead, rolling me onto my side against the tailgate. It bounced across the field worse than my grandfather's wagon. My head banged against the steel floor and I was tossed into the air when the truck dropped into a hole. I hadn't made a sound. Terrified and starved for air, I blacked out.

My head banged again and I opened my eyes. My face was wet. I'd been crying. The truck was travelling over uneven ground again. Something poked me in my side. It hurt. I wiggled and tried to lift free but it moved with me. I reached down and found one of my pistols hanging loose from my holster. I pulled on it but the front sight caught in the threads of the sack. With a yank it came free, tearing a small hole. I brought it up in front of my face and ripped another hole and another. The truck came to a stop and I slid forward, dropping the gun somewhere under my arm.

The tailgate was lowered and I was tossed to the ground. The air was knocked from me again. I gasped like a fish out of water.

"Make sure you get yourself a mouthful. You're going to need it."

The man rattled around in the truck then came back. Somehow, I could feel him smile. He kicked me and I started to cry.

"Yep. When I was your age, my daddy used to toss me in a hole. First, he'd beat me until I couldn't stand and then he'd say, boy, ain't nothing going to make you a man quicker and toughen you up better than spending a few days doing nothing but thinking." He laughed. "That hole was blacker than the inside of a coffin and smelled worse than pig poop. That's where you're going. I'm going to give you a chance to think about all the trouble you've caused me. And maybe, just maybe, if I remember where I put you, I'll come back in a few days and look you up."

He walked behind me. Ten, eleven, twelve steps. I heard the sound of a shovel being pushed into the Earth. I was frantic. I reached into my holster, pulled out my other pistol and began ripping holes in front of my face. He started to hum.

When I'd made a hole big enough, I poked my fingers through and ripped it larger - big enough to see the stars overhead and tree branches to my left. Other than the sound of him singing and his shovel being pushed into the ground, it was quiet. I imagined a hole with the dirt being piled to the side and worms and grubs wriggling about. I started ripping again with my gun until the hole was the size of my head. I prayed for enough time to widen it and pull it over my shoulders.

"I don't know about you kid, but I could use a drink of water."

He dropped his shovel and walked past me. I pulled the edges of the bag together. I didn't want to think about what he'd do, if he found I'd been trying to escape.

He came back, kicked me again and laughed. I began to bawl.

"Here you go." He poured water onto the bag, over my head. "If you suck hard enough, you should be able to wet your lips." He snorted and went back to work.

"Another few minutes and I'll have this hole ready. You got anything you'd like to say before we part company?"

I didn't answer. Tears were running down my face. I dragged the gun's sight furiously across the material. It came open halfway down to my stomach.

"Cat got your tongue? I'm not going to ask you again. Do you have any apologies or last words you'd like to say?"

I stuck my head out, sat up and pulled the material down over my shoulders to my waist. My gun was still in my hand.

He turned and looked at me - a dark figure against the bright moon, which hung directly behind him.

"Why you little son of a gun. Where do you think you're going?"

He raised his shovel and stepped towards me. I pointed my pistol at him.

He stopped. "What the… Where did you get that?

I reached between my legs for the other, rose and kicked free of the bag. I trained them both on his chest.

He began to laugh. "Why those are just play toys you had in that itty-bitty holster of yours." He shook his head. "I got to admit, for a little fella, you sure got sand." He glanced over his shoulder at the hole he'd dug. "Almost going to be a shame, tossing you in there."

I started shaking and my stomach pushed its way into my throat. The smell of wet clay clogged my nostrils. I leaned forward and gagged as I began to lift from the ground.

"Hey! Where do you think you're going?"

He rushed towards me. A few more feet and I'd be away. He raised his shovel to swing and I fell forward, face first into a putrid abyss.

22

Captured!

Tika peeked between the curtains and waited for Sweetpea to leave. The moment his feet disappeared above the window, she slipped outside. She planned to follow him, to learn where he came from.

Fortunately, tonight, Sweetpea didn't shoot into the sky and disappear in a flash of light. Instead, he floated towards the trees on the other side of the river. Tika closed her eyes and concentrated, willing her feet to leave the porch. Nothing happened. She stepped onto the wet grass, her heart pounding as she focused on what he'd said.

'Just believe you can do it.'

Tika closed her eyes, relaxed and leaned onto her toes. The weight of the world slipped away as her feet left the ground. She was doing it. She was flying again.

Sweetpea was no longer in sight. Tika soared above the house and searched the horizon for his trail of lights. There was nothing. She sailed to the spot above the trees where he'd seen the truck and glanced down. Sweetpea was sinking to the forest floor. What was he doing? Had he returned to meet someone? Perhaps the men on the horses?

Tika circled the thick canopy and spotted a lone figure, moving through the underbrush. The other riders and their horses weren't visible. A dark truck was parked along the edge of the field. Something didn't feel right. She shot back to warn Sweetpea. He hadn't come here to meet someone! He was on his hands and knees, struggling to his feet. Tika's warning cry caught in her throat as the shadow raced forward and struck him. The dark figure must be Orv! He'd returned and captured Sweetpea!

Tika watched in horror as her friend was struck again then carried to the truck and tossed into a bag in the back. She followed it across the field and down the highway, onto a narrow lane that led into the woods. Tika was frantic. Somehow, she had to rescue Sweetpea. When the truck slid to a stop, she darted into the treetops and watched as he was tossed to the ground.

Terror gripped her as the man took a shovel and began to dig. Orv was going to kill and bury her friend! She had to do something.

Sweetpea's head popped from the bag. Somehow, he'd made a hole big enough to peer through. Tika waved wildly, although she doubted he could see her. Sweetpea ducked back inside and cried out as he was kicked again.

Tika left her hiding spot. If she flew high enough and circled behind him, could she swoop down and lift him into the sky, the same way he'd rescued her? She knew she had to try.

As Tika flew nearer, something shiny flashed in the moonlight. The bag was now around Sweetpea's waist. He wobbled to his feet, his toy pistols in his hands. Orv stepped forward and raised his shovel. Sweetpea began to rise into the air but something was wrong. He was climbing too slowly. He bent over and wretched as Orv swung, knocking the pistol from his hand into the box of his truck. Tika swooped down and glanced at the shadow, just as a loop of rope shot into the air. The man wasn't Orv! It was somebody else.

The loop opened above Sweetpea's head and started to fall. Tika pushed it aside and the shadow screamed as she grasped beneath Sweetpea's arms. She carried him deep into the forest, before dropping next to a narrow stream.

Sweetpea gagged. Tika rolled him onto his side and splashed cold water onto his face. He opened his eyes.

"You're safe now. I've got you. The bad man can't hurt you." Tika lifted his head into her lap. His pistol was still in his hand. She tried to take it from him but his grip tightened. "It's okay, you can keep it. Lie still. You're safe."

Sweetpea looked up, his eyes wide. "Tika?"

"Yes. I've got you. I flew us into the forest. Nobody can hurt you."

Sweetpea struggled to rise then lay back down. "I'm going to be sick again. The bad smell's trying to get me."

Tika didn't understand. Sweetpea must believe he's still in the bag.

"You've got to help me," he gasped. "I've got to go home. I have to hurry. If the bad smell gets a hold of me, I don't know where I'll go." He staggered to his feet.

Tika ducked under his arm and held it across her shoulder. "Sweetpea, I don't know what you mean. What bad smell? You're not in the bag anymore. You're safe."

He shook his head. "You don't understand. We have to hurry." He pulled his arm free and leaned forward to rise, before falling to his hands and knees.

Tika grabbed him and helped him to his feet. "Okay," she said. "I flew us here, I should be able to carry you home." She didn't think it would be a problem. When she'd flown him into the woods, he'd felt light as a feather. "But you're going to have to help me. I don't know which way to go. I don't know where you live."

Sweetpea pointed into the sky. “Take me above the trees. If I see the moon, I'll know which way to go.”

Tika ducked under his shoulder and wrapped her arm around his waist. With her other hand, she held onto his. She closed her eyes and said a silent prayer before lifting into the sky. As they rose, she glanced down. There was no trail of lights behind him. She was flying for them both.

“That way,” he pointed.

Tika banked to follow his directions.

After flying across grassland, forests and farmland, a wide river appeared in the distance. The moonlight shimmered on its surface. Below them, an immense forest stretched between two towns and to the shore of a large lake that faded into the distance.

“Hurry. I don't feel good,” Sweetpea said. “ The smells almost got me. I don't know if I can make it much further.” His head began to drop. “You have to follow that river, past an island....” His voice faded and his head hung limp.

“Sweetpea, open your eyes!” Tika cried. “You have to help me. I don't know which way to go.” She released his hand and lifted his head. “Sweetpea!” she shouted.

His eyes popped open and his body went rigid. “I'm not going into the ground!” he screamed. “You can't make me.”

Sweetpea's arms flailed as he struggled to break free. Tika clutched at the front of his shirt. He pulled at her wrists and the buttons popped open. He fell.

“Sweetpea, no!”

Tika turned and dived. Far below she could see him tumbling through the air. Sweetpea rolled onto his back and reached up for her as she shot forward. Terror shone in his eyes. He dropped into a thicket of trees. Tika swooped down between the branches and found herself in a clearing filled with thousands of flowers.

"Sweetpea," she cried. "Where are you? Where did you go?"

He didn't answer.

Tika looked wildly about. At the far end of the clearing, a group of horsemen was riding into the trees. In the arms of the lead rider was Sweetpea. His body lay limp. Tika shot forward and called out his name. As the last rider entered the trees, they disappeared.

23

A Good Cry

Colleen had to admit, Daniel was right - walking in the Misery did provide a completely different experience than bouncing through it in a wagon, down a rutted lane.

She stopped where the path turned to follow the Thames, short of the clearing. An errant breeze rippled across the surface of the water and shook the magnificent Tulip tree standing beside her. It ruffled from top to bottom, setting up a muted flute composition that vibrated through its trunk. Colleen placed her hand upon it and listened, fascinated as the scent of wildflowers washed over her. Reluctantly, she pulled away and continued down the path, until she sat cross-legged in the center of the glade.

The beauty Honor had created was more breathtaking than she remembered. The vibrancy of the colors - the casualness of the setting - the architect's hand hidden in the offhand manner of her presentation. The only order visible in the placement of the roses, bordering the outer edge.

Colleen closed her eyes and breathed in, allowing the bouquet of aromas to sedate her, until she was shaken roughly awake by her husband.

"Colleen." Gus's hand was on her arm. "Danny's yelling. Jack's having another hallucination."

In the boys' room, Jack was on his side in his bed. His brother was bent over him.

" He's choking," Danny cried. "I rolled him over but it doesn't help."

Colleen dropped next to Jack. His hair was soaked with sweat and the smell of vomit was heavy. His lips were turning blue.

"He's choking, Gus. Quick, slap him on his back." She stuck her fingers in Jack's mouth to clear his airway, as Gus struck him firmly between his shoulders.

"Is he going to be okay?" Danny sobbed.

Colleen wiped her fingers on the sheets as Jack took in his first full breath. It rattled deep in his chest. "Roll him onto his stomach." She lifted his head and cradled it in her lap. "Everything's going to be okay. Mom and Dad are here. You're going to be alright."

Jack's body went stiff. His arm swung back and he struck her across the face. Colleen's glasses flew to the floor. Jack's toy pistol was in his hand. He raised his arm again and Gus grabbed it and pulled the gun away.

"He hit me," Colleen gasped.

Danny picked up her glasses. "You're bleeding, Mom. On your nose and in the corner of your eye."

"Here, let me take him," Gus said. He held his son firmly in his lap as Jack fought furiously to break free. "Sweetpea, it's okay, I've got you. There's nothing to be afraid of." Jack continued to kick and squirm. "Jack," Gus said, sharply. "I've got you. It's okay."

Jack threw up down the front of his pajamas and screamed. "I'm not going in the hole. You can't make me. Tika, help!"

Colleen grabbed his hands. "Jack, it's Mom. You're not going anywhere. Nothing bad's going to happen." She pressed his head against her chest and rocked him back and forth. "It's okay. I've got you."

His body relaxed and his eyes popped open. They were dull and unfocused. "Tika?"

"No. It's Mom. You're safe."

Jack began to bawl, his body convulsing as he was wracked by heavy sobs.

Colleen began to cry too, as Danny and Gus wrapped their arms around them.

"I've got to clean up," Gus said. "I'll bring back a couple of warm washcloths."

He returned with his shirt off and wiped clean Jack's face and hands. Colleen laid Jack on his back, took off his pajamas and dressed him in the clean pair Danny had taken from his drawer.

"I'll change his sheets too." She sniffed. "He can have a bath in the morning."

"I'll grab some clean ones, Mom," Danny said.

"Here, take him, honey. When I'm finished, I'll come get him."

Gus's eyes met hers. Neither of them spoke. He carried Jack into the living room.

After she made Jacks' bed, Colleen had a shower. She was shaking so badly, she didn't want anyone to see her. The hot water that normally calmed her did little good. Her hands were still trembling as she dressed. Colleen looked in the mirror. The cut across her nose and into the corner of her eye was beginning to discolor. She went into the living room. Gus shook his head. Jack was still wide-awake.

Colleen sat next to him and rubbed his back. "Are you feeling better?"

Jack looked towards her, his eyes vacant, as though focusing would force him to acknowledge that something terrible had taken place.

"Do you think you're ready for bed?"

Jack shook his head and whispered, "The badman tried to bury me." Tears poured from his eyes. "He tied me in a bag and dug a hole and then he hit me and kicked me."

Colleen couldn't help herself. She began to cry again. "Oh sweetie, it was just a dream. I'm so sorry." Tears burst from her eyes like pinched grapes as she hugged him.

Jack buried his face in her hair. "Mom, I don't ever want to go to sleep again. I don't want to close my eyes. There's something bad inside of me that wants to take me away."

Colleen stroked his temple and kissed his forehead. "Tonight, you can sleep with your father and me. Will that help you feel better?"

Jack shook his head.

The four of them ended up in one bed. Danny came in when Jack didn't return. Colleen lifted the sheets and he slid in. Danny had never slept with them before, not even as a child. He lay with his back towards her, his arm across his brother.

"Mom?" he whispered.

"Yes, honey?"

"When Uncle Reg poured oil on Jack's head and we prayed for him to get better, something inside of me told me that I had to look out for him. And that when I get older, I'm going to be a pastor."

Tears welled in Colleen's eyes. She didn't think she had any left. She buried her fingers in the back of Danny's hair.

Colleen believed in the power of a good cry. An invitation she wisely extended to her boys. "Let it all out," she'd encourage. She saw no shame in displaying emotion. Colleen viewed it as therapeutic, a chance to wipe the slate clean and to think clearly again. Plus, by cheering them on, she knew she'd quickly learn just how much pain they were really in. It seemed crocodile tears turned into smiles at her urging, while real tears would rival Niagara. Now she lay curled in her bed and cried silently, until her heart was dry, her senses sedated and all that remained was her ability to think.

"Dear Lord," she murmured, "How could I have been so blind?"

The neurologist's diagnosis of Jack's addiction the previous month had blindsided her. Her initial shock replaced by a blanket of shame. This wasn't supposed to happen. She was his mother. She wasn't supposed to let it.

"Oh, Jack."

Colleen hadn't been prepared for a child such as him. He was so overflowing with energy. On the run from the moment he woke until his eyelids closed each evening, he'd played and frayed upon her nerves until finally each night she lay awake, wondering how much more she could take.

He reminded her of a summer thunderstorm, at the end of a sweltering day. A thunderhead that kept crashing and blowing, electrifying the air until it left you begging for the respite of a rain that never came.

Danny had given her such a false impression of motherhood that Honor had nicknamed him her 'Little Farmer.' "At his happiest drawing milk and spreading manure," she'd chuckle, as he lay in her wasted arms.

Then came Jack, a tiny force of nature. Colleen wished that everyone who commented at the energy that radiated from his body, could for one day have to keep up with the demands of the inexhaustible supply.

She remembered just before his fifth birthday, making an appointment with Dr. Wilkes, when all she'd really wanted was someone to talk to. He'd surprised her by asking if she'd bring along Jack.

Wilf examined Jack's reflexes, eyes and ears. He laid him on the table and worked his way down his spine to his toes, examining his growth. Finally, he held onto his hands, palms down, frowning as Jack fidgeted from foot to foot.

"Okay, that's it." Wilf opened the door. "Sheila, could you take Jack into the waiting room please. I'd like a moment alone with his mother."

Jack burst around the nurse and out of sight.

Dr. Wilkes closed the door and sat on his silver stool. "That's quite the little fellow you have there." He smiled. "He's as healthy as a horse."

Colleen's shoulders dropped.

"Colleen, do you remember being this tired before you had Jack?"

"Lord, no," she sighed.

"Well it's only natural for you to be on edge. I can only imagine what that little tornado's putting you through. Colleen, Jack's hyperactive. Extremely hyperactive."

She stared into his eyes.

"He's running all day?"

She nodded.

"Won't nap in the afternoon? Has trouble sleeping at night?"

She nodded again. "What exactly is hyperactive and how do we get rid of it?"

Wilf smiled. "There is no cure. Your son just has extra energy to burn." He lifted his feet to the bottom rung of his stool. "I could prescribe a sedative to help him sleep but I won't. As he gets older, he'll slow down. For now, just allow him to run and tire himself each day. He's healthy, he's not hurting anyone, and I promise, soon you'll be wondering how you made it through all of this."

"I'm wondering already, but at least now I know why. I thought I wasn't being a good mother."

Wilf patted her hand. "Listen. I can't think of anyone better suited to handle that little guy than you. Most mothers would have seen me a long time ago." He opened the door. "Now, I need you to collect your son before I lose a receptionist." He smiled as she walked by. "And remember, if you need to talk, just call. If we're closed, you can ring me at home."

Colleen sniffed and wiped her eyes with her pillowcase. That day so fresh in her mind. Almost four years ago, but it seemed like yesterday.

"Well, Wilf," she whispered, thinking of everything they'd been through, first the disease in Jack's legs and now his addiction. "It sure hasn't turned out the way we'd planned. None of us can be very happy with how we've failed him."

Colleen's heart ached as she recalled what she'd told Gus the day after Jack first took his medication.

'I've finally been given the Sweetpea I dreamed of.'

24

Tailor Tape

Going to bed with my parents didn't help. There was no way I was closing my eyes. I was so afraid that the smell of wet clay would return and I'd disappear once again inside my head. So, all I'd been doing was thinking, until finally I came up with something I needed to find out. Sneaking from the room shouldn't be a problem. I felt like I was inside a Three Stooges episode.

On my right, Dad was snoring louder than you'd believe possible. Every few minutes he'd reach a crescendo and the bed would shake when he'd jerk himself almost awake. Then his breathing would stop for a count of ten and he'd start it all up, all over again. I was in awe. On the other side, my mother was trying to keep pace. What the heck? How was this possible? I didn't think girls snored. Whatever happened to *'sugar and spice and everything nice?'* And then there was Danny. He couldn't keep his dang nose out of my left ear. Every third breath he'd exhale and his lips would open with a little 'puh,' like a bubble bursting in a bowl of hot porridge. The tickle expectation alone was driving me nuts. I crawled over the sheets and left the room.

My mom's cloth tailor tape was in her sewing basket, inside the hall closet. I took it with me and sat on the front porch. There was something that needed measuring - my head.

I wrapped the tape around my head, above my eyes, pinched it together then took it off. Eighteen and one half inches. No way. The circle was too small. I measured again and again, each time with the same result. Something wasn't making sense.

I went back inside and got a safety pin, fastened the tape together at the mark and slipped it back on. It fit perfectly. I closed my eyes and it remained in place. How was this possible?

With my eyes open, I swung my head in tiny circles. It felt a little bigger than it measured, but I could live with the difference. However, the moment I closed my eyes it became huge. If I wanted to, I could place the entire universe inside. The tape should shoot off like an elastic band around an inflating balloon. I closed my eyes again and tried to imagine my brain inside. I could do it but it was difficult. In fact, I found I could picture a picture of a brain inside, easier than picturing my own.

How could there be so many things about myself that I didn't understand?

I imagined the inside of my mouth. Wiggled my tongue from side to side and felt my teeth and gums. Eyes closed or open, the size remained the same - just enough room and a little more for a bite of food. So, what made my head so special? Why did it grow so big when I closed my eyes?

From everything I'd ever read and learned, I knew that other than dreaming, there was nothing my body did for no good reason. So, the only conclusion had to be - God made it this way, for a purpose. Obviously not just to hold my brain, but perhaps also my imagination? Could that be what my nightmares were? My imagination killing time while I slept? If so, why did I have no control over it and how could I disappear?

So far, I could only remember three dreams I'd ever had - the flying dream I told Pauly about and the two I'd had with

Tika. I remembered nothing from any of my nightmares. In fact, for the first time, I realized that I had few detailed memories from any point in my life. Sure, I remembered Mom and Dad and Danny and Pauly and Grandpa and the other people I saw all the time. But when I tried to remember specifics, like last years' birthday, or going to school when I was six, seven or eight, I came up empty. Why all of a sudden was I beginning to remember things? Was I just beginning to experience what everyone else had been, for their entire lives? And why did the end of last night's nightmare still terrify me so much? I shuddered at the taste of fear that remained in my mouth.

There was a noise. Three houses down at Cecil's, a man was putting a box into the back of a pickup. From the glow of the porch light past, I could see it was the person who'd helped me in his driveway. He turned. I couldn't tell if he saw me. It was too dark. I waved but he didn't wave back, he turned and walked away. Maybe he was having trouble sleeping too?

My train of thought had been interrupted. What had I been thinking about? Oh yeah, my dreams.

Pauly said my dream about Tika was a true dream. That didn't make sense. For it to be true, didn't I need to be able to fly? And not only that, how could someone I'd met in a dream be real? I needed answers.

I went inside, grabbed a couple of encyclopedias, took them outside and sat on the top step and opened them to the D's. Unfortunately, the first book didn't contain much information, other than that dreams were thought to last only a few minutes. I opened the next one but it was pretty much the same. It seemed scientists didn't know or couldn't agree why we dreamed. I flipped through the next couple of pages. One thing became clear - people long ago placed much more importance in what took place during their sleep than we do today. Many cultures believed that a person's soul or spirit actually left their body and visited the place they travelled to. Native Americans believe that while dreaming, they can visit their ancestors or contact their guardian spirit.

What?

I read the line again.

Native Americans believe that while dreaming, they can visit their ancestors or contact their guardian spirit.

Didn't Grandpa say that's what Tika had asked me, when I thought she'd said garden spirit? How could I dream about something I'd never heard of before?

I was looking in the direction of the Big Chief Drive-in, at nothing in particular, when a voice said, "Jack, what are you doing outside so early? It's only five o'clock."

I turned. My mom was standing behind me. I hadn't heard the door open or close.

"And what's that you're wearing around your head? Is that my measuring tape?"

Dang. I still had it on.

"Nothin'."

"What do you mean, nothin'? It's around your head." She took it off. "Why, you've even pinned it together to hold it in place."

She dangled the tape at arm's length and looked at me like I was nuts. This wasn't good. I wanted to disappear. I could think of nothing to say that would make me appear less foolish.

"I just wanted to put it on, is all." My face began to heat up.

Mom's smile changed when she sensed my embarrassment. It softened, becoming almost supportive. She rubbed the top of my head and slipped the tape back on. She was going to let this one go. How come Danny inherited her inability to not laugh, but not this nicer trait? I felt instant relief.

She sat beside me and looked at the book on my lap.

"What are you reading?"

"Nothin'." I looked at my feet, willing them to lift and shuffle me away.

She picked up the top one. "You're reading about dreams. Did you find what you were after?"

Well, I needed to talk to someone. Looks like she's gonna be it. "Mom, how can I dream about things I don't know?"

"What do you mean? What don't you know?"

I pointed at the page, to the spot where it mentioned Native Americans and the spirit world.

"What am I looking for?"

I put my finger under the line. "Remember when Grandpa said Tika asked me if I was her guardian spirit? How could I dream about something I'd never heard of before?"

Mom read the paragraph. "You must have heard these words before but don't remember."

"No, I thought Tika said garden spirit. Grandpa's the one who said guardian spirit. What's a guardian spirit?" I looked up at her. Her eyes had dark circles around them. She looked like a raccoon. "What happened to your face?"

"I banged my nose. It's nothing. What was it you asked?"

"I don't know what a guardian spirit is."

Mom closed the book and thought for a moment. "A guardian spirit is like an angel. Someone who watches over and protects you."

"Tika thought I was an angel?" I hadn't expected that. I don't think I'd ever been considered an angel before.

Mom put her arm around me. "Sweetpea, the girl in your dreams isn't real. You've just been having nightmares."

That wasn't right. When Tika was the only person in my dream, it was wonderful.

"No, Mom." I tried to explain again. "I thought Tika asked me if I was her garden spirit. Grandpa was the one who said guardian spirit. If I'd read or heard about guardian spirits before, I would have known that's what she said."

Mom didn't answer.

I leaned against her and wrapped my arm around her waist. "Mom, I'm really scared. What if Pauly's right and I had a true dream? What if Tika's a real girl? Last night the badman didn't come back to get me. He wants to hurt Tika. That's what he told her." I shivered. "What if the next time he comes back, he gets a hold of her? I've gotta do something. I've got to find her."

25

The Bracelet

Daniel looked at his watch when the phone rang. Seven-fifteen. He picked it up in the middle of the third ring.

"Hello?"

"Good morning, Daniel."

It was Colleen. Her voice sounded tired and strained.

"Good morning, Colleen. Is everything okay?" Daniel felt no need to mince words. There was no other reason he could think of for such an early call.

"No," she sighed. "Last night was our worst."

Daniel waited for her to continue.

"Jack hallucinated again. He woke up vomiting and screaming that a badman hurt him, and was trying to bury him in a hole." Colleen's voice cracked. "Daniel, it was the worst experience of my life. I've never seen anyone so frightened."

Daniel sat at the table. Rested his forehead in his palm. "I didn't have a good feeling when you left. How's he doing this morning? Any better?"

"No, that's why I'm calling. We're not going to church today. Everyone's too tired and Gus and I have been talking." She paused. "We've decided to show Jack your bracelet."

Oh. He hadn't expected this. "Are you sure?"

"Yes. If you'd seen how terrified and lost he was, and the questions he's been asking. He thinks the girl in his dream is real and in danger. He says he has to find her."

Daniel wasn't surprised. Hadn't he'd attempted the same thing for almost eighteen years?

"We'd like you to be here, when we show it to him."

"Okay." Daniel's mind was spinning. He couldn't tell if it was from fear or anticipation. "I'm going to have a cup of coffee first and a bite to eat."

"Take your time. There's no need to hurry. We'll see you when you get here."

"Okay, Colleen. I'll be there before noon."

26

Winchester

Rose stepped onto the porch. Low grey clouds blanketed the morning sky. With a rumble, they opened and rain began to fall. She reached out from the shelter of the awning and felt the raindrops cold against her skin. This past week she'd sensed a change in the weather. Soon hot summer days would be forgotten, replaced by the cloudy skies and brisk autumn winds that always seemed to soothe her. She closed her eyes. This was the time of year she felt closest to her forbearers.

Rose imagined scouts returning to the village from their search for the buffalo. Summer camp being loaded onto travois and the people moving to the site of the hunt. Braves on mustangs riding close to the massive beasts, driving arrows between their flank and rib cage to bring them down. Women skinning and dressing the meat. Hides made into bedding, clothing and tent coverings. Horns into dishes, ladles and spoons. Hair into rope and leads, and dung collected to fuel fires, or ground into fine powder to prevent diaper rash. The people had wasted nothing.

"Grandmother?"

Rose opened her eyes. The white cross on the church stood out in sharp contrast against the dingy sky.

"Yes, Tika?"

"I dreamed of Sweetpea again."

Rose already knew this. In the middle of the night she'd been awakened when Tika cried out the boy's name. Rose found her granddaughter weeping and tossing in bed, her blankets kicked to the floor. After rearranging them, she'd sat next to her, singing softly until she quieted.

Rose turned. Tika was wearing her bracelet, choker, and the light blue dress Bud had purchased for her the previous Easter. Her hair was braided into ponytails. Her beauty took Rose's breath away. She opened the screen door, stepped inside and took her granddaughter's hands.

"Tell me about it."

Tika looked down in embarrassment. "I was on the roof of the church again, below the cross. I was crying because of Uncle Bud. When Sweetpea came, he was a little boy again. He told me that it wasn't my fault. He said if I hadn't told you about Orv, that Orv might have hurt me."

Rose put her hand beneath her granddaughter's chin and lifted her face. Tika averted her eyes. "There's no need to feel ashamed. I believe it's true. If you'd said nothing, Orv may have hurt you." Rose stroked Tika's hair. "Tika, your uncle loves you very much and his only wish was to protect you. You did no harm to Bud. He was injured by Orv. It was not your doing."

"I know but that doesn't make me feel any better."

Rose squeezed her. "You've become a very special young lady. I'm proud of you."

They stood together in each other's arms.

"Grandmother, Sweetpea also showed me how to fly. It was easy. He said all I had to do was believe, and when I did, I had no problem at all. It was wonderful. I wasn't even scared."

Rose chuckled. "As you get older, you'll find you can do many things once you believe you can." She held Tika's shoulders and stood back. "Bud's going to be very happy to see you today. You look wonderful in your dress. It matches well with your bracelet and choker."

"There's more, Grandmother."

An unexpected stab of fear pierced Rose's chest.

"I know it was just a dream but - Sweetpea made me promise to tell you that he saw Orv's truck last night, hidden in the trees, on the other side of the river."

Rose's knees weakened.

"After Sweetpea brought me home, I followed him, to see where he came from. He returned to the trees and was captured. I thought it was Orv but it wasn't. It was another man. He hurt Sweetpea and took him into the woods to bury him." Tika's lips began to tremble. "But I saved him, Grandmother. I had to. He couldn't fly, so I had to help him. But something happened when I was carrying him home. He began to fight me and pulled my hands away. He fell into the trees of a big forest. I tried to catch him but I was too late. Sweetpea disappeared into a field of flowers and I saw the horsemen carry him away."

Rose pulled her into her arms.

"I don't know what happened to him, Grandmother. I don't know if he's okay".

Could it be true? Had Orv returned? And who was this other man? Rose suspected her granddaughter's dreams to be much more than they appeared, especially after her description of the boy flying away. And now Tika had also seen the horsemen. She needed to speak to Carter right away. The police were so certain that Orv had fled. The thought of him still in the area, and near their home, frightened her. She remembered his threat to Tika. *'I'll be coming back for you.'*

Rose looked at the clock above the sink. Where was the deputy? He should have been here by now. They'd planned to go to church together, then into the hospital in Jefferson to visit Bud.

"Tika, did Sweetpea say anything else?"

"Yes," Tika replied, pulling back and looking her in the eye. "He made me promise to ask you to call my mother. He said that if she knows Uncle Bud's been hurt, she'll come as quickly as she can."

Rose nodded. She hadn't told Tika that she'd called Helene from the hospital, the day Bud was injured. She hadn't wanted to give her false hope. That had been a mistake. Tika should have been told. She had the right to know.

"I did call your mother, child. From the hospital. I wasn't able to speak with her, but I left a message." She squeezed Tika's shoulders. "I too believe Helene will come, if she can. Her and Bud have always been close. I've been waiting to hear from her."

"Thank you, Grandmother." Tika smiled. "She'll come, I know she will. Sweetpea said so."

"Carter will be here soon. Put your shoes on and bring our coats from the closet. It's raining and there's a cool breeze."

Rose started towards the phone. She heard a car door shut. She opened the screen door as the deputy stepped onto the porch.

"Good morning," Carter greeted. He slapped his wet hat against his leg. "I'm sorry I'm late." He looked into the sky. "What a miserable morning. I think we're in for an all dayer."

"Good morning, Carter." Rose looked past him at Orv's home. "Before you come in, I hate to ask this of you, but could you check next door? I think it's possible Orv returned last night. After we spoke. He may have parked in the trees across the river."

Carter put his hat back on. "Why do you say that, Rose? Did you hear something?"

"No, I promise I'll explain afterwards." She pointed to the small stand of trees above the falls. "I believe he may have parked there and crossed below. If so, you may find tracks." She tried to smile. "When you return, I promise I'll have a hot cup of coffee waiting for you."

"Give me five minutes. I'll check his house first."

The deputy walked across the driveway and disappeared behind Orv's home just as the church bells rang, calling worshippers for the morning service.

Rose and Tika were sitting at the table when Carter returned. He walked past the door and a couple minutes later returned. He beat the rain off his hat again, before stepping inside.

"You're right. I found tire tracks in the trees and footprints under the kitchen window." He shook his head. "He must have snuck back for his money and handgun. He couldn't have been very happy."

Carter didn't say it but it was obvious from the look on his face that he was furious with himself, for allowing Orv to get so close.

"What should we do? He has to be nearby. Do you think that's the only reason he returned?"

"I don't know. I wish I had an answer for you." Carter glanced at Tika. "I've radioed the sheriff. We're going to search the area again." His eyes narrowed. "Rose, do you think Bud might have any idea where Orv's been hiding? I know they hunted together a couple of times. Maybe Bud knows of an empty house or shack that Orv might be using?"

"I don't know. You'd have to ask him."

Carter turned in the doorway. "I'm afraid I'm going to have to pass on that coffee, and we're going to miss church. We need to drive into the hospital. I need to speak with Bud and radio back anything I learn."

"I think that best also," Rose said. She picked up her coat from the back of the chair. "Come, Tika." She didn't want to spend another minute in the house, knowing Orv was nearby.

The rain continued all the way to Jefferson City, rising back into the air in a fine mist from the wheels of the traffic. No one spoke. Rose sat in back, considering Tika's visions, for now she was sure that's what they'd been. She wasn't surprised. She too had been blessed many times with visits to the dream world. The first when she wasn't much older than her granddaughter.

Rose remembered the young man in the forest who'd injured himself with his rifle. Over the years, she'd thought often of him, wondering if he'd recovered and how his life had progressed. Daniel, she remembered. She'd been led to him during a wild winter storm by the same horsemen who led Sweetpea to her granddaughter. Rose smiled as she recalled the tall warrior telling her his name. It hadn't surprised her to find her guide in the spirit world to be the same man her grandmother had relied upon to find the herd. Rose knew of the power of the sacred hoop. She was aware that the physical and spiritual worlds were connected and on the same plane, and that all creatures lived on after physical death. Rose closed her eyes and gave thanks for the many blessings her family had received.

Rose and Tika waited under the awning at the entrance while Carter parked his car. Rose shivered and took her granddaughter's hand as a feeling of great apprehension settled over her. Everything seemed to turn grey, as though the drizzle had washed all color from the day into the glassy puddles scattered upon the pavement. She wondered, as she watched

Carter run towards them between the parked cars, if the news of Orv's return had hit her harder than she realized. Something didn't feel right. Her thoughts turned to Bud and Helene. She needed to see her son. Rose opened the door, ushered Tika inside and held it for Carter.

"I'm sorry I took so long," he said. "I just received a radio call from Sheriff Neall. A couple of officers from Jefferson City are on their way here to speak with me. Something to do with Orv."

She didn't respond.

"Rose, are you okay?"

"I don't know. I don't feel well." She turned and walked quickly down the hall. "I need to see my son."

The nurse behind the counter recognized them when they turned the corner. She rushed out from behind her desk.

"Mrs. Flowers. We've been trying to contact you. I was hoping you were on your way." She took Rose's elbow and steered her through the door of the waiting room.

Rose was alarmed. "Is there something wrong? Where's my son?"

"I'm sorry," the nurse said, motioning for her to sit.

Rose shook her head. She wished to remain standing.

The nurse took her hand. "Your son experienced minor pain during the evening. This morning his discomfort increased, so we called Dr. Westshot." She glanced at Tika and Carter. "He's being prepped for surgery. Please, have a seat. I'll tell the doctor that you're here. I'm sure he'll be in right away to speak with you."

Carter stepped forward and put his arm around Rose. The news hit her hard.

Rose swayed as though her world had been shaken. Bud had been doing so well. What could have changed? "Yes. Please. I'd like to speak with him right away."

"I'll tell him you're here."

"Rose, please, sit," Carter said, leading her to the couch. "Is there anything I can get for you?"

She shook her head. Tika sat beside her and took her hand.

"Uncle Bud's going to be okay, Grandmother," Tika said. "Sweetpea promised me."

The door opened and Dr. Westshot came in. Rose began to stand.

"No, please." He sat on the edge of the table. "I've only a minute. As you're aware, Bud experienced discomfort during the night. The nurses were monitoring his vital signs around the clock." He paused to take a breath.

"This morning he began experiencing chest pain, a rapid heart rate and shallow breathing. He became anxious." Dr. Westshot took Rose's hand. "He went into shock. I suspect that he's bleeding internally and fluid has built around his heart. I'm going to attempt to drain the fluid, using a needle and catheter. Of course, I'll also have to find where the blood is coming from. If that doesn't work, my only recourse will be surgery. My nurses are waiting." He stood. "I promise, the moment I know anything, I'll have someone give you a full assessment."

"Thank you, doctor." For Tika's sake, Rose knew she had to appear strong, although her heart was beating wildly in her chest.

Dr. Westshot turned in the doorway. "Mrs. Flowers, I promise I'll get to the bottom of this, and I happen to be darn good at what I do."

Rose nodded, put her arm around Tika, closed her eyes and began to pray.

The room remained silent as the gravity of the situation settled upon them. This was unexpected. Yesterday they'd been assured Bud would be released tomorrow, or the day after at the latest.

Tika squeezed her hand again.

"Grandmother?"

"Yes?"

"You don't need to worry. I know Uncle Bud's going to be okay. Sweetpea told me." Tika smiled. "He promised, Grandmother. That's what he said."

The nurse returned with a pitcher of water. She set it on the table then left.

Rose thought of the day that Bud had been injured, and the talk she'd had with Tika about her great grandmother. Could the boy really know her son would be okay? As much as she wanted to believe, it was difficult. If Bud didn't pull through, Tika's trust in herself and her dreams would be shattered. Rose chastised herself. Hadn't she been convinced on the way in that Tika's dreams had been much more than just dreams? And now here she was questioning herself. What would have happened to the people of the village if Wakanda had been so full of doubt?

"Rose?"

"Yes, Carter?"

"At the house, you told me you'd explain how you knew that Orv had returned." The deputy was sitting tall in his chair, his hat in his lap. He smiled faintly, as though embarrassed to question her.

Rose liked Carter. He was a good man but many people didn't accept native beliefs. But she'd given him her word and knew that she wouldn't have, had she not respected him.

"Tika, could you please ask the nurse where the chapel is located?"

"Yes, Grandmother."

Rose waited until the door closed then turned her attention to the deputy.

"I apologize, Carter, but first I must ask for your confidence in what I am about to tell you."

He leaned forward. "Of course. It will remain between us."

"Thank you." Rose gathered her thoughts. "For as far back as my people remember, the woman in our family have been blessed by the great spirit, Wakan Tanka, with visions from the dream world. After Orv attacked Tika, she withdrew and began having nightmares. She wouldn't speak of them. Bud and I believed it was because she missed her mother." Rose glanced toward the window.

"The night before Bud's injury, I gave Tika a bracelet and choker that has been passed through our family, and showed her how to pray to the eagle, to ask him to accept and carry the burden of her fears, so she could find peace in her sleep. Since that night, she's been visited in her dreams. Last night she was told that Orv had returned."

"You're telling me Tika dreamed that Orv came back?"

"Yes."

"Son of a gun." Carter's face reddened. "I mean, of course I believe you. There's no other explanation but - son of a gun." He shook his head. "I have to be honest with you. Over the years, I've heard many stories about you. Many people say you have the gift of seeing, that often you're aware of events before they take place. Up until now, I've never put any stock in it." He looked at his hat. "Truth be known, I've never questioned native beliefs. I've always wondered why some people can't picture being part of a world much larger than what we see." Carter smiled. "Thank you. Thank you for trusting me enough to share this. I promise it will remain between you and I." He studied her face. "One last question?"

"Of course."

"After the doctor left, Tika said that Bud was going to be okay. Is that another of her visions? Do you believe this too?"

Rose bit her lip. Had she not been wondering the same thing?

"Carter, let's just say that I want to believe Bud will be fine. For Tika's sake as well as his."

Carter nodded.

A moment later, Tika opened the door. Two officers were standing behind her.

"Grandmother, the nurse said the chapel is around the corner, at the end of the hall." She pointed to the left. "And these policemen were at the counter, looking for Deputy Carter. I told them that I knew where you were."

Carter rose to his feet as Tika held open the door.

"Thank you," said the taller of the two officers. His face was expressionless. He stepped forward and shook Carter's hand. "I'm Officer Baines, Jefferson City police, and this is Officer McRae." He stepped aside so the other officer could shake Carter's hand. Officer McRae was carrying an object wrapped in a heavy cloth. He glanced at Rose.

Carter introduced her. "This is Rose Flowers and the young lady is Tika. How can I help you?"

"I spoke with your sheriff this morning," Officer Baines said. "He told me that you were on your way to the hospital. I wasn't aware that the man who'd been stabbed is your friend."

"Yes," Carter replied. "I've known him all my life. Rose is his mother and Tika's his niece."

Officer Baines took off his hat. "I'm sorry ma'am. I hope your son is doing well?"

"He will be fine," Rose said.

The two officers looked at each other.

"Would you mind if we sat?" Officer Baines asked. "We may have information regarding the individual that injured your son."

"Of course not," Rose replied.

"Could I ask that the young lady please wait outside?"

Rose glanced at Carter who nodded. "Tika, would you mind waiting in the chapel? I'll come for you, after we've finished."

"Yes, Grandmother," Tika said. She closed the door.

"Okay," Officer Baines began. "I'll get right to it." He opened his notebook. "Last night at approximately twelve forty-five, one of our officers attempted to stop a vehicle about eight miles outside of town. He was responding to a call when it passed him at a high rate of speed, going in the opposite direction with its lights off." He glanced at his colleague, who nodded.

"By the time the officer came to a stop and turned his vehicle around, he'd lost sight of it. Approximately five miles later, he came upon it laying on it's roof, at the bottom of an embankment. It appeared to have struck a sign and left the road. When the officer reached the vehicle, he established that it was carrying a single occupant, who appeared to be either unconscious or deceased." He looked at the floor.

"Unfortunately, the fuel tank had ruptured and it had begun to burn. The officer suffered third degree burns to his hands and one arm in an unsuccessful attempt to extricate the occupant." He glanced at his notebook. "The fire department arrived on the scene approximately sixteen minutes later. By that time, all that remained of the vehicle was a burned-out shell."

No one spoke.

Officer Baines cleared his throat. "The vehicle was a 1962 Ford pickup, wearing plates from a '59 Chevrolet. It appears to have been dark green in color. When Officer McRae read the report this morning, he realized that it might be the truck from your bulletin from last Friday, although the plates don't match. Unfortunately, the coroner believes it will be impossible to positively identify the driver, due to the intensity of the fire." He turned to Officer McRae. "Tom."

Officer McRae leaned forward and placed the package he'd been carrying on the table. "This rifle was found in the truck. We're hoping it may help to identify the driver. Your original bulletin said the suspect was armed and dangerous, and included updated information you provided about a rifle. We'd like you to examine it and give us your opinion." He unwrapped the towel. "Unfortunately, as you can see, there's not a great deal left. The stock is burnt away and most of the finer hardware melted."

Carter bent and examined what remained. "May I?"

"Of course. We were unable to retrieve any evidence from it."

Carter picked up the rifle and turned it in his hands. All that was left was the barrel, chamber, magazine, and bolt. The trigger guard and trigger were missing and the sight had melted into a misshaped nub. He wet the corner of the cloth in the pitcher of water and cleaned the steel magazine above where the trigger had been. He held it close to his face, examined it then cleaned the other side and peered closely at it too.

The two officers glanced at each other.

"I'll be back in a moment," Carter said. He lay the rifle down, left the room and returned a couple minutes later carrying a pair of glasses. He smiled. "Magnifying, he said. "I figured sometimes a surgeon must need help to see clearer." Carter put the glasses on, picked up the rifle and closely examined both sides again. He sighed, lay it down in his lap, removed the glasses and sat back in his chair. "It's Orv's."

"If you don't mind, how can you be sure?" Officer McRae asked. "We've examined it and were unable to find any identifying features."

Carter handed him the glasses. "It's an 1890 model Winchester .22, long rifle. Bud told me yesterday that it was a very desirable gun in its day and still highly collectable. If you look on the magazine, above where the trigger had been, on the right side, you can faintly make out a name that he noticed someone had tried to sand off. That name was likely engraved by or for the original owner, over seventy years ago."

Carter handed Officer McRae the rifle. The officer put on the glasses and held the gun close to his face.

"Well, I'll be," he exclaimed. "There does appear to be something there, but I can't make it out."

Carter leaned back in his chair. "I believe you'll find that it says, '*Daniel S. Trapper*'."

27

The Past Meets the Present

Daniel pulled into his son's driveway. No one was outside waiting for him. It felt odd wiping the interior without at least one of his grandsons standing by. He took his time, performing the ritual by rote, his mind buried in thought. The passenger door opened.

"Sheesh." he jumped. "You trying to send me to an early grave?" He sat back and took a deep breath.

"Sorry, Dad," Gus apologized. "I thought you saw me."

"I might have, if I hadn't been in another world."

His son slid in and closed the door. "Before you came in this morning, I wanted to warn you that Colleen doesn't look like her normal self."

"What do you mean?"

Gus sighed. "Last night when Jack was hallucinating, he hit her. He had his toy gun in his hand. He caught her across the nose. This morning she's sporting a couple of world class shiners."

"Oh, for heaven sake."

Gus shook his head. "Dad, it was unbelievable. I don't know how much Colleen told you on the phone, but if I hadn't seen it with my own eyes, I wouldn't have believed it. Jack was screaming and swinging so wildly, I could barely restrain him. I hate to think how badly he might have hurt her if I hadn't been there."

Daniel sat back. He made up his mind. "Son, I don't believe it's a good idea to show Jack the bracelet. Since Colleen called this morning, I've been doing a lot of thinking. The way I figure it, we're in a no-win situation. If the bracelet isn't the same, it won't change his mind, he'll still believe the girl in his dream is real. And if it is the same, it will only convince him. Either way, it's impossible for him to ever really know. But if he never sees it, perhaps in time he'll forget."

"He's not going to forget, Dad. He's been crying all morning. There's nothing we've been able to say or do to change his mind. He's convinced that she's real." Gus stretched his legs and stared out the front window. "Let me ask you a question. After your accident, if you hadn't found the bracelet, would you have forgotten about Rose? Would you have come to believe that you walked out of the Misery under your own power? That she was just a figment of your imagination?"

"No."

"Well, Jack's dream is every bit as real to him, as Rose is to you." Gus rubbed his forehead. "No. I don't believe we have a choice. We have to show it to him. Even if all it does is help us get a handle on the situation." He cleared his throat. "Besides, I hate to admit it but he's got me starting to wonder."

"Oh, she's real all right," Daniel said.

Gus looked at him in surprise. "You honestly believe that?"

"Yes. Son, you asked me a question, now let me ask you one. When's the last time you sat in a thirty-six-year-old vehicle, named after a person who doesn't exist, having a conversation about someone from a dream?"

Gus snorted. "You and your homespun logic."

Daniel chuckled. "Well, I'm sorry, but I have no doubt that Jack's Tika is every bit as real to him, as my Rose is to me."

Colleen was waiting for them on the back porch. Gus hadn't exaggerated. She looked like she'd been on the losing end of a bar room brawl. Her face was drawn tight and there were ugly bruises around both her eyes. Daniel could also see that she'd been crying.

His son attempted to put his arm around her but she turned away. "Colleen, what's wrong?" he asked.

"Jack saw the bracelet. I left it on the counter while I was doing dishes. I didn't hear him and Danny come in. He took it out of the bag." Colleen looked at them both. "All he did was make a little squeak. When I turned around, he was as white as a sheet. And then he did the most remarkable thing. He closed his eyes, leaned forward and began to fall flat on his face. He wasn't even going to put out his hands to stop himself. Luckily Danny caught him just before he hit the floor, then all Jack said was that he wanted to lie down, so I took him to his room and came to get you."

She looked Daniel in the eye. He wanted to reach out and comfort her.

"Daniel, it was a mistake. Jack should never have seen it. Danny said that he thinks Jack thought he could fly."

When Daniel opened the door to his grandson's bedroom, Jack rolled over and faced the wall. Daniel sat beside him and put his hand on his shoulder. The boy flinched and moved further away.

"What's the matter, Sweetpea? You don't want to talk about it?"

Jack shook his head. "You lied, Grandpa. Mom told me it was your bracelet. You knew Tika was a true dream but you didn't tell me. When you asked me what it looked like, you already knew."

Daniel looked out the window. He tried to gather his thoughts, attempting to put himself in the boy's shoes. "I didn't lie to you, son." He got up, moved across the room and lay on his back on Danny's bed.

Jack peeked at him in surprise, then rolled back over.

Next door a lawn mower fired up. It began to growl up and down the yard, chewing and spitting out the morning silence. Daniel waited. His grandson didn't disappoint him.

"Grandpa, why didn't you tell me you had a bracelet just like Tika's?"

It was a question Daniel figured he'd be asked. "I wasn't sure that it was the same, Jack. I found that bracelet over sixty years ago, a ways from here and a long time before you were born."

"But why does it look the same?"

Daniel closed his eye. "Native people believe the eagle has great power. I imagine many bracelets and items made over the years had a similar design."

Next door the mower sputtered, ran rough then died. Out of gas, Daniel suspected. He fought back the urge to glance outside and confirm his guess.

Jack rolled onto his back. Daniel opened his eye and waited.

"Grandpa, how could I dream about something I don't know? I didn't know you had a bracelet like that, and that the eagle was powerful. How could I dream about that?"

"I don't know."

Jack rolled over to face him. Daniel continued to look at the ceiling. The boy was asking him tough questions. He'd obviously been thinking things through.

"Grandpa, do you think Tika's a real girl?"

Shoot. Daniel figured at some point he might be asked this, but not so soon. He hadn't had time to prepare an answer.

He wasn't ready. "I don't know, Jack. I suppose it's possible, although I've never heard of such a thing." He'd blinked.

"Yes, you have, Grandpa. Pauly dreamed of me before I was born. Before he even knew where babies came from. You can ask Mom. He told her."

"I've heard that, Jack. But I'm not sure that maybe Pauly wasn't just *wishing,* that his best friend was coming along."

"That's what his dad said too," Jack acknowledged. "But what about when Tika asked me if I was her guardian spirit? I'd never heard those words before."

Daniel rolled onto his side to face his grandson. "Sweetpea, you're asking me tough questions. I'd be lying if I told you I have all the answers. I've had dreams myself that have made me stop and wonder. I don't know what else to tell you."

Jack rolled onto his back. "Grandpa, what if Pauly's right and I had a true dream? What if Tika's a real girl? The badman said that he was gonna come back and hurt her. She's my friend and I'm really scared. I have to help her but I don't know how."

Daniel got up and sat beside Jack. Tears had pooled in his grandson's eyes and his hands were shaking. The look of despair on his face tore at Daniel's heart. He covered both of Jack's hands within his and squeezed. Sweetpea was wearing the bracelet.

28

Together Again

Tika sat at the back of the chapel. She knew she'd been asked to leave because the policemen wanted to speak about Orv. Her hope was that he'd been captured, but she couldn't help but wonder about the package they were carrying. If Orv had been caught, what was it they needed to show Carter?

Tika thought about Sweetpea. Although she'd been terrified for him when he fell, she didn't believe he could be injured. After all, he was either her guardian spirit or just a boy that her mind had made up. Someone who didn't exist couldn't be hurt. At least that's what she hoped, because she hadn't felt that way when the man struck him. Besides, hadn't she seen the horsemen ride off with him into the trees? Tika wished she'd been able to follow, to make sure he was okay. She fingered the choker about her neck.

How was she supposed to determine what was real in her dreams and what they meant? Her grandmother said that only the person who had them could say what they really were. Perhaps since Sweetpea had promised that Bud would be okay and her mother would return, she'd soon know if he really was her guardian spirit.

The chapel door opened. The top of a person's head poked in. They didn't enter. They seemed to be looking for someone. Tika rose to her feet but before she could call out, the door closed. She ran to it and stepped into the hall. The back of a familiar figure turned the corner and disappeared. Tika's heart began to pound. She took off running.

"Mom!" she yelled.

When she reached the corner, the nurse at the counter was smiling. Her mother had turned to face her.

"Tika?"

They ran into each other's arms. Sweetpea was right. She'd come home.

"I didn't see you in the chapel," her mother cried. "Where were you?"

"At the back, behind the door," Tika bawled.

Her mother knelt and straightened her ponytails over her shoulders. "I can't believe how much you've grown. You're not a little girl anymore."

Tika pushed inside her mother's arms and wrapped herself around her body. She'd been praying so hard for this day. Her mother kissed the top of her head and squeezed her as they rocked back and forth.

"It's okay, sweetheart. I promise, I'm not going anywhere."

Tika closed her eyes and lost herself in a swell of emotions. She didn't want to ever let go. "Have you come back to stay?" she asked, afraid of the answer, but more fearful of not knowing.

"Yes," her mother answered. "I'm better now, Tika. Much better." She squeezed her again and kissed her. "Where's your grandmother?"

"She's in the waiting room with Carter and some police officers. Uncle Bud had to go into surgery."

"I know. The nurse at the counter told me when I asked where you were."

Her mother held onto her shoulders and stepped back. "I can't get over how much you've grown and how beautiful you are." She gave her another kiss and took her hand. "Come. Show me which room your grandmother's in."

The two officers were leaving as they walked down the hall. They were still carrying the package. When Tika stopped in front of the door, her mother bent, hugged and kissed her again.

For the first time Tika realized how wonderful her mother looked. Helene's hair was braided and she was wearing a bright colored top like she always used to. There was also a trace of happiness around her eyes, something that had been missing for a long time. Tika couldn't remember her looking so young and alive. The sadness that had aged her after the accident, seemed to have been washed away.

"How's your grandmother holding up? Have you been able to help her?"

"Yes. She's worried about Uncle Bud though. But I told her he's going to be okay." Tika smiled. "She's going to be really happy to see you, Mom. This morning she told me she was sure, that if you knew Uncle Bud had been hurt, you'd come home."

"Well," her mother put her hand on the door, "Let's go see her."

Tika's grandmother never said a word. She just rose and met Helene halfway. As they hugged, she smiled at Tika and reached out to pull her close. Carter had a big grin too and he winked at her. Finally, they all stepped back, holding each other's hands.

"I can't tell you how happy I am to see you, Helene. Now I know Bud's going to be okay, because we're together again," Rose said. She smiled down at Tika. "Have you noticed what a beautiful young lady your daughter has become?"

Helene smiled. "Yes. The nurse at the counter told me she was in the chapel. We've already had ourselves a good cry."

Carter cleared his throat.

"Oh, I'm sorry," Rose said. "As usual, Carter's been a blessing, driving us back and forth to visit Bud."

"Hey, Carter," Helene said. "Do you think you'll ever get tired of taking care of the Flower children?"

Carter laughed at the inside joke. He'd grown up with Bud and Helene. They'd always been close. So close that at times he'd almost come to think of himself as her older brother. "You know, until today, I never realized how alike the three of you look, and how beautiful you all are. Come here, Helene."

She laughed and stepped into his arms.

The door opened and Dr. Westshot came in. "I'm sorry to interrupt," he said. He took in the commotion. His eyes settled upon Rose. "Mrs. Flowers, I'm happy to inform you that your son is doing well and is in recovery."

The three women turned and hugged him at the same time. The doctor tried to lift his hand to push up his glasses but gave up and hugged them in return.

"I must say, passing along good news to you ladies, certainly has its rewards."

Everyone laughed. After they released him, Carter shook the doctor's hand.

Dr. Westshot turned to Rose. "The knife nicked a small blood vessel in your son's chest. It bled just enough to put pressure against his pericardium, which caused his discomfort. I've drained off the fluid, patched him up, and he's as good as new. I'll have him home to you in a couple more days. Oh, and before I forget." Dr. Westshot dug into his front pants pocket and pulled out a piece of paper. "Before going into surgery, Bud asked me to give you this, deputy. He said it's directions to a hunting shack, where the man you're searching for may be hiding."

Carter's brow furrowed as he read the note. He looked at Helene. "Do you have a car?"

"Yes, I borrowed one from a friend. Why?"

"Are you spending the night in Medicine Falls?"

"Yes."

"Good. I think I know where this is. I need to radio the sheriff and have him meet me. When you leave, can you drive your mother and Tika home?"

"Of course."

"Thank you." Carter turned and hugged Rose. "When you see Bud, tell him thanks and that I'm glad that he's okay. Tell him I'll speak with him as soon as I can."

Rose nodded. "Okay, and Carter, after you're finished today, I'd like you to come to the house for supper. We can update you about Bud's condition."

"It's a date." Carter glanced at Helene. His face reddened. "I mean - oh you know what I mean. And don't forget to tell Bud about Orv. I know it's not going to be what he wants to hear but..."

"Don't worry," Rose said. "I'll hold dinner until six. Will that give you enough time?"

"Six it is. I'll see you then." Carter picked up his hat and left.

29

The Lights in The Sky

Danny found Pauly sitting in his mother's garden. Parked around him in the soil were a half dozen of his Tonka construction trucks, but he wasn't playing with them. He was staring into the cornfield through the wire fence that edged their backyard.

"Hey, Pauly. What are you doing?"

His friend didn't turn to look at him.

"Thinking."

"Oh. What are you thinking about?"

"Sweetpea."

Danny sat, stirring up a puff of dust that settled like smoke into the leaves of the plants. In front of him sat a yellow front end loader, its bucket loaded with dirt. He picked it up and pretended to examine it, trying to figure out how best to proceed. He decided to just jump in.

"How come you're thinking about Jack?"

Pauly didn't answer him.

Danny set the toy down and crossed his legs. In the front yard, Mr. Cook fired up the lawn mower again. It roared then settled into a steady drone.

"Pauly, I need you to tell me about true dreams and I promise I won't tell anyone, and nobody can hear us."

Pauly looked down, his lips pressed together.

Danny had seen this face before. When Pauly didn't want to talk, you had to push him. "I know you think Jack's in danger and so do I. And you're the only person who can help me protect him."

Pauly glanced at him.

"Please. Tell me what you know and why you think he's had one."

Pauly emptied the dirt from the loader into a red dump truck. He pushed a handle that tilted the box, the tailgate swung open and the dirt poured to the ground.

"Please."

"I can't. Fatboy and Mom told me not to talk about it anymore."

"I know, but that's only because they don't believe, and don't think Jack's in danger."

"Do you believe in true dreams?" Pauly asked, without looking up. "Have you had one?"

"No."

"Then why do you believe?"

"I don't," Danny admitted. "But I know you do, and you said somebody wants to hurt Jack. And last night in his sleep, a man hurt him real bad."

Pauly looked into the cornfield again. "I know."

Danny was shocked. "What do you mean you know? How?"

"I heard him scream and saw the lights come on in your room."

"Oh." Danny hadn't thought of that. Their houses were close together, the windows only a few feet apart. He decided to try a different approach.

"Pauly, do you know Grandpa's at our house right now, in our bedroom, talking with Jack?"

"No."

"Do you know that this morning, Jack found a bracelet Grandpa gave Mom and Dad, that looks just like the one the girl in his dream was wearing?"

Pauly's forehead wrinkled. Danny thought that one might get him thinking. He waited.

"Where did Grandpa get it, Danny?"

"I don't know. I didn't get a chance to ask him. When he came in, he went right in to see Jack. That's why I came outside to look for you. So we could talk." Danny slapped the back of his neck and scratched a mosquito bite. "Do you know what Jack tried to do when he saw the bracelet?"

Pauly closed his eyes.

"He tried to fly, Pauly. Why would Jack think he could do that?"

His friend remained silent.

"I know," Danny answered for him. "Because now he thinks he's had a true dream too. Why does he think that? Did you talk to him?"

"Just a little bit."

"What did you tell him?"

Pauly kicked the dump truck onto its side. "I'm not supposed to talk about it, Danny. If I do, I won't be a good boy anymore."

Danny decided to push him again. Harder this time. "Pauly, do you want to see Jack get hurt? Because that's what I think's gonna happen if we don't do something. And so do you." He hated having to scare his friend but Jack was his brother, and he needed to learn what Pauly knew. Pauly's lips began to tremble. Danny felt terrible.

"I didn't tell him anything," Pauly whispered. "I just asked when he had his flying dream, if he saw lights shooting across the sky."

"Light's in the sky? What does that have to do with anything."

Pauly looked at him like he was nuts. "Because that's what true dreams are, Danny. When Jack said that he saw lights shooting up from the ground and across the sky, I knew he had one." Pauly stared him in the eye. "*The light's he saw were other people, flying in their true dreams.*"

"What? How do you know that? Have you had a flying dream?"

"No."

"Then how do you know about these lights?"

Pauly remained silent.

Danny considered it. If Pauly never had one, he had to have either dreamed about seeing people fly, or somebody told him.

"Did somebody tell you about these lights?"

"No."

"Have you had dreams about seeing people fly?"

"Yes."

"Did they make lights in the sky?"

"Yes."

"Were they true dreams?"

"Yes."

"How do you know?"

Before he could react, Pauly seized his wrist. Danny was shocked at the strength in his grip. He tried to pull free but his arm wouldn't budge. He looked up. Pauly's eyes were wide and full of pleading.

"Because it was Jack, Danny! I tried to tell everyone but nobody would listen." Pauly squeezed harder. "When Jack came to me in my dream before he was born and told me we were going to be best friends, he could fly. And when he flew away, there were thousands of tiny lights following him."

30

Burlap

Carter glanced at his watch before stepping onto the porch. It was shortly after noon. Before he could knock, the door opened.

Rose looked out. “Oh, it’s you, Carter. I thought I heard something.” She looked at him oddly. “You’re awful early. We just arrived home.”

Carter slapped his hat against his leg and followed her inside. Helene and Tika turned from the counter. They were both wearing one of Rose’s calico aprons and were preparing lunch.

“Well, Carter Winslow,” Helene needled. “I’ve never known you to be early in my entire life.”

Carter nodded and tried to smile.

“You left your vehicle running, Carter,” Rose said.

“I know. I’m sorry, but I wanted to stop by and let you know that I don’t think I’ll be able to join you for dinner this evening.” He looked down and kneaded the brim of his hat while he chose his next words. “I just came from the shack Bud sent me to, and I’m heading into Jefferson City to speak with him.”

“So, was Bud right? Had Orv been out there?”

“Yes. We found a few of his things but mostly empty beer bottles and cigarette butts.” Carter looked questioningly at her and tipped his head towards Tika.

"It's okay. When Helene drove us home, I told them about Orv. They know what happened."

Carter nodded and struggled to hold her gaze. "There's something else I need to tell you." He looked down at his hat again. "We found more out there."

"Carter, what's wrong? I've never seen you this upset before. Please, have a seat. Can I get you something to drink?"

"Water would be fine. Thank you." He sat and covered his knee with his hat.

Rose poured him a glass and he drank half before setting it back down. From the corner of his eye, he saw Helene wrap her arm protectively around Tika's shoulders.

Carter cleared his throat. "You're going to be hearing about this on the news later today, but I wanted to make sure that you heard it from me first." He glanced at the table. "And I'm sure there'll be reporters coming by, looking to speak with Bud."

"Carter, what is it? What's wrong?"

He looked into Rose's eyes. There was no easy way to say what he had to. No way to cushion the shock. "After I left the hospital, I met the sheriff and he followed me to the shack. I knew roughly where it was. Same as Bud, I came across it a number of years ago." He finished his water. "After we searched the place, I went outside to radio in. The sheriff wanted someone to come out and take pictures and collect evidence. When I went back inside, he was lifting a section of floor that he'd noticed was hinged. He figured there might be a cache underneath. You'll find one in most hunting shacks." He rubbed his hands over his face.

"I helped him prop it open and climbed inside. It isn't a normal sized cache. Someone dug it out. It's a little over three feet deep and almost the same from side to side. At the bottom, I found a burlap sack, some rope, and a pair of children's running shoes. In the corner was a metal lunch bucket." He glanced at Rose. Moisture built behind his eyes. He blinked.

"The lunch bucket was open. Under the lid, a boy's name had been scratched. Likely by his parents." Carter picked up his hat and kneaded the brim. "It was the name of a child who went missing in Jefferson City, in November of 1965. I'm sure you'll remember. There was a state-wide search for him, until a farmer found him on a country road two weeks later, badly beaten and almost froze to death."

"Oh, dear Lord," Helene exclaimed. "I remember that. And this is the man who tried to hurt my baby? Who lived next door and almost killed my brother?"

"Helene," Rose cautioned. "Let Carter finish."

Carter looked at her. This woman never ceased to amaze him. Had she already grasped what he and the sheriff hadn't, until just before the state police arrived? He turned and looked at Helene.

"We can't be sure this was Orv's doing. The day he injured Bud, your mother told me that he moved in next door in November, and that he hadn't been living in the area. Of course, that could just be his story but that places him here days after the child was taken. That's why I need to speak with Bud." He set his hat on his head. "Yesterday Bud told me he was with Orv at the shack, the day Orv purchased his rifle from a man he met near there. I need to find out who this other person is. In the meantime, the state police are out there now, searching for more evidence."

"It was a different man," Rose whispered.

"What's that, Rose?"

"Nothing, Carter. I was just thinking out loud."

The deputy stood. "I'm sorry for having to back out of dinner, but I'll likely be needed out there until late this evening. If I return to town after speaking with Bud, I promise I'll stop by and let you know if we've learned anything new."

31

A Badman

Terry was becoming more angry and anxious by the minute. Everything he was stealing from Cecil's house, he'd loaded in his truck hours ago. He should have left by now. Hanging around was asking for trouble. The only thing keeping him was his desire to grab Sweetpea.

He lit another cigarette and looked out the bedroom window. Two doors down, the older Trapper boy and the retarded kid were still sitting in the garden. Terry wondered what they were talking about and where Sweetpea was. He hadn't seen the little bugger since early this morning, when he'd caught him snooping from his front porch.

Terry's hands balled into fists. "What kind of name for a boy is Sweetpea anyways?"

Every since Friday morning, when he'd first seen Sweetpea on his bicycle, then been almost run over by him after hiding behind the bushes, Terry wanted to hurt the boy. If only Sweetpea's father hadn't been following down the sidewalk, he'd have gagged, bagged, and taken him right there and no one would have been the wiser. All the valuables in the house could have waited. Sweetpea was the real prize.

Terry punched the wall and looked at his watch. Twelve o'clock. Another half hour and he had to go. It was a forty-five-minute drive back to Bothwell and the guy he was selling everything to said he'd meet him outside the pool hall at one-thirty. *'And if you're not on time, forget about it.'* That gave him a half hour to grab Sweetpea, stash him in the hole and then drive into town.

One hundred and fifty dollars was all that he was getting for everything he'd taken from the house. Or two hundred if he threw in the pistol he'd found in the closet. Either way it wasn't a lot of cash, so he was leaning towards keeping it, to replace the rifle he'd sold in Missouri. The way Terry figured it, he never knew when he might come across another weapon and at least this time he had a choice. That hadn't been the case when he'd needed the cash for gas and food while he was holding the kid beneath the shack. Oh well, there was nothing he could do about it now. Hard to believe that had been almost two years ago. Damn, he wanted Sweetpea. He took another pull on his cigarette, dropped it and ground it into the carpet.

Terry's only redeeming quality was that he was evil and he knew it. After each abduction, it sickened him to know the cruelty he was capable of inflicting upon a child. So, he'd slink away, to an abandoned shack or cabin in the backcountry, to self-mutilate and promise himself that it had been his last. Until the shame of the abuse he'd suffered as a child would begin to build again, driving him back into the open, to vent his pain upon another. Terry blamed his depravity upon his father.

'Momma's boy,' that's what he'd been called before each beating, and before being locked for days in the hole beneath the ground.

'Someday you'll thank me for this boy, because there ain't nothing going to toughen you up quicker than spending a few days down there doing nothing but thinking.'

And that's exactly what Terry had done, thought of nothing but how he wanted to thank his old man with a bullet, before finally concluding that he didn't have the courage and running away. But then a funny thing happened - somehow the old man's perversion became his.

Terry began to despise the weakness he perceived not only in himself but also in others, particularly young boys. Until finally he took his first and doled out the same punishment he'd received, before dropping the child off a couple weeks later, beaten and in tears, out in the country, in front of a farmhouse. Somehow his and his father's circle had become complete. Terry had become what he despised most. Over the next eleven years he took and released five more boys. The last in Jefferson City, Missouri, when he'd almost lost control and took the boy's life. He cursed his old man.

Ten days ago, when he'd returned home, it was with the single intent of killing him. But the moment Terry saw his father, he'd discovered he was still terrified of him, despite the old coot being wasted down to a bag of bones from the cancer eating his insides. Terry decided he'd wait for him to die. It shouldn't take long. Even his father's doctors couldn't figure out what was keeping him alive. There was nothing left of the old man but a bad smell and a river of tears. Then Terry would take whatever he wanted and hit the road. In the meantime, he couldn't stand hanging around. Everything about the place left nothing but a bad taste in his mouth.

Terry shook his head and looked out the window again. The older Trapper boy was nowhere in sight and the retarded kid was stumbling along the edge of the cornfield, his arms flailing as he carried on an animated conversation with himself.

Terry sneered. "Where are you, Sweetpea?"

All he wanted was for the kid to ride his bike one more time down the driveway, then he'd grab him. He'd already laid out a bag and rope on the tailgate of his truck. But if Sweetpea didn't show soon, Terry was going to have to come back for him. A risk he didn't particularly want to take, although for Sweetpea he'd make the exception. Just the thought of listening to him bawl and carry on for his momma brought a smile to his face. He looked out the window. The retarded kid had opened the gate and was almost at the back of the house.

"What?"

Terry watched him walk to the porch, look up then shuffle in his awkward gait around the corner. Terry ran into the washroom and looked out the window between the two houses. The boy was nowhere in sight. He went to the front door, parted the curtains and looked out. The kid was standing at the rear of his truck. In his right hand was the bag and rope he'd set aside for Sweetpea.

Terry opened the door. "What do you think you're doing?"

The boy turned. On his face was a look of sadness and fierce determination.

"You are a badman."

"What?" Terry was flabbergasted. Who the heck did this kid think he was, talking to him like that? Somebody had to be putting him up to it. Likely they were watching right now, to gauge his reaction. Probably Sweetpea's older brother. Terry glanced about. They appeared to be alone.

"You're not supposed to be in Mr. C's house and you want to hurt Sweetpea."

Terry felt like he'd been punched in the stomach. His insides turned to water. "What the hell are you talking about and who do you think you are?" For the first time in years, his hand had been caught in the cookie jar.

"You are a badman," the boy said again. "You broke four rules. You're lying. You're taking things that don't belong to you. You said bad words, and you want to hurt Sweetpea. That's why Mr. C's things are in your truck and you got this." He held the bag and rope at arm's length, like a prosecutor providing a jury with damning evidence. "I'm telling Fatboy." The boy bent, looked at Terry's license plate then turned to walk away.

"Wait." Terry's mind was spinning. How did this kid know what he was up to? And how had he put him on defense so easily? "I'm not taking anything and I'm sure not here to hurt anyone. This is my uncle's house. He asked me to stop by and pick up some things for him. That's why the bag's there. To carry stuff in."

Damn. He couldn't believe he'd just told him that Cecil was his uncle. Now what was he going to do? Whatever it was, it better be quick or he was in trouble. "Stay there and I'll prove it to you. I've got a letter from him. It's on the front seat of my truck."

Before stepping off the porch, Terry glanced toward the highway. Fortunately, there was no one in sight and he'd parked so that his truck was hidden behind the thick bushes and ash tree in the center. He walked quickly to the driver's door and smiled as he opened it.

"It's right here."

He reached behind the seat and grabbed his small leather sap. It was shaped like a beaver tail and weighted with lead. He turned and brought it down hard on top of the boy's head.

Amazingly the kid didn't fall but staggered and fell against his truck. Terry raised it to strike again but the boy reached up and grabbed his wrist. Terry went wild with fear. His arm felt like it had been caught in a vice. He tried to pull free but the boy stumbled against him, dropped the bag and grabbed at his shirt front. Terry reached up with his free hand, took the sap from his other, and swung it against the side of the boy's head. This time the kid's eyes rolled and he crumpled face first to the ground. A bright spray of blood burst from his nose onto Terry's shoes and the concrete.

Terry grabbed an old tarp from the bed of his truck, covered him quickly, then rolled him into a tight bundle. With the rope the boy dropped, he tied both ends, then picked him up and threw him into the back. Terry jumped inside, started the engine and pulled onto the highway.

Next to the stain of blood on the driveway was a broken toy six-shooter, that had been lying inside the tarp.

32

Questions

Bud wasn't used to being confined and despite the pain in his chest, he wanted to go home. Of course, Dr. Westshot would hear none of it. After today's setback, he said that Bud needed two more days under his personal observation, and then he might consider allowing him to depart.

Bud smiled. How many times had he paid this price? The doc obviously wasn't willing to take another chance on disappointing his mother. Bud had witnessed her effect on others before. Somehow Rose's stoic bearing drew upon the fiercest loyalty. An attribute he'd never observed to the same degree in anyone else.

Bud's stomach growled. They hadn't been feeding him enough to keep a bird alive. He lifted his head to read the clock, the door opened and Carter stepped in.

"Hey." The deputy smiled. "How are you?"

"Carter. It's good to see you."

His friend walked to his bedside and the two men shook hands.

"Doc says I can only stay for two minutes, and I had a heck of a time getting that from him."

Bud chuckled. "It's called the Rose effect."

Carter smiled. "Been there, done that. You have to admit, she's quite the lady." Carter looked him over from head to toe.

"It's sure good to see you. That was quite the scare you gave us this morning."

"I scared myself," Bud said. He nodded toward the door. "You come in by yourself?"

"Yes, I just left your house. The ladies were making lunch." He put his hand on the chair next to the bed. "You mind?

"No, I've been eyeing that myself. I'm getting sick of this bed."

"You'll be up soon enough." Carter sat and took off his hat.

"Huh." Bud pressed his palm against his upper chest, winced then looked at his friend. "Before I forget, I want to thank you again, Carter. I've been told several times that if you'd waited for the ambulance, I wouldn't be here."

"You're welcome, but like I told you before, it's your mother and Tika that deserve your thanks. They had more to do with keeping you alive than me."

Bud nodded. "Mom told me about Orv this morning. I can't say I feel sorry, but that's sure one hell of a way to die."

Carter chewed his bottom lip. "So, she told you about his rifle?"

"Yes. I hate to admit it but that was the first thing that crossed my mind." He sighed. "There's fifty dollars I'll never see again."

"And you saw Helene?" A faint smile played on the deputy's lips. "She sure looks terrific, doesn't she?"

"Yes, and Tika's got her mom back. I can't tell you how happy that makes me. When I think of what that son of a..." Bud clenched his fists. "Have you been out to the shack, to see if Orv had been there?"

"Yes. That's why I came in to speak with you. I've got a few questions."

"Go ahead. As you can see, I'm not going anywhere."

Carter looked him in the eye. "It's not good, Bud. We found things out there that I doubt will ever leave me."

Bud waited for him to continue.

"Inside the shack, we found a cache beneath the floor. At the bottom, I found rope, a pair of shoes and a lunch bucket from the boy who went missing two years ago from Jefferson City. The one they found out in the country, beaten and half froze to death. The sheriff has called in the state police. They're out there now, searching for more evidence."

Bud closed his eyes. His jaw muscles tightened. "As peculiar as I found Orv, I never would have thought that of him."

"Well, if it's any consolation, we're not sure yet that it was him. The child went missing about the same time he moved in next to you."

Bud looked up at him. "You're wondering if it might have been the fellow he purchased his rifle from?"

"Yes. It's a possibility. Is there anything you can tell me about the man?"

"Like I told you yesterday, Orv said he met him while he was out scouting turkey. He said the fellow had a game rifle that he wanted to sell and Orv asked if I'd go with him and take a look."

"What was your gut feeling about this other person? Do you remember what he looked like, his name or where he was from?"

Bud shook his head. "He seemed decent enough. I never pushed him for information. I do remember Orv asking him where home was and him pointing north." He closed his eyes and tried to picture more. "I'd say he was Orv's age. Maybe a couple of inches shorter. Thin, with straight brown hair down to his shoulders. That's about it."

"Did he have a vehicle? Do you know if he was staying at the shack, or how he came to be there?"

"No. I didn't see a car or truck around and it just looked like an abandoned hunting shack. I don't know if they decided to meet there because that's where they'd first met or…" Bud felt the blood drain from his face. "Carter, you don't suppose the boy was inside while I was out there?"

"I don't know, Bud. And there's no way you could either. Do you think you'd recognize this fellow if you saw him again? If we came up with a photo?"

Bud closed his eyes. His mind was spinning. "I believe so." He remembered something else. "As we were walking back to Orv's truck, Orv said something about never trusting a man with green eyes."

"Green eyes? Is that it?"

Bud nodded then looked at his friend. "Carter, Mom said you found papers in Orv's house. That he'd been living under an alias. Have you learned any more about that?"

Carter looked at the floor. "Yes, and it all kind of ties in with what we found at the shack. But I wanted your opinion first." He grimaced. "Sheriff Neall talked to the authorities where Orv came from. They believe he killed his father when he was fifteen. They said his old man was a mean one. Beat Orv on a regular basis. So bad that he wound up in the hospital a number of times with broken bones, but always with an explanation. They think Orv finally had enough and set fire to the house, after he'd beat him to death with a hammer. By the time they figured it out, Orv was long gone. That was almost eighteen years ago."

Bud closed his eyes. "I'll never understand the evil a man can do to a child. I know it creates a lot of anger. Do you think that might explain Orv taking the boy?"

"That's what I'm beginning to think," Carter said. He rose and put his hat back on. "I have to be getting back and you need to get some rest. Thanks for your help, Bud. I'll let you know if we come up with anything new."

They shook hands again.

"Carter, Mom said that you're going to have dinner tonight at the house?"

The deputy sighed. "I was planning to. Before this." He looked down at the floor. "When I stopped in, I told her that I didn't think I'd be able to now. I believe I may have made a mistake. I could use being around some friendly faces."

Bud put his hand on his friend's arm. "Then give her a call. Let Mom know you've changed your mind. I know Helene would be happy to see you."

33

Where's Pauly?

Gus saw the pistol in Cecil's driveway first. When he bent to pick it up, he noticed a curled splash of blood next to it. He looked up at the house. The inside door was open but there were no vehicles in the driveway. Gus pressed the doorbell. There was no answer. He went around back. A lower corner window in the door was smashed. He turned the handle. It was unlocked. He stuck his head inside. Glass crunched beneath his foot. This wasn't good.

"Hello," he called. "Is there anybody home?"

It remained silent. Gus went back out front. On the other side of the road, Danny and Jack were riding their bicycles down the sidewalk, searching door to door for their friend. Gus walked home and found Colleen on the phone in the kitchen. She was asking one of the neighbors if they'd seen Pauly. He waited for her to hang up.

"Any luck?"

Colleen shook her head.

Gus handed her the pistol. "I found this in Cecil's driveway, next to some dried blood."

Colleen's eyebrows lifted. "Blood?" She examined the gun. It was silver with a white plastic grip. Jack's initials were scratched into the butt. "This is Jack's. What was it doing there?"

"I don't know. But the front door to Cecil's house is open and I found a window smashed in the rear. Someone had broken in."

Colleen's eyes widened. "Have you told Glenn?"

"No. I wanted to talk to you first. Do you know where he is?"

"He was going toward the school. Danny and Jack went the other way."

"Okay. I'm going to find him, pick him up and take him to Cecil's, then bring him home. Before I come back, I'll make sure the boys are on their way."

"Gus, do you think something's happened to Pauly?"

"I don't know. But it doesn't feel good." He opened the door then turned. "I think it would be a good idea when we return, if you're with Hazel."

"I was just thinking the same thing. I'll go over right away."

Gus jumped in his truck, backed onto the highway and drove toward Baldoon School. Half way down, on the opposite side of the road, his neighbor was talking with Stan Kildare in his driveway. When Gus pulled in the two men turned and looked at him. Glenn walked over and Stan gave him a quizzical smile and a half wave. Gus nodded.

"Any luck?" Glenn asked as he opened the passenger door. "Did your boys find him?"

"No, jump in. There's something I need to show you."

His neighbor slid in and closed the door.

"I found something at Cecil's," Gus said, as he backed out. "I can't be sure it has anything to do with Pauly, but you need to know."

He pulled into Cecil's driveway, showed Glenn the blood and told him about Jack's gun. Glenn knelt to examine the stain. When he looked up, his eyes were wide with fear.

"But we can't be sure this has anything to do with Pauly. Can we?"

"No. But I found a broken window in the back door. Someone has broken in."

Gus went with Glenn to the rear of the house.

Glenn turned the door handle. "I'm going inside," he said.

"I'll go with you."

Every room was a mess. The closets and drawers open, the contents strewn onto the floor. Someone had thoroughly gone through everything.

Glenn's face turned pale. "Have you called the police?"

"No. I wanted to show you first."

Glenn looked at him. "Gus, I don't remember seeing Pauly playing with a pistol today. Are you sure Jack didn't leave it out front?"

Gus shook his head. "Jack hadn't been out of the house. And there's still the matter of the blood."

"What am I going to tell Hazel?"

Gus put his hand on his neighbor's shoulder. "I don't know, but we can't be sure that anything has happened. We need to get the police out here. Colleen went next door to be with Hazel. I told her I'd bring you home."

Glenn nodded and they walked out to the truck.

"I want to tell Danny and Jack to come home first, Glenn. It'll only take a minute."

When the police pulled into the Cook's driveway, it seemed half the people in the neighborhood came over and gathered in their front yard.

Gus went out and told them that Pauly was missing. A suggestion was made that they split into groups, to search the neighborhood.

Constable Goodall, the officer with the Ontario Provincial Police, asked Gus and Glenn to accompany him to Cecil's. Hazel insisted on going too, while Colleen stayed with the boys.

After examining the blood and the broken rear window, the constable went into the house. A moment later he returned and called for backup. Within minutes, three more patrol cars pulled into the driveway and a half-dozen officers went inside.

Gus's heart became so heavy, he couldn't stand still any longer. He left Glenn and Hazel in the backyard and wandered around to the front of the house.

A long line of vehicles had parked on both sides of the highway. Every driveway, front yard, and the parking lot of the drive-in was filling fast as a steady stream of vehicles came down the road from Wallaceburg. It looked like a couple of hundred people had already gathered on the Cook's and his front lawn, murmuring among themselves and looking towards Cecil's. Gus was overwhelmed.

"Glenn, Hazel, come look."

His neighbors walked out front and stood beside him.

"The whole town's coming, to help you find your son." Gus's voice caught in his throat. "They must have been calling each other."

Glenn and Hazel embraced.

Gus looked back at the crowd. Colleen was waving to him from their front porch. "I'll be right back," he said.

As he walked down the sidewalk, Brad Benson, the owner of the Big Chief restaurant, called out to him from the edge of the crowd. "Gus, any word yet about Pauly?"

Everyone became silent.

"No." Gus stopped and looked over the concerned faces. "They're searching Cecil's right now, to see if they can learn anything."

"Okay," Brad said. "Please let Hazel and Glenn know that we're here for them, and that as soon as we can get organized, we're going to split into groups to search from the plaza to the river. Tell them we won't stop looking until we can bring Pauly home."

"Hazel and Glenn will appreciate any help you folks can provide. I'll also let the police know what you're planning. I'm sure they'll have suggestions." Gus paused. "And please, everyone, say a prayer for Pauly. He's a good boy and his parents need him home, safe and sound."

"We'll find him," someone shouted from the crowd. "Yes," others called out. "We'll find him."

Brad stepped forward and squeezed his arm. "We'll do everything we can, Gus." He turned and raised his hands. "Okay, folks. We're meeting across the road and forming into search parties. We'll need group leaders and volunteers."

Gus continued down the sidewalk. He stepped onto his porch and gave Colleen a hug. "This is unbelievable," he said, as he watched the crowd move across the highway. He looked at Colleen. "You wanted me?"

Colleen squeezed his hand. "Honey, Danny's in his room. He's upset. He says he has something he needs to tell you."

Gus stopped in the doorway to his boy's room. Danny was sitting on the edge of his bed with his hands in his lap. He didn't look up.

"What's wrong, son? Your mother said you wanted to speak to me?"

Danny clenched his hands and kept his face lowered. "Today when Grandpa was here, I went outside and talked to

Pauly. I made him tell me why he thought a badman was after Jack, and why he believed in true dreams." Danny lifted his head and his bottom lip began to quiver. "I didn't mean to do anything wrong, Dad. I was just worried about Jack."

Gus could tell that his son was on the verge of tears. This wasn't like Danny.

"It's okay, Pauly's going to be fine. He's likely just wandered off and lost track of time."

"No," Danny said. "I heard Mom talking about Jack's gun and the blood you found in the driveway. I think Pauly knew someone was at Cecil's. He always knows everything that's going on in the neighborhood. Remember the other day when Jack almost ran into a man over there? I think Pauly knew about that too."

Gus could have kicked himself. He'd forgotten all about the person who'd helped his son. He needed to go back and tell the police. They were going to want to speak with Jack, since he was the only person who'd seen the man.

"I forgot all about that," he said, turning to leave.

"Wait, Dad, there's more." Danny looked down at his hands. "I think Pauly maybe thought the man Jack saw, was the badman from his dreams. I think he might have went over there to tell him to leave Jack alone."

Gus's heart sank. It all made sense. Pauly wouldn't think twice about doing whatever he needed to protect his friend. That might also explain why Jack's pistol was there. Pauly likely took it with him, thinking he could frighten the man.

"The pistol. Do you think Pauly took it with him?"

Danny shook his head. "No. Last night when Jack went to sleep, he wore his holster with both guns. He never left the house today, until we went to look for Pauly. I don't know how it could have got over there."

34

The Hole

Pauly couldn't keep his eyes open. It scared him too much. He hadn't known such blackness could exist. It disoriented him, as though he'd fallen in his sleep and stopped halfway to the ground. Up and down and all around seemed to surround him from every direction.

Pauly rolled onto his back. Behind him, his hands were stuck together, and he couldn't pull his feet apart. He drew his knees up and sat with his hands behind him on the floor. It was dirt. Cold and moist and heavy smelling, like the container his mother threw the weeds into that she'd pulled from the garden. He opened his eyes and shut them quickly. Somehow, he could sense more light and felt safer with them closed. Pauly wished he could touch his head. It hurt and his left ear too. A layer of crust covered his upper lip. He stuck out his tongue and tasted it. Steel.

"Mom?"

His voice lingered and filled his ears. He called again, softer this time.

"Mom?"

Pauly liked the way it sounded but not the awareness that it travelled nowhere. There was no echo. It seemed to just drip from his tongue and hang about.

He reached back as far as he could and found nothing. With his hands pushing down, he dug in his heels, lifted his butt and slid back. Although it terrified him to move, he had no choice. There had to be something solid around him. He slid back a couple of inches at a time until his fingers brushed against a wall. Loose pieces sprinkled to the floor. More dirt, cooler and wetter than the floor. Pauly slid back one more time and his back touched. He leaned against it. It was too cold. He drew away, but at least now he knew he was somewhere. He'd try to figure out where, after he'd built up the courage to search for more walls.

He'd been right. The man in Mr. C's home had planned to hurt Jack. And even though he was the one who'd now been taken, knowing his friend was safe brought comfort to him. His decision to confirm his suspicion had been correct. Pauly didn't like to make mistakes. His father said if a person thought things through, they'd almost always make the right decision. He had that to hold onto. Now he needed to do some more good thinking and figure out what his next step should be.

Pauly knew he was in a hole inside the earth. That didn't frighten him. After the workers left for the day when they were building a new house by the school, he'd slid down the wooden ramp into the hole for the basement. Even when he looked up and realized how difficult it was going to be for him to climb out, he hadn't been scared. Of course, that hole had been open with the sun shining down, but the way he figured it, if the house had been on top, he'd still have been in the same hole. Pauly decided to look at this situation the same way. He was in a hole, no different from any other, and now he had to figure a way out.

Above him he heard a noise. Three footsteps. They stopped and heavy objects were slid across the ceiling. Pauly opened his eyes and looked up. His stomach flopped and turned as a wave of dizziness rolled over him. A thin crack of light appeared. Someone cursed and something heavy was thrown to the side. A moment of silence, then a portion of the ceiling began to lift. It stopped after forming a square. The silhouette of a person's head and shoulders appeared from the left. Pauly squinted. It made no difference. The only light came from behind. Instinctively though, he knew who it was.

"So, you are awake," the man said. "I didn't think you were. I figured the moment you came to, you'd start bawling for your momma."

Pauly recognized the voice. He was right. It was the man from Mr. C's.

"So why aren't you crying? You figure you're some kind of tough guy?" The man snorted and spat at him. "You little bugger. You have no idea how much trouble you caused me today, snooping around and accusing me of things I didn't do. Plus, you cost me a lot of money." He spat again. "A lot of money. So, what am I going to do with you? You're not even the person that's supposed to be down there."

Pauly smiled. It wasn't something he planned, it just happened when he realized what the man meant.

"Did you just smile?" The man laughed and shook his head. "Boy, you ain't got the good sense God gave a goose. What's your name?"

Pauly lowered his head and looked at his surroundings. Now that there was light, he could see what the inside of the hole looked like. It appeared to be a little taller than him and about the same distance from end to end and side to side. In the corner, nearest his right foot, was a blanket rolled into a ball. In the opposite corner, what looked like a steel hook hung from the ceiling. There was a hat or something on it. That was it. Nothing else.

"I asked you a question and if you're smart you'll answer me," the man said, angrily.

Pauly looked up. "I don't like you. You're not a good person. You're bad. You hurt people and you wanted to hurt

Sweetpea. He's my best friend, so I'm not talking to you." He looked again at the hook, to remember where it was.

"Why, you little bugger. Who the hell do you think you are?"

The man stomped away and cursed some more. Something heavy crashed to the floor, he returned, reached forward and slammed the door. Pauly was swallowed in darkness again. More cursing and stomping and it became quiet. Pauly closed his eyes. Somehow, he could still see the square of light, the man's outline and the hook against his eyelids. He'd noticed before that he could sometimes do this and wondered how. He wished he'd asked his father. Pauly saved his thought with a big number one.

The footsteps returned. Pauly looked up slowly this time. The square opened and the silhouette returned. The man appeared to be holding something. He swung back and forth a couple times before a wave of cold water splashed down. Pauly sputtered and turned his face. He was drenched from head to toe.

"Ha," the man snorted. "Now you're not so tough, are you? Now I'm only gonna ask you one more time. What's your name?"

There was nothing Pauly was more afraid of than water. A recurring nightmare he had since he was a child, was of falling in water and not being able to get up. It was never deep. Just enough that with his hands on the bottom, he couldn't lift his head high enough to breathe, or to get his feet beneath him. It terrified him.

"Pauly," he muttered, as he began to shiver.

"Pauly," the man laughed. "That's better. Trouble is, now because you're so stupid, you gotta spend the night down there cold and wet. Do you think the next time I ask you something, you'll answer me quick and won't waste my time?" He waited for Pauly to respond. Pauly lowered his eyes and looked straight ahead. The man cursed. He disappeared and a moment later lowered a ladder over the edge, climbed down and stood over him.

"Lift your face."

Pauly continued to look straight ahead.

"I said lift your damn face."

The man slapped him and Pauly fell onto his side. He struggled to sit back up. Tears trickled down his cheeks.

"Dang, you're a hard-headed little bugger," the man shouted. "Now I'm only going to tell you one more time. Lift. Your damn. Face."

Pauly slowly raised his head and looked into the man's eyes.

The man stepped back as though he'd been struck. With shaking fingers, he ripped a length of tape from a roll and pressed it across Pauly's mouth. He turned and scurried up the ladder. Quick footsteps and silence filled Pauly's ears. Minutes later, the man returned, pulled the ladder up and slammed the door. The heavy objects were slid back in place. A couple more footsteps, then nothing but silence.

Pauly closed his eyes and began to work his way over to where the blanket was. The floor was slippery now. It also smelled terrible, like decaying wet clay. He turned and reached out with his fingers. The blanket was thick and damp. He released it and slid back to his second wall. If he'd figured right, the hook should be directly in front of him, in the opposite corner.

35

A Field of Flowers

When Mom left our room, Danny and I rolled onto our sides to watch her go. She stopped in the doorway and turned to look at us. It was the worst thing she could have done because it was exactly what I needed her to do, and from the look on her face it was clear - she was as frightened to leave our sight as I was to be out of hers.

"Goodnight, Mom," Danny said.

I wanted to jump out of bed and punch him right in the gut. Didn't he understand that the moment he said that she'd leave, today would be over, we'd be alone, and Pauly still wouldn't be home?

Mom tried to smile. A hand reached inside my chest and squeezed my heart.

"Goodnight, boys," she said, before pulling the door closed.

I waited until just before it clicked. "Goodnight, Mom."

Danny rolled onto his back. I stayed where I was, glaring at him. For two reasons - I wanted to whack him, but I also wanted to make sure that he didn't disappear too.

Today had been by far the worst day of my life. After our dad called us home, I'd spent the entire time wandering between the living room and kitchen, answering questions from policemen or listening to strangers talk about the search. Every word was a reminder that Pauly was missing. Why did they need to keep talking about it? Wasn't it obvious from our mother's crushed postures, shaking hands, red eyes, and the reluctance of everyone to look them in the face, that we knew he was missing? We were the people who loved Pauly the most, knew him best and felt worse about the hole his disappearance left. We didn't need any reminders.

It finally got to the point where I couldn't take it anymore. All the non-stop activity built to a frenzy inside of me. My muscle spasms and shakes returned and I began to move from chair to chair between the rooms, sniffing to detect the smell that always dragged me away. Until finally, I became sick and my mom had to rush me into the washroom and hold my shoulder's while I threw up.

Then Mr. Cook and our dad came home. The sounds of Pauly's mother's grief resounded through our home, signalling to everyone that the search was over and wouldn't resume until morning. Strangers filed out, their shoulder's slumped and heads lowered as they were forced to accept that he hadn't been found. If I could have, I would have closed my eyes and disappeared for a while, but I didn't because I couldn't be sure when I'd be allowed to return.

Danny's blanket rose and fell. I found myself matching my breathing to his. Then I realized I couldn't hear him anymore and since seeing doesn't always equal believing, I waited until he breathed in, then I breathed out. Much better.

Danny continued to stare at the ceiling.

I decided to ask him what I'd been wanting to since Pauly had disappeared but had been too afraid to, after I felt Mrs. Cook shaking while she sat next to me on the couch.

"Danny, do you really think that a badman got Pauly?"

Danny didn't answer. He wasn't going to be fair. This was something I needed to know.

"Danny, please? Do you?"

He closed his eyes and pressed his lips together. I waited.

"Yes," he finally said.

"Why? Why would anybody want to hurt Pauly? He's never done nothin' to no one."

Danny lay still for a moment then rolled over. He stared at me. I knew that he was going to say something but the way he looked at me made me feel like I wasn't being very smart.

"Jack, when Pauly talked to you yesterday about your flying dream, did he ask you if you saw lights shooting across the sky?"

"Yes." Why did Danny want to know that?

He lifted onto his elbow. "Well? What did you tell him? Did you see them?"

"Yes. But what does that have to do with anything?"

Danny pulled his covers off and sat on the edge of his bed. "Because today when Grandpa was talking to you, I went outside and asked Pauly to tell me about true dreams. He said the lights you saw were other people, flying in their true dreams, and that's how he knew you had one."

Danny paused, thinking he was giving me time to understand. There wasn't enough in the world.

"He also told me that when he dreamed of you, before you were born, and you told him that you were going to be best friends, *that you were able to fly and there were bright lights following behind you."*

What? Why hadn't Pauly ever told me that? And why didn't I remember?

"Pauly said I was flying?"

"Yes. He said almost every night when he's sleeping he sees bright lights, and sometimes the people that are flying come down to talk to him. That's how he knows when he's had a true dream."

My thoughts started pushing and shoving and butting in front of each other. There were too many trying to be heard. I rolled onto my back and covered my face with my pillow. I wanted to scream.

The bright lights meant that my flying dream was a true dream?

The first time I'd seen Tika, when she'd been trying to get away from Orv, there'd been tiny lights sparkling beneath her feet. And when I showed her how to fly, when we were on top of the church, bright lights followed her into the sky. Plus, Tika told me that there were lights behind me when I flew. I wrapped my hand around the bracelet on my wrist. If Pauly was right, then Tika was real and so was Orv! I had to do something. Orv was going to come back to hurt her! I pulled my pillow down and squeezed it in my arms.

"Danny, then Tika's a real girl and the badman's going to hurt her! I have to do something. I have to find her."

Danny shook his head. "No, you have to find Pauly. You've got to try to dream about him. He's the one that needs your help right now."

"But how, Danny? How can I find him? I don't know where he is."

"Jack, Pauly said you flew to him before you were born and he sees people flying all the time. Maybe if you're thinking about him when you go to sleep, and if I keep talking to you about it, you'll fly to him again. You have to try."

But I was too scared. What if I did find him? How could I help? I was too little and the badman might catch me.

Danny read my mind. "You don't need to save him. You just have to find out where he is, so we can tell Mom and Dad."

"But I'm too scared," I whined. "When the badman caught me, he hit me and kicked me and tried to bury me in the ground." I could feel the muscle that held my bottom lip release. It started to dangle.

"Jack, Pauly's your best friend. You have to try. Don't worry, I won't let anything bad happen to you, and you can come back right away."

Danny was right. I did have to try. Our dad told the policeman that he thought Pauly went to Cecil's to tell the badman to leave me alone. But I didn't know how to fly to whoever I wanted to. I'd only found Tika because the men on the horses had led me to her.

"Jack, tonight when you go to sleep, you've got to think about Pauly as hard as you can while I keep talking to you." Danny stood and lifted my gun belt from the bedpost.

Not this again. There was only one left in the holster.

"Here, put these on. We've got to do it the same way as before."

I never did fly. One moment I was listening to Danny's voice and the next I was sitting on the church with no idea how I got there. My eyes were wet. I wiped them with the sleeve of my pajamas and looked into the sky. It was covered with clouds being lit from inside by lightning.

The hair on my arms and my brush cut tingled as a bright ball burst right above me and shot down. I covered my head, bent my neck, and closed my eyes. It blinded me then faded away. Nothing bad happened. I peeked out and Tika was standing in front of me.

"Sweetpea, I was praying that you'd be here! I've been looking all over for you."

I never said a word. I just jumped up and hugged her.

"I was so worried," she said. "I dreamed that you came to my window and tapped on it, but when I went outside you were gone."

I'd been to Tika's house? Why didn't I remember that? I squeezed her again then turned to wipe my eyes. I felt like a baby.

"What's wrong, Sweetpea?"

"Tika, a badman hurt my friend today and took him away. I've got to find him. And last night after you went home, I went back to the trees to make sure Orv left, but he was hiding and he caught me. He hurt me real bad and tried to bury me."

"I know, I followed you. Don't you remember? I picked you up and flew you away after he knocked the gun out of your hand."

Tika had saved me? I thought I'd escaped by myself. When I woke up the last thing I remembered was rising into the air and throwing up from the smell of wet clay.

"You saved me?"

"Yes. I carried you into the woods but you got sick and said that you had to go home. So I helped you fly because you couldn't. But when I was carrying you, you started to fight me and you fell. You landed in a big forest. In a field full of flowers." Tika's eyes widened, full of wonder. "Sweetpea, is that where you live?"

Why would she think that? "No, I woke up in bed and I was sick because I thought Orv had come back to hurt you."

"He did. In the morning, I told my grandmother and they found his tracks in the trees."

My stomach flipped. A terrible thought came to me. Why hadn't I thought of it before? Oh no, Pauly… It hadn't been the man from Cecil's who'd taken him, Orv must have followed me home!

My stomach climbed into my throat and I moaned.

Tika grabbed my hand. "Sweetpea, what's wrong?"

"Tika, Orv must have followed me home! He's the person who took my friend."

"No, Sweetpea, you have to listen." Tika squeezed my hand. "When we went to the hospital today to visit my uncle, a policeman told us that Orv had been killed in an accident last night. His truck went off the road and caught on fire. They know it was him because they found his rifle." She looked into my eyes. "Besides, it wasn't Orv who hurt you. When I flew down to pick you up, I saw him. It was a different man."

It hadn't been Orv? Although I'd never seen him clearly, I'd been sure that it had to be him. Something else came to me. "Tika, what did you say happened to my gun, before you flew me away?"

"The man knocked it out of your hand with his shovel. It landed in the back of his truck."

I reached down. The grip of the left one fell naturally into the palm of my hand, but the right one remained missing. It landed in the back of his truck? How could that be?

"Tika, after the man took Pauly today, my dad found my other gun on the ground, next to some blood. How could it be there?" I needed time to think.

I sat with my back against the steeple. Tika sat beside me and took my hand again.

"Tika, what did the badman look like?"

"He was short and skinny and had long hair. I only saw him for a moment. That's all I remember."

I knew of only one man with long hair - the person at Cecil's who'd kept me from falling off my bike. But he'd been nice. Nothing was making sense. What was I going to do?

"Tika, how am I going to find my friend? I don't know where to look."

"Why don't you ask the men on the horses to help you?"

"I don't know where they are."

"Maybe they're still in the forest? I saw them carry you away last night, after you fell."

"I was with the men on the horses?"

"Yes." Tika tilted her head as though she were surprised I didn't know. "Sweetpea, the leader was carrying you. I tried to follow but they rode into the trees and disappeared. I thought maybe they were taking you someplace for help."

"Do you think they might still be there? They were the ones that helped me find you. Maybe they know where Pauly is? Could you show me where you saw them?"

Tika stood and helped me to my feet. "I was going to look for you there, if I didn't find you here. Come on. Let's go."

We leaned forward and lifted into the sky.

36

Daniel

After Carter went home and Tika went to bed, Rose sat in the living room with Helene and told her about Tika's visits to the dream world. At first Helene sat quietly, her eyes glistening as she learned about the boy who'd helped her daughter. Then she too questioned whether it had been just a dream, before breaking down when Rose told her of Sweetpea's warning and Orv's tracks being found in the trees.

"I should have been here," Helene cried.

"No. Don't blame yourself. Orv was a wicked man. We couldn't keep an eye on Tika all the time. He would have waited for another opportunity." Rose patted her daughter's knee. "Besides, everything is okay now. Bud's getting stronger and we're all thankful you've returned."

After Helene went to bed, Rose opened the door to Tika's room. Her granddaughter was lying on her side sound asleep, her covers pulled beneath her chin. In her arms was her pillow, her right hand wrapped protectively around the bracelet on her left wrist. Rose entered and sat in the chair next to the bed.

What she hadn't expressed to Helene, was her fear for the boy from Tika's dreams. Since learning about the child in the cabin, and Tika telling her that Sweetpea had been injured by an unknown man, Rose had been unable to find peace in her thoughts. Her heart had become heavy and burdened with fear.

Who could this other man be? Did he present a danger to Tika's friend? And what about Orv's rifle? Rose didn't believe in coincidence, and although she'd never learned Daniel's full name, she believed the rifle might once have been his. Was the young man she'd rescued in the woods over sixty years ago and the boy who visited her granddaughter connected? If Daniel were still alive, he'd be an old man now. Sweetpea could be his grandson. She wished she'd spoken to Tika before she went to sleep and told her to warn Sweetpea if he came again to her dreams. Rose closed her eyes. She prayed to the eagle to find Daniel and deliver her fears.

37

Honor

Daniel lit the burner on the stove beneath the tea kettle and prayed once again for Pauly's return.

"Dear Heavenly Father, please shield Pauly from danger. Comfort him and give him the strength he requires, until he can be returned safely to his mother and father. Amen."

Daniel's insides were in turmoil. He didn't believe in coincidence, and the fact that Pauly had warned his grandson about exactly what seemed to have befallen him was tormenting him. Why hadn't he listened to the boy when he'd tried to tell them that Jack was in danger? Because Daniel was sure that Jack's dream, Pauly's abduction and his rescue were connected. If only he could figure out how.

When the water came to a boil, he poured himself a cup of instant coffee, carried it outside and sat on the porch in Honor's rocker.

A waxing moon hung low in the late summer sky, its luminous light challenged by a thin wisp of clouds moving across the western horizon. It was going to be a night of little shadow. Of a darkness neither complete nor insufficient. Along the outer edge of the cornfield the Misery rose like an impenetrable wall. Daniel leaned back in his chair and sipped from his bitter brew.

That the answers lie within the Misery, he was sure. But he didn't know how. What was it Honor used to tell him?

'Where things begin, Daniel, is often where they end.'

Daniel upbraided himself. On his way back to the farm from his son's home, before he'd learned of Pauly's disappearance, he'd made plans to camp tonight in the clearing, the same as he'd done as a young man. But when Gus called him after supper, Daniel had picked up his books instead. Despite knowing the answers that he searched for weren't inside. He should have followed through on his initial plan.

Daniel lay his head back and thought of his wife. "I need you, Great Honor. What words of wisdom could you give me, my darling?"

He closed his eye and his favorite picture of her flashed in his memory. It was from the day he'd approached her after spring services in Newbury. She'd turned, smiled and brushed his hair from his temples.

I can't believe how well your scars have healed. It's certainly given you a most rugged, handsome look.

Honor had accepted him back into her heart so openly.

Daniel set his coffee cup on the table next to the chair and sighed as the weight of sleep began to descend upon him. As he lay his head back, he was sure he could feel Honor by his side.

What do I do my darling? Where do I look for the answers?

His breathing settled into a soft rhythm. Daniel could feel himself sinking.

Daniel, you have to open your mind and your eye. Remember the circle.

I'm trying, my darling. Fingers poked him in the side. He shifted in the chair and smiled.

Daniel, the circle. You have to open your mind and your eye.

Daniel dreamed of an elderly woman, her face creased with the lines from a thousand smiles and great wisdom. Her eyes were large, her cheekbones high. Her long gray hair was braided into ponytails that lay across her shoulders. She smiled at him.

He was reminded of someone. Stiff fingers poked him in the side again. Harder this time.

Daniel, open your eye!

He jerked awake. Crossing the sky were two shooting stars, their long tails stretching far behind. They descended and soared above the tops of the trees before plummeting into the Misery. For a split second, in their brilliant afterglow, he was sure that he saw the outline of a group of men on horseback, riding along the edge of the trees.

38

Cecil

Cecil was having a hard time staying awake. He clicked off the cruise control, straightened his seat back and lowered his window. The cool night air rushed in, chilling and reviving him as the Caddy's lights and engine continued to bore through the darkness. Up ahead he could see the glow from the lights of the city of Waterloo. He had a little over one hundred miles to go. Cecil turned off the radio and worried about what he might find ahead.

After the police called him at his cottage and told him what had happened at his home, he'd packed his clothes, shuttered the windows, and made plans to leave in the morning. At the time, returning right away hadn't seemed the prudent thing to do. It was late afternoon, almost a six-hour drive back from Bobcaygeon, and there was nothing he could add to shed light on what had transpired. As he'd told the constable, he had no idea who might have broken into his home or taken Pauly. He was every bit as confused as they. And yes, if he thought of anything, he'd certainly let them know.

Then everything changed after his brother called.

Clarence wanted to make sure that he'd been contacted. He told Cecil he'd learned about what had happened on the radio. Cecil told him yes, he'd spoke with the police and would be returning in the morning. Then he'd been forced to listen while his older brother shared his view about the world going to hell in a handbasket, and how because of his cancer, he was almost happy he wouldn't have to witness much more. As usual their conversation became a one-sided rant, with Clarence rambling on and him trying to figure a way out.

"I'm sorry, Clarence," he finally interrupted. "I've a long drive ahead of me tomorrow and plenty to do beforehand, including buttoning up the cottage."

"No problem. I just wanted to make sure you knew what's been going on. You know, I never thought I'd see the day when a man couldn't leave his door unlocked or his valuables unprotected. It's got me starting to wonder how safe I am, out here alone on the farm. Nowadays it seems a person never knows who's might be coming down their lane, or what their intentions are."

"I suppose you're right," Cecil agreed, hoping his accedence might help end the call, and fully aware that his brother had expressed no concern for Pauly. "I'll tell you what. When I get back, we'll get together and talk about it."

His brother paused. Cecil couldn't recall that happening before.

Clarence's voice returned, flat and cold. "Well, before you do, I guess I should let you know that my boy's back."

"What?" Cecil was stunned.

"Yeah. He dirtied my doorstep a little over a week ago. Dead broke and as sorry looking as ever."

"I'm surprised," Cecil said, and he was. Completely. It had to be thirteen, no fourteen years since his nephew ran off. At the time, not much of a surprise. Clarence and the boy had never got along. Sheila, Clarence's second wife and the boy's mother, used to say that the two of them mixed like water and oil, and no matter how hard she tried, the thick one always came out on top. Cecil smiled ruefully at her analogy.

Unfortunately, in his estimation, she'd described quite well how Clarence had mistreated his son. Clarence always had been too damn demanding, especially after Sheila passed and there'd been no one to challenge his charge that their son was effeminate. Cecil shook his head. He too had to shoulder some of the blame. How many times had he considered asking to take his nephew in and raise him? And how many times had he kicked himself for not having done so?

"So, how is he? Is he looking good?"

"Well." Clarence paused again. "Okay I guess, if you like the looks of the longhairs. Let's just say he's back. So far, he's only been by a couple of times, to borrow money. He hasn't shared any of his plans with me." He sighed. "In all likelihood, I'll end up having to mother him again. Until I die."

Cecil shook his head. It was obvious the old feelings had already boiled to the surface. "Well I'd sure like to see him. I've often wondered what he's been up to. Is he there now? Could I speak with him?"

"No, I have no idea where he is, or where he's been staying. The last time he stopped in was three or four days ago, for more money. He did ask if I knew where you were living though. I told him you'd moved again and gave him your new address. Next time I see him, I'll let him know you asked."

"Okay, thank you."

Cecil couldn't believe the boy had returned. Although he supposed if he'd been home, his nephew likely would have stopped in by now to visit. It was no secret that he and the boy were closer than he'd ever been with his father.

"Well listen, Clarence. If you see him, tell him I'm happy to hear he's home. And thank you for your call. I'll see you when I get back."

"Okay. Good enough. I'll expect to hear from you." His brother hung up.

It wasn't until later in the afternoon, when he was putting his suitcases into the Caddy's trunk, that Cecil's first dark thought came to him.

Longhair.

Funny how Clarence used that word to describe his son's appearance. Didn't the police say the man seen at his home was slight and short with hair to his shoulders? Cecil supposed that description fit many others. He wondered how long a man's hair had to be for Clarence to consider him a *longhair?* And how could he call back and ask, without looking the fool?

Then another thought struck him. Clarence said his son had been home for over a week and he'd given him Cecil's new address. Hadn't he figured, if he'd been home, his nephew would have stopped in by now? Cecil knew that was the truth. He couldn't pretend otherwise. Suddenly it seemed too big a coincidence his home being broken into and Pauly being taken. Cecil shook his head. What was he doing? Why was he thinking these things? He'd never known his nephew to be a thief, let alone someone capable of harming a child.

Cecil lowered his face into his hands. He knew why. If it were just the items taken from his home, he could wait until morning to return and find out. But Pauly was missing. Cecil's conscience would never allow him to sleep, wondering if his notions might be correct. He needed to return right away.

Cecil was sure that he knew where his nephew would be staying. That his brother seemed to have no idea, surprised him. The boy was likely where he used to go, to get away from his father. The one place it cost him nothing to stay.

Cecil considered his position. He didn't believe he had enough to go on to justify calling the police. Plus, he wanted to take into consideration how his nephew would feel if he were wrong - being accused of such an abhorrent act would certainly drive the boy away for good.

No. If he left right now, he could drive back tonight and look for him. If he was where he figured he might be, he'd speak with him to either confirm or rid himself of his suspicions.

Cecil looked at his watch. If he hurried, he could be there shortly after midnight.

39

Sunkwa

Flying with Tika was wonderful. We held hands as we rose into the clouds cloaking the town, losing sight of each other momentarily before popping free above.

I looked back and realized I'd been wrong. What I'd thought had been lightning illuminating the clouds from inside, were stars shooting through or above, on their way into the sky or back to the ground.

I wondered if Pauly was right - if each star really was a person flying in a true dream? And if they were, did any of them know that the stars shooting past were other people? Or did they believe, as I once had, that they were simply dreaming - unaware that the heavens were full of people travelling about to meet one another in shared dreams.

I watched Tika. Now that I believed she was real, I couldn't imagine her not being my friend. She looked so happy and beautiful. It seemed so natural to be flying beside her that for a time, as I enjoyed her smile and exclamations of joy, I forgot everything that had happened and where we were headed. If Tika hadn't squeezed my hand as she began to descend, I think I would have continued on around the world.

I looked about. Far ahead was the river with the island I passed on my way to her home. Directly below was a large forest. It stretched between two towns and to the shore of a lake that seemed to fold out of sight in the distance. Why hadn't I noticed this before, when I'd been flying by myself?

Tika released my hand and pointed down. "We have to follow that little river. The open spot where I found you was right beside it."

I looked down at a narrow waterway winding through the trees like a thin snake. It continued across open fields, before joining a small lake near the island.

"We have to stay high. If we go too low, we'll fly right past."

I followed Tika down through wispy clouds until we levelled, then she shot in front of me, rolling and banking as she traced the line of trees. Other than the sound of the wind rushing past my ears, tugging at the collar of my pajamas, it was silent. Tika's trail of lights twisted and turned like a sparkler through the night.

"There," she exclaimed, looking back over her shoulder and smiling as she pointed ahead. "I see it. It's around the next bend."

I looked down. In front of us a narrow path ran from the trees to the water's edge before turning to follow the river.

"I can smell the flowers," she said.

I sniffed. Tika was right.

She dropped quickly and came to a stop, hovering above the water. I floated down beside her and tried to look through the trees lining the bank.

"Did you see the riders?" I whispered.

Tika shook her head.

We drifted forward until we were standing on shore. I peeked between the branches. I was amazed. I knew this place. This is where Grandpa had brought us the day before in his wagon. Danny and I had played here in the water, while Pauly sat on the shore above. How could this be the place where I'd fallen?

"Tika, this is my grandfather's special place. He used to come here with my grandmother before she passed. Her name was Honor. She planted these flowers."

Tika smiled at me. "I thought this is where you came from. It's beautiful."

"No. You don't understand. My Grandpa lives on a farm over there." I pointed in what I hoped was the right direction. "Before we came here yesterday, I'd never seen this place before." Tika tilted her head. I could tell that she didn't understand what I was trying to say. My face began to heat up. "Tika, I'm not a guardian spirit. I'm just a boy. My real name is Jack. My nickname is Sweetpea." I lowered my eyes. "My brother helps me have flying dreams - because I'm too scared to fall asleep."

"You're not my guardian spirit?"

"No. I'm not an angel."

"But I don't understand. If you're not my guardian spirit, how do you fly with the men on the horses? You said they led you to me, and I saw them carry you after you fell."

I reached out and took her hand. "They did lead me to you, when I was flying in my dream. I saw them riding through a field and flew down beside them. When you cried, the leader pointed me towards town so I could help you."

Tika looked at our hands. "But how did you know my Uncle Bud was going to be okay and that my mother would come home?"

I felt terrible. I'd been so concerned about finding Pauly that I'd forgotten all about her troubles. "I'm sorry, Tika. I just knew that you loved them, so I wanted your mom to come home and for your uncle to get better." I looked down at the ground because I knew she was going to be mad at me.

"Sweetpea?

"Yes."

"Look at me."

I shook my head. "No, I don't want to." I was too ashamed.

"Please, Jack?"

Uh oh, she used my name. Now I knew she was angry. When my mom called me Jack, it almost always meant trouble. I closed my eyes and forced myself to lift my head. When I peeked out, Tika was smiling.

"I'm glad you're a real boy. It doesn't matter if you're not my guardian spirit. I still think you're wonderful. You helped me and my grandmother said you're my friend too." Tika took hold of my other hand. "Sweetpea, the reason I came to look for you tonight was to thank you. My mother came home today and my Uncle Bud is going to be okay."

"Really?"

"Yes." Tika let go of my hands and hugged me. "When my grandmother gave me my bracelet and choker, she said it would help me find peace in my sleep. She also told me that *only I* could say what my dreams meant." Tika pulled back and looked me in the eye. "I'm the one who said you were my guardian spirit. You tried to tell me you weren't, but I wouldn't listen. I'm much happier that you're a real boy, because now I have a best friend."

I laughed. Tika made me feel so good.

"Tika, when we were flying here, I was thinking how glad I am that you're real, because you're my friend too." My face felt like it was about to burst into flames but I continued. "Before I met you, I never wanted to be hugged or kissed by a girl before."

Tika leaned forward and kissed my cheek.

We both laughed and I kissed her back. I would have done it even if Danny was there. I didn't care anymore if he thought liking a girl was funny. That was his problem.

And that's the moment I heard the horses.

Maybe it was all the John Wayne movies or the hours spent watching Rawhide and Bonanza, or maybe it was an echo buried in genes inherited from a distant ancestor - for somehow, I knew the sound of their pounding strides before they broke from the trees at the end of the clearing. Before their bobbing heads and wind-pulled tails lifted into view, as they thundered over the crest of a small hill, turned as a flock and charged towards us.

Later, I realized that I hadn't been afraid. I hadn't thought to hide. I simply stepped from the trees with Tika's hand in mine, and accepted their appearance with a mixture of amazement and relief.

The lead rider raised his hand and the group came to a halt in front of us, the horses blowing hard from their furious charge.

There were five men, dressed in breechcloth and leggings. The leader alone wore his breastplate of leather, fringed and decorated with beads. I could see that Grandpa was right. What I'd thought were sticks now looked like polished tubes of bone. On his thighs, his leggings were dyed in stripes of red and black and in his right hand was a long-feathered lance. His white horse, with its beautiful brown tail and mane, was much taller than the others. His men spread out beside him, each on a horse of a different color - a roan, black, buckskin and bay.

I smiled and squeezed Tika's hand. Even though the leader looked fierce, I knew that he was nice because he'd helped me make sure that she was safe. Plus, Tika said that he'd carried me after I fell. I waited for him to speak.

He slid from his horse and stood in front of us, the tip of his lance between his feet. He was the biggest person I ever saw - tall, slender and powerfully built with dark eyes set deep in his stony face. He looked first at Tika, then me.

"Sweetpea, you should not be here. It is not time."

I was amazed. How did he know my name? And what did he mean it wasn't time?

Tika stepped forward and held out her hand. He swallowed it within his and waited for her to speak.

"My name is Tika," she said. "My grandmother is Rose. You are the man who rode with Wakanda to save the people of the village. She told me about you. She said you are a great warrior named Sunkwa."

Sunkwa smiled. "Yes, and in your face and heart, I see your great grandmother. I also see you are wearing her necklace and bracelet." He nodded toward me. "As is Sweetpea." He reached out and slid up my pajama sleeve.

Tika's eyes narrowed. I could tell that she was surprised. She let go of his hand and turned the bracelet on my wrist until the eagle faced her.

"Sweetpea, how did you get my grandmother's other bracelet? She told me she lost it. I've never seen you wearing it before."

"My grandpa gave it to me today," I stammered. "He said he found it a long time ago."

Sunkwa turned and raised his hand to the riders. They dismounted and moved to the edge of the water. He put a hand on our shoulders. "We must talk."

Sunkwa led us to the far end of the clearing, to where the flowers grew. He sat cross legged and motioned for us to sit in front of him, next to the tree with the scar on its trunk. He told us the story of how he and Tika's grandmother had rescued my grandpa, and how her bracelet came to be left behind. As he talked, Tika and I held hands. Her eyes shone in the moonlight. When Sunkwa finished, he turned and looked at me.

"Sweetpea, why have you come here?"

I couldn't help it, tears began to well behind my eyes. I lowered my head so he couldn't see them. "I came to find you," I blurted. "Today a badman took my friend. He wanted to hurt me but took Pauly instead. I need you to help me find him, like you helped me find Tika."

Sunkwa sat silent. I looked up. His face was turned toward the sky. I glanced at Tika. She put a finger to her lips and shook her head. I waited. After a moment, Sunkwa looked at me.

"I cannot lead you to him." He leaned forward and put his hand on my shoulder. "Sweetpea, you must listen to my words. I know the boy you search for. He has a strong spirit. He too knows that you search for him. But he also knows that the man who took him must first be found, or his evil will continue." Sunkwa stood and pulled us to our feet. "I know this will be difficult, but you must leave the dream world and return here tonight with One Eye. Once he is here, you must tell him to speak to the man who purchased his rifle, before it was sold to Orv. Only then may he find what he searched for before he was injured. In this way, you may also be able to stop the man who wishes to hurt your friend. Do you understand?"

"I don't," I said, as tears ran down my cheeks. "Sunkwa, why can't you just take me to Pauly? He's never hurt anyone."

"Sweetpea, do not despair. You must remain strong. Tell One Eye my words. But not before he is here. If he asks you why he must wait, tell him your words come from Sunkwa, then he will know. Can you remember this?"

"Yes." I fought back the urge to whine and tell him that he wasn't being fair.

"One last thing," he said. "Come."

Sunkwa turned and led me into the flowers. Once we reached the middle, he told me a story about my grandma and grandpa. Then he whispered something that he wanted me to tell Grandpa. I didn't understand but promised I would. He squeezed my arm and we walked back to his horse.

As though a signal had been sent, his men returned. With his lance in his hand, Sunkwa leapt to the back of his horse. The men mounted, turned and followed him into the trees.

Tika and I were alone.

"I have to go now," I said. "Do you want me to fly back with you to your home?"

Tika shook her head. "No. You need to find your friend."

I slipped the bracelet off my wrist and handed it to her. "I think my grandpa would want your grandmother to have this back."

Tika lifted my arm and slid the bracelet back on. "No. I think she would be much happier knowing he's given it to you." She paused. "Sweetpea, when will you visit me again?"

I don't know why but I felt frightened that this might be the last time I was going to see her. And from the look on Tika's face, I could see that she felt the same way.

"I'll try to visit whenever I can. Wait for me on the church. If I don't see you there, I'll come to your window."

Tika laughed and kissed my cheek. "That's what you said the last time when you left." She took my hand. "Sweetpea, the next time I see you, I want to tell you a story my grandmother told me about circles."

"I'd like that."

Tika raised my hand and used my sleeve to wipe her eyes. "Goodbye. Jack." She leaned forward and left the ground. "I'll pray for you and your friend."

"Goodbye, Tika."

Tika shot straight into the sky, in a ball of light that flew so high, I lost track of it among the other stars. I wiped my eyes on my pajama sleeve but didn't do a good job. I used the same spot that she had.

40

Pauly

Terry turned off Highway 79 onto the gravel road that ran past his father's farm. Up ahead on the left, at the end of a long lane, sat his house, the main barn and a couple of outbuildings, just past what the old man called the back eighty - a square section of land he sowed each year in field corn.

Terry turned off the trucks lights, eased off the gas and rolled by. Small pebbles, picked up and thrown by the tires, pinged inside the wheel wells and against the undercarriage. He kept an eye on the windows and held his breath. The old man was a light sleeper, and the last thing Terry wanted was for him to look out and see him crawling past.

Tonight had been a complete waste of time. For three hours, he'd sat in the parking lot across from the pool hall, hoping the fellow who'd said he'd buy everything would show. It had been a long shot but Terry needed the money and to be rid of the stuff in his truck. And now here he was, late at night, pockets still empty, driving without headlights down a country road in a vehicle still loaded with stolen goods.

Terry shook his head. It was all Pauly's fault. If only the kid hadn't stuck his nose where it didn't belong, he'd have made it into town on time like he was supposed to. But after dropping the kid in the hole, Terry had been ten minutes late and the fellow had already left.

He had to get rid of Pauly. So far, the kid had brought him nothing but bad luck. And not only that, truth be known, Pauly scared the hell out of him. Pauly wasn't like the others Terry had chosen. He was much tougher. There was no way he'd ever be able to break him. Pauly's strength of will reminded Terry of his father. He'd recognized it the moment the boy looked him in the eye after he'd slapped him. If the ladder hadn't already been leaning against the trapdoor, Terry doubted he'd have made it outside before throwing up.

So now he had to figure out how he was going to do it. He couldn't let Pauly go like he'd done with the others. He'd told the boy that Cecil was his uncle. It wouldn't take long for the authorities to find him and he'd wind up in jail, and Terry wasn't about to let that happen.

Inside the glove box was the pistol he'd taken from Cecil's home. But he wasn't crazy about firing it in the woods at night. The sound would echo off the trees and draw attention. No, his best bet would be to dig a hole, tie the kid's hands and feet, then roll him into it. After he backfilled it, he could sit on top and listen to Pauly suffocate. Terry smiled. Maybe then he'd get the boy to cry for his momma.

After crossing Highway 2, Terry turned off the road at the end of a fence row, drove through a shallow ditch and onto a lane that led into the trees. In the moonlight the narrow path was easy to follow. Occasionally tall grass or branches from the scrub brush scraped along the bottom and sides of his truck. Five minutes later he was at the cabin. He pulled around back, parked among the trees and lit a cigarette. Leaning against the back wall by the fire pit was a shovel. Terry knew of a small clearing next to the river, about five minutes walking distance. The trees there were thin enough to make it an easier place to dig. There'd be fewer roots to cut through. He'd have a couple of beers first, walk Pauly out and then dig the hole. Terry could see no reason why he should have to carry him.

41

The Misery Calls

Daniel made up his mind, he was heading into the Misery. He wished he'd went earlier like he'd planned. There was no way he was spending the night in the house now. Not after seeing the riders. He knew he'd never be able to sleep. Daniel didn't consider himself a fool. He knew it was possible that he hadn't been fully awake and had imagined them, or in the dim light his eye may have played a trick, but at this point in his life it made little difference. Something was drawing him into the Misery, and after everything he'd experienced within its trees, he'd learned long ago to follow his intuition.

Daniel packed his cooler and set it on the kitchen table. Behind him on the stove the tea kettle began to whistle. He spooned instant coffee into his thermos, filled it with hot water and put it inside, along with another of drinking water. The only other thing he wanted to take was his lantern. It was hanging on a hook in the barn, next to a container of kerosene he kept handy in case of emergency. He'd grab it before starting the tractor.

Daniel pulled on his hiking boots and a sweater then looked for his Tiger's ball cap. It was on the back of the utility room door. He put it on, picked up his gear and turned out the kitchen light. As he reached to open the door the phone rang. He set everything back down and answered it.

"Hello?"

"Hey, Dad. I'm sorry to be calling so late. I hope I didn't get you out of bed."

It was Gus and from the sound of his voice, this wasn't a call he wished to be making. A feeling of dread washed over Daniel. He closed his eye and steeled himself.

"You didn't. I'm still up. Are you calling with word about Pauly?"

"No. Nothing yet." Gus sighed. "I'm calling about something else and it's kind of awkward, so I'm going to need you to bear with me."

"Well, give me a second. I was just in the middle of something. Let me take a seat at the table." Daniel slid into a chair and took off his cap. "Shoot."

Gus cleared his throat and laughed nervously. "It's probably a good idea that you're sitting. I'm not sure how to begin, so I'm going to just say it." He paused. "Jack had another flying dream tonight. He says he needs to speak with you. He said he flew to the Misery with the girl from his dreams."

"Her name is Tika," Sweetpea shouted in the background. "And she's not a dream girl."

"Sorry," Gus said. "Dad, Jack says her name is Tika and she's not a dream girl." He paused again. "He says the two of them flew to the Misery tonight to talk to a native man, who was there with other men on their horses."

Daniel's heart skipped a beat. What in tarnation? He lifted the lid on his cooler, took out his thermos of coffee, poured a cup and sipped. "Go on."

"He said the leader of the men told him that he has to go into the Misery tonight, and that he's supposed to bring you."

Daniel was speechless.

"Dad, are you still there?"

"I am. Did he say why?"

"He says it has to do with Pauly. He said he went there to find the riders, so he could ask them for their help."

Daniel rubbed the side of his face. "Son, I'm at a loss for words. I don't know what to say. I suppose you'd like me to speak with him?"

"I think you're going to have to."

"Tell Grandpa he has to listen," Danny yelled. "Tell him it has to do with true dreams."

"Did you hear that?" Gus said. "Danny says it's important that you listen. He said he helped Jack have another true dream."

"Okay. But before I speak with him, is there anything in particular you'd like me to say? Obviously, the boys are upset."

"I don't know." Gus sighed. "Just play it by ear, I guess. I wasn't going to call but Danny insisted. I don't know what else to tell you."

"Okay, put Jack on. But don't stray far from the phone."

"I won't."

Daniel could hear Gus pass the receiver to his son. "Grandpa says he'd like to speak with you."

When Jack came on the phone, his voice was full of excitement.

"Grandpa?"

"Yes, Sweetpea. What's going on? Your father says you've got something important to tell me?"

"We have to go to the forest tonight. You and me. To the place where Grandma planted the flowers. I talked to the leader of the riders. He was there with Tika's grandmother when you got shot. She's the person who owns the bracelet you gave me."

His grandson spoke so quickly, it took Daniel a moment to grasp what he'd said. "Whoa, slow down. Start at the beginning again and say it slower this time."

"I flew to the forest tonight with Tika, and talked to the man who found you after you got shot. He said he was there with Tika's grandmother. He said the bracelet you gave me today was hers."

Daniel's heart raced. "Sweetpea, how do you know about my accident? Did you overhear your mother and father talking about it?"

"No." Jack sounded exasperated. "Grandpa, the man told me. He said after you got shot, Tika's grandmother and him found you."

Daniel's mind was spinning. "Sweetpea, put your father back on."

"You gotta listen to me," Jack pleaded. "The man said that we have to go there tonight, to the place where Grandma planted the flowers."

"Why? What are we supposed to do when we get there?"

"I'm not supposed to tell you." Jack began to cry. "Grandpa, you gotta believe me. The leader made me promise not to say nothin' until we get there."

"Calm down. I believe you. Now hand the phone to your father. I need to speak with him."

Gus came back on the line. "Sorry, Dad. He's pretty upset."

"Gus, I have to ask you a question. Did either you or Colleen say anything to Jack or Danny about what I told you the other day?"

"No. We figured you must have, when you were talking to him about your bracelet."

Daniel rubbed his scars. "I didn't tell Jack anything, other than the fact that I found it." He could hear Danny questioning Jack in the background.

"Why didn't you tell Grandpa the man's name?"

"I didn't have a chance to. He wanted to talk to Dad." Jack was crying harder now.

"Boys, you have to keep quiet,' Gus said. "I can't hear your grandfather."

"You were supposed to tell him," Danny said. "The man told you."

"Dad, I need to talk to Grandpa again," Jack wailed. "I forgot to tell him something."

"Just a minute," Gus said.

"No, I have to talk to him now."

"Dad, give me a second."

Daniel could hear Gus talking to Jack. "Sweetpea, tell me what you want to say and I'll tell your grandpa for you."

"No. Only I'm supposed to. The leader told me."

Gus came back on the line. He sighed. "Jack says he's got something more to tell you."

"I heard. Put him on."

"Grandpa?" Jack blubbered.

"Calm down, Sweetpea. What do you need to tell me?"

"The leader said if you don't believe me, I'm supposed to tell you his name. It's Sunkwa."

Daniel's felt the blood rush from his head. He gripped the edge of the table to steady himself. A roaring sound filled his ears. His throat tightened.

Gus came back on the line. His voice sounded like it was coming from the end of a long tunnel. "Dad, did you hear him?"

Daniel heard…

He was lying on his back in the snow. Rose's warm palm was pressed against his forehead. She was pointing to a tall man, impossibly dressed in moccasins, breech-cloth, tan leggings and breastplate. In his hand was a long-feathered lance.

"Sunkwa, will lift and carry you to his horse. I will sit behind and hold you. We will take you to the home of your people. Do not be afraid."

Tears streamed down the side of Daniel's face. He tried to find his voice.

"Dad, I can't hear you. Are you still there? Is everything okay?"

“I’m here,” Daniel forced out in a strangled whisper. “Gus, we need to do what Sweetpea says. You need to get out here as quick as possible.”

42

Circles

Tika didn't return to her bed after leaving the clearing. Instead she flew to the church, sat with her back against the steeple and cried. She felt so ashamed.

Today should be the happiest day of her life - with the return of her mother, Uncle Bud's recovery, her grandmother's joy that they were all together again and Orv no longer a threat. But all she could think of was herself, and that she might never see Sweetpea again.

These last couple of days and the adventures they'd shared in the dream world had been fantastical. She'd learned so much about herself and felt so many new feelings. Tika feared that without Sweetpea in her life, she might never view the world again in the same way. Together they'd overcome so many situations, by such wonderful means, that hope had built inside her for the future.

She wiped her eyes and looked into the sky. The heavy clouds that had blanketed Medicine Falls were gone. Now brilliant moonlight shone and silvery stars glued to black paper flickered between cotton-ball clouds. Tika marvelled at the depth of the heavens and the hundreds of stars shooting past, their long tails glittering in their wake. Each one reminded her of their flight to the forest - of meeting Sunkwa, the warrior's story about the rescue of Sweetpea's grandfather, and Jack's friend, who was now in danger. Tika stood. There was no time to feel sorry for herself. She needed to speak with her grandmother. To tell her everything that she'd learned. Tika leaned forward and flew to her bed.

When she knocked on her grandmother's door, the inside light clicked on. Her grandmother opened it, looked into her eyes and took her hands. "You've been crying. Something has scared you. Come."

Tika couldn't help herself. Tears spilled down her cheeks. Her grandmother's concern was always so genuine.

"Tell me what is wrong," her grandmother said, as she sat her on the edge of the bed and patted her hands.

"Tonight, I found Sweetpea on top of the church," Tika whispered. "He'd been looking for me. He was afraid that after Orv came back, he might have hurt me."

Her grandmother handed her a tissue from the night table and waited as she dried her eyes.

"He was crying because a badman has also taken his friend." Tika looked into her grandmother's face. "He didn't know what to do. So we flew to the field of flowers where I saw the riders, to ask for their help"

"Did you see the men?"

"Yes. Somehow, they knew we were coming. After Sweetpea told me his grandmother had planted the flowers, they rode from the trees." Tika tried to smile. "It was Sunkwa and the men who helped Wakanda find the buffalo. He told us that you and him rescued Sweetpea's grandfather, in the forest a long time ago, after he shot himself."

Her grandmother smiled. "I thought the boy might be Daniel's grandson."

"He is, Grandmother. Sweetpea's not my guardian spirit. He said his real name is Jack. He thought I'd be mad at him but I told him, I'm the one who's supposed to know what my dreams mean. Besides, I'm happy he's a real boy."

Her grandmother chuckled. "I'm proud of you. So, did Sunkwa help him find his friend?"

Tika looked down and shook her head. "No. He said he couldn't. Sunkwa said the man is evil and must be stopped. He told Sweetpea to leave the dream world and return to the forest tonight with his grandfather. He said they have to find the man who purchased his rifle, then find what he'd been looking for before he was shot." Tika looked at her grandmother. "Sunkwa also told us that Orv's rifle, once belonged to Sweetpea's grandfather. Grandmother, how can that be? How can Sweetpea and his grandfather and you and me and Sunkwa and Orv and his best friend, all be tied together?"

Her grandmother pursed her lips and smiled. "Tika, you know. We've talked about this many times. It is the circle." She took her hand. "When you dreamed of Sweetpea, do you not remember telling me how he turned into a ball of light when he flew away? And have you not wondered about the other lights moving about in the heavens?"

"Yes." Tika smiled. "They're beautiful. At first, I thought they were shooting stars, but now I don't believe so. Sometimes they fall to the ground and other times they shoot into the sky."

Her grandmother patted her hand. "As do you, each time you fly. Tika, the lights you see are other people sharing in their dreams, as you and Sweetpea have. The Great Spirit wishes it to be this way. We must all learn that we are connected and come to understand that everything we do harms or helps another." She smiled. "You and Sweetpea have been given a great gift. Most people never learn the people they dream of are often real." She turned the bracelet on Tika's arm so the eagle was facing them.

"Since Carter learned of the boy held at the cabin, my fear has been that your friend is in danger. Now the person who harmed the child and who harmed Sweetpea in his dream, has taken his friend. Sunkwa must be aware of this. This is why he cannot take Sweetpea to his friend. If he were rescued before the man is caught, the man will continue to harm others. Sunkwa must believe that only Daniel can stop him. Only then can our circle be completed." She squeezed Tika's hand.

"Come, before we return to our beds, let us ask the eagle to deliver our prayers to Wakan Tanka. Let us pray for the return of Sweetpea's friend and for Daniel's success."

43

The Rifle

I'd never been out this late before travelling anywhere other than home. Normally Danny and I would be sitting on the backseat fighting to stay awake, looking out at the stars and needing to pee the moment we arrived. This was a whole new experience and I had to admit, I was feeling pretty grown up.

I looked over the seat at the clock in the dash. It said 11:15 and we'd just turned onto Highway 79, or Nauvoo Road as the locals call it. Grandpa told me that most people have no idea it was originally a wagon trail blazed in the mid 1800's by Alvinston Mormons, heading to Nauvoo, Illinois, the city built by the Latter-Day Saints. They thought it began as an old hunting trail, created by a fictitious tribe they named the Nauvoo. Grandpa laughed and said it's funny how people will make up the darndest things to satisfy themselves.

Danny leaned over and looked at the clock too. Dad glanced in the rear-view mirror. On his face was the same doubtful expression he'd been wearing when we left home.

"Are you boys still sure you know what you're doing?"

I waited for Danny to answer. Instead my brother looked at me. This was the first time I felt under such pressure to perform. Something told me that if this was going to be a part of growing up, I wasn't going to like it much.

Fortunately, Mom saved me. "Honey, don't you think it's a little late to be asking that again? In another minute, we'll be at the farm."

Dad looked at the road and sighed. "You're right. But if this isn't the most doggone thing I ever heard of, heading out in the middle of the night to a forest because of a dream. I still can't believe Dad said to hurry."

"That's because Jack proved his dream was true," Danny said. "I didn't believe it either until Pauly explained it."

"So, Sweetpea," Dad said, without looking back. "Tell me again what we're supposed to do, once we get there."

This had to be the eleventh time he'd asked me the same question.

"I already told you. Me and Grandpa have to go to where the flowers are, then I'm supposed to tell him what Sunkwa said."

Dad shook his head and didn't say another word until we pulled into Grandpa's lane.

All the outside lights were on and Grandpa was sitting in his rocker on the porch. He'd already pulled Rosie from the barn and parked her next to the house. By the time we came to a stop, he was halfway across the yard.

"That was quick," he said, when we opened our doors. "Seems like I just got off the phone with you."

Dad answered him over the roof. "Well, you said to hurry, so we did. I see you've got Rosie ready to go."

"Yep. All we have to do is get in. I've packed everything we'll need." Grandpa closed Mom's door and gave her a hug. "Hello, Colleen," he said, then he turned to Danny and me, "Come here you two." He bent and gave us a squeeze. "How are you boys holding up? Are you okay?"

"Yes, Grandpa," we answered at the same time.

"Well, Jack," he said, rubbing my head. "This is your play. You tell me what I'm supposed to do and then let's get it done. Where are we heading?"

"I told you. We have to go into the forest, to where the flowers are."

"That's it? There's nothing we need to talk about first?"

"No. Sunkwa told me not to say anything until we get there."

"Okay."

"I have a question, Dad," my father said.

"Go ahead."

"This Sunkwa, is that really the name of the man who rescued you?"

"Yes."

"And you're not wondering how Jack dreamed of him?"

Grandpa rubbed his chin. "Son, at my age there isn't a whole lot left that surprises me. It seems the older I get, the less I know and the more questions I have."

"So, you're just going to accept it?"

Grandpa opened Rosie's driver's door. "Jump in and I'll tell you a story on the way that might answer you."

Danny, Mom and I, sat in the rear. Grandpa started Rosie and we pulled onto the highway.

"When you called tonight, I was halfway out the door," Grandpa said. "Another minute and you'd have missed me. I'd made up my mind to spend the night in the clearing." He rolled his window part-way down. "Earlier I'd fallen asleep on the porch and dreamed of your mother. She kept telling me to open my mind and my eye, and then it felt like somebody poked me in the ribs." He looked at Dad and smiled. "When I did, danged if I didn't see two shooting stars fall into the Misery, and a group of men on horseback, riding along the edge." He looked ahead. I could hear his chin begin to flap.

Dad looked at him. "And you're sure you weren't still dreaming?"

Grandpa sat silent for a moment then spoke so low I could barely hear him. "Son, based on the dreams Sweetpea's been having, what he told me tonight and where we're headed, does it really make a difference?"

"The shooting stars were Tika and me, Grandpa," I explained. "When you're flying in a true dream, that's what everybody looks like."

Grandpa nodded his head. "And that doesn't surprise me a bit. Not one tiny bit." He slowed and turned onto a gravel road. "We can't take Rosie down the trail, so we're going in by a different route. Often times, late in the year, Honor and I came this way." He shifted and stepped on the gas. "We're going in along the river. We'll have a short walk. I brought along my lantern and also threw a bag of wood in the trunk, so we can build a fire."

Just after we crossed the highway and before we came to a wooden bridge, Grandpa turned left onto a lane that unless you knew existed, you'd never see. The car bounced along and things began to bang in the trunk. Danny and I laughed as we were shaken from side to side.

"Just a bit further," Grandpa said. "The river bends up ahead. We'll walk to where it cuts back in. The clearing's there."

A minute later we stopped and climbed out. The forest was silent. Rosie's headlights lit a narrow path that wound over a slight rise, into the trees and out of sight.

"I'll carry my lantern; you boys bring along my cooler and the firewood." Grandpa smiled at Mom. "Colleen, I threw a couple of lawn chairs in the trunk. If you wouldn't mind bringing them."

Danny and I grabbed a handle on each end of his cooler and Dad threw a burlap sack of wood over his shoulder.

Grandpa turned off the headlights then he and Mom led the way. About halfway there, bullfrogs in the reeds along the river started to croak and call to one another. Danny and I snickered when Mom jumped and looked nervously into the trees. You'd have thought the noise was coming from a herd of hungry hippos.

In the moonlight the clearing was beautiful. There was just enough light to see clearly yet cast faint shadows. Mom gasped and stopped to take in the view.

"It looks exactly like it did in my dream," she whispered, before she followed Grandpa and set up the chairs.

Grandpa hung his lantern on a branch along the river and lit it.

"Throw the wood over here, Gus. I'll get a fire going and then Sweetpea can tell us what we're supposed to do."

Dad dumped the wood on the ground and Grandpa built a pyramid with it. He lit it with a wooden match. Once the flames started to crackle and lick into the air, he pulled his cooler over and sat on it. Mom and Dad sat too, while Danny and I spread a blanket.

"Well, Sweetpea," Grandpa said, after we finished. "I'm ready whenever you are."

I sat cross-legged next to Danny and tried to remember exactly what Sunkwa had said. "There are three things, Grandpa. But one I'm not supposed to tell you until later."

He leaned forward. His chin stopped flapping and he turned his head so that his good eye was on me.

"Sunkwa said first you have to talk to the man who bought your rifle, before it got sold to Orv, and then you've got to find what you were looking for, before your accident. He said if you do that, we might be able to find Pauly."

Grandpa's good eye narrowed. The marble one stayed wide open. It felt like he was sighting down a gun barrel on me.

"Say that again." He closed his good eye and cupped his hand around his ear. I tried to remember the words as best I could.

"Sunkwa said I'm supposed to tell you that you have to talk to the man who purchased your rifle. Before Orv bought it. And then you gotta find what you were looking for, before you got shot. He said if you did that, we might be able to find Pauly."

Grandpa raised his other hand and rubbed both sides of his face. "Sweetpea, you're going to have to help me out here. I've never heard of this Orv before. I don't believe I know anyone by that name."

"He's the badman who was chasing Tika in my flying dream. Remember when I told you he grabbed my foot when I picked her up and flew her to the top of the church? He got killed last night in an accident when his truck rolled over and caught on fire. That's how they found your rifle."

Grandpa looked at the tops of the trees. His left eye sparkled in the moonlight. I'd never seen it do that before. I glanced to Danny to see if he'd noticed. His eyes were glued upon him also.

"Jack, I have no idea who purchased my rifle. My brother sold it at the hardware and I never saw it again."

"Wouldn't the store have records?" Dad asked.

"It was the old store, son. It closed almost forty years ago, after Mr. Taylor died. There's no way of looking into it now. He didn't leave any family."

"Well, it likely sold local," Dad said. "There has to be someone who knows."

Grandpa shook his head. "No, and that's not the only problem. This fellow told Jack, I have to find what I was looking for, *before my accident.* The only thing that could be is the old outlaw hideout. If I couldn't find it sixty-three years ago, I doubt I'll find it now."

"You have to try, Grandpa," I pleaded. "Sunkwa wouldn't have told me to tell you that for no good reason. You must know who bought it. You just don't remember. You gotta try. We gotta find Pauly."

Grandpa leaned forward. "Sweetpea, I don't know who bought it and I never did. And the old outlaw hideout was just a story the boys at school talked about. I don't know if anyone ever learned if it was real."

I stood. My head was spinning, my hands shaking and I felt like I was going to throw up. "No! You're doing it again! It's just like Tika's bracelet and her calling me a guardian spirit. How could I dream about Sunkwa and your rifle and the outlaw, when I never heard of them before? You're not trying. You don't care about Pauly. You're not trying to help me find him."

Before I'd stopped talking, I felt ashamed for what I was about to say, but I'd lost control of my mouth. I couldn't bear to look at anyone, especially Grandpa. And I didn't want them to see me. I turned and ran through the flowers, back onto the path we'd came in on. Mom and Dad called my name. I pretended not to hear and ran down the trail, wiping my eyes with my fingers. The bullfrogs stopped croaking. A branch slapped me in the face. Dad called my name again. I tripped over a root and stumbled forward, almost regaining my balance but I'd reached the edge of the hill and started to fall. I put my hands out to keep from landing on my face and ran into someone.

"Hold on, little fellow."

I crashed into a man's chest. The top of my head whacked his chin as he stumbled backwards, landed on his rear then rolled onto his back with me still in his arms. I kicked and screamed as hard as I could. All I could think was - the badman had me again.

The man's arms tightened around me. "Whoa, I got you."

That was the last thing I wanted to hear. I pushed my knees into his stomach, trying to get to my feet. I heard a 'whoosh' as I pushed all the air from him. His grip loosened and I was grabbed from behind and lifted. As I hung in the air, my feet continued to kick like a dog dreaming about chasing a rabbit.

"I got you," Dad said. "Calm down. You're okay."

He set me down and looked at the man on the ground.

"Cecil?"

Our neighbor struggled to sit up. He leaned back with his hands on the ground behind him as he gasped for air.

"Here let me help you up," Dad said, as he reached out.

Cecil shook his head. "Give me a minute, Gus," he wheezed. "I've got to catch my breath."

Grandpa, Mom and Danny came running up. Mom's eyes widened as she looked first at me, then Cecil sitting on the ground.

"What happened? Is everyone okay?"

Grandpa stepped forward. "Cecil? What are you doing out here? You're the last person I'd expect to see. Here, let me help you up." He bent and put his arm under Cecil's, while Dad grabbed his hand and the two of them pulled him to his feet. Cecil bent forward, put his hands on his knees and breathed deeply.

"I thought that was your car, Daniel," he gasped.

Dad looked first at Grandpa then at Cecil. "Dad, I wasn't aware that the two of you knew each other."

"Of course, we do," Grandpa said, over his shoulder. "I've known Cecil all his life. He's Clarence's younger brother."

"Clarence?"

"Cruikshank," Grandpa said. "The farm on the corner of Hagerty Road. Just yesterday you and I stopped and closed the door to his cabin." He looked at Cecil. "I believe the wind blew it open."

"Well, I apologize," Dad said. "I didn't know Clarence had a brother. I would never have put two and two together."

"Well, Clarence is ten years older than me, Gus," Cecil explained. "By the time you came along, I was already up north, working for the hydro. We never met until a couple months ago, after I retired and moved into the neighborhood."

Dad turned to Grandpa. "Dad, it was Cecil's house that was broke into. And where the police believe Pauly was taken."

Grandpa looked at Cecil, a puzzled expression spread across his face. You could tell he was trying hard to put things together. "Cecil, are you able to walk?"

Cecil nodded. He looked at me and smiled. "Sweetpea, you scared the living daylights out of me. Popped out of the trees like a frightened doe, right into my arms. Dang near gave me a heart attack."

Grandpa took his arm. "Come on. We've got chairs set up around a campfire. Let's get you into a seat." He walked with Cecil down the path.

When we stepped from the trees into the clearing, Dad squatted next to me. "Are you feeling better?"

I nodded. My legs were sore and wobbly, my hands were shaking and I felt embarrassed, but otherwise I was fine. Mom and Danny walked with me to the fire.

"Do you want to sit with me?" Mom asked.

I shook my head, let go of her hand and sat on the blanket next to Danny.

Cecil and Grandpa walked around the other side of the fire. Dad leaned two new pieces of wood against the flames then sat. Grandpa opened his cooler, filled a paper cup with coffee and handed it to Cecil. He put the lid back down and slid the cooler in front of him.

"Here, have a seat."

"Thanks," Cecil said. He sat and looked about the clearing. "Daniel, Clarence told me what your wife created here. This is the first time I've seen it. She did an amazing job."

"Thank you" Grandpa smiled. "Honor sure enjoyed it." He paused. "We both did." He looked down at Cecil. The puzzled look returned to his face. "So, what brings you into the Misery at this time of night?"

Cecil gazed into the fire. "I was at my cottage this afternoon when the police called. They told me what happened, so I packed and came home." He looked at my dad. "Gus, has there been any word about Pauly?"

"No."

Cecil shook his head. "Clarence also called, to make sure I knew about it. He told me his boy was home, so I thought on my way by, I'd stop in to say hello. I didn't realize I'd be this late. When I crossed the bridge, I saw the light from your fire and thought maybe Terry was out here camping." He looked at Grandpa. "If you don't mind my asking, what are you folks up to? It's a little late to be out picnicking."

Grandpa glanced at me. I'd never seen such a sad look on his face. I felt terrible. I tried to find the courage to tell him how sorry I was, but I came up empty.

"It's a long story," Grandpa said. "Truth be known, we're trying to find Pauly."

"And you thought he might be out here?" There was a look of both incredulity and shock on Cecil's face.

"We don't know," Grandpa replied. He put his hand on his chin, rubbed it and looked at the ground. No one spoke for a moment. And then Grandpa did the most remarkable thing. He glanced at me and he winked.

"Cecil, I've got a story I'd like to tell you," he said, as he walked over and stood behind me. "Stand up, Sweetpea."

For a moment, I thought he might spank me, but I did as I was told. I figured if that's what he wanted to do, I deserved it.

Instead, he sat cross-legged and pulled me into his lap, before wrapping his arms around me.

"Cecil, you know Jack. He's just about the finest boy you'll meet. He's also Pauly's best friend. They love each other like brothers." Grandpa paused. "Earlier tonight, when Jack went to bed, he dreamed that I might be able to find Pauly. I know it sounds fantastic but he told me things that got me wondering. So, I asked his mom and dad to come to the farm, and then we drove out here." He squeezed me. "Unfortunately, he's asked me a couple of questions I can't answer, and I'm afraid I'm letting him down."

"You're not letting him down, Daniel," Mom said. "We knew before we came out here that this was a long shot. And Gus and I both know you'd do anything for the boys."

"Thank you, Colleen, but please, let me finish my story." Grandpa kissed the back of my head. "Cecil, you mentioned what a wonderful creation Honor put together here and I'd like to share with you why. Sixty-three years ago, I had my hunting accident in this clearing. Tonight, Jack told me things about my accident, that he shouldn't know. Then he told me there's two things I need to do for us to find Pauly." Grandpa paused again. "He said the first thing I need to do is talk to the man who purchased my rifle, after my accident. But I don't know who that might be. My brother sold it in Bothwell and I never saw it again." His arms tightened around me. "Now, unless I miss my guess, I'm thinking you might be the man to help me."

Cecil squinted at him. No one made a sound, other than a lonely frog that croaked down by the river. Cecil took a sip from his cup then held it in his hands between his knees. I could see they were shaking.

"Daniel, my father purchased your rifle. I remember him trying to sand your name off the magazine. When I got older, he gave it to me."

I could feel Grandpa's head nod.

"Well, Jack says that rifle was recently sold to another fellow, by the person who took Pauly."

Cecil closed his eyes. "Son of a…" He stood, tossed his coffee to the ground and strode to the water's edge.

Grandpa lifted me from his lap and stood. He walked over to Cecil and put his hand on his shoulder. "I'm sorry," he said. "It was your nephew, wasn't it?"

Cecil kicked a rock from the bank into the water and nodded.

44

Forsaken

Pauly couldn't stop shivering. The cold from the wet ground had leached into his bones, sealed in by his damp clothes. Every part of him was in agony. The spasms in his muscles made his body feel like it was being stretched in a thousand directions. Especially across the tops of his shoulders, from his arms being pulled back and his hands tied. And his feet. They hurt too. Earlier they'd fallen asleep but now they were awake, cramping and biting at him. He moaned and a drop of blood escaped from the bottom of the tape covering his mouth. He'd bitten into his lower lip, to keep from crying out.

Pauly had never felt forsaken before. He was used to the pain from his spasms, but this was a million times worse. His fingers felt curled into claws and every joint in his body seemed twisted and frozen. Pauly wished he could stand but knew that even if he could, the pain would be too intense. He tried to relax. It helped momentarily but then his muscles stiffened again.

Pauly had never complained about his condition, other than not being able to go to school. But he knew if his mother or father were present, he'd cry uncontrollably.

He pressed his eyes closed and tried to think of his best friend. He pictured Jack's face and heard the sound of his voice. Pauly tried to remember the feel of Fatboy's arm around his shoulders and his mother's touch when she massaged his legs.

He found if he concentrated hard enough, for short periods of time he could manage the pain, but then it would return worse than before. He wanted to go home. Tears trickled down his cheeks.

The only thought that he found he could hold onto for any length of time was that help was on its way. It had to be. People had to be looking for him. He was sure of it. Over the years, he'd had so many dreams and learned of so many things that he was sure were going to come true, he knew this couldn't last forever. He had that to hold onto - his belief in true dreams. Otherwise this pain wasn't going to end and he couldn't bear the thought.

Pauly opened his eyes. For some reason that also seemed to kick start his sense of smell. The odor from the wet clay ground beneath him was sickening. It enveloped him. It smelled of decay. There was a noise above. Footsteps. Pauly lifted his head. His shoulder muscles felt like they were about to tear.

The heavy objects were pushed to the side again. Pauly heard a grunt and a curse. A sliver of light appeared as a piece of the ceiling began to lift. It formed the square again. A light was hanging above it. The man's shoulders and head appeared from the side.

"You ready, you little bugger? It's time for us to leave." The man held out his hand. There was a silver pistol in it. "I'm coming down there to help you up the ladder. If you give me any trouble, I'm going to shoot you and leave you down there. If you understand, nod your head."

Pauly lowered his head and closed his eyes.

"I'm not asking again, Pauly. If you'd like, I can shoot you from up here. Now, do you understand?"

Pauly nodded.

45

The Cabin

Daniel had one more question for Cecil, but he knew that his friend needed a moment to collect himself. He opened his cooler and poured four cups of coffee. He handed Colleen and Gus one, set another on top then sipped from his, after sitting on the blanket between his grandsons.

"Cecil, I poured you another coffee. It's on the cooler. We need to talk."

Cecil picked it up and sat. He didn't look up. "Daniel, how did you know Terry had your rifle?"

"I didn't."

"But you knew I did."

"No, I didn't know that either. I guessed."

Cecil looked at him. "How?"

"You said that Clarence told you his boy was home and you were going to drop in. That didn't make sense. You wouldn't have come through the Misery on this side of the clearing. You'd have taken the side road east. You drove right past it and it leads directly to your brother's farm. Plus, you said that you saw the light from our fire. With the bend in the river, there's no way it can be seen. Also, Jack told me I had to come to the Misery tonight to *speak to the man who purchased my rifle.*" He took a sip from his coffee and smiled. "I figured after you showed, it wasn't likely we'd be having any more company. So, I got to wondering why you said what you did."

He set his coffee down.

"I think when you learned that Terry had returned, you figured it might be him who broke into your home and took Pauly. Otherwise you wouldn't have come home tonight. That's also why you drove into the Misery the way you came. You planned to check the cabin to see if he's there. When you and Jack ran into each other, you were as surprised as he."

"You're right," Cecil replied, staring at the ground between his feet. "If it had just been my house, I'd have come back tomorrow. But with Pauly missing and Terry back, I began to wonder." He rubbed his forehead. "Clarence said that he told Terry where I was living now. He also said he'd let his hair grow, so he fit the description." Cecil looked up at him.

"I hope you don't think less of me, Daniel. I thought of calling the police, but you know how hard Clarence was on Terry. That's why he ran off. I wanted to talk to him first, to give him a chance to clear himself. I didn't want to make a false accusation and drive him away again. Not after all these years."

"I understand," Daniel said. "You were caught between a rock and a hard place. Plus, it's family." He finished his coffee and stood. "I've got one more question for you. When I had my accident, I was out here looking for the outlaw hideout. A couple of the boys at school said it was nearby. Jack told me that for us to find Pauly, I've also got to find it tonight. Do you have any idea where it might be?"

"I don't. I'm sorry," Cecil said. "I heard the stories too. When I was a youngster, I even did a project on it at school. I went to the newspapers in Newbury and Bothwell and looked up everything I could find. I learned that the outlaw's last name was Shaw. He was a thief, broke into homes and small businesses. But I don't know if he was ever caught, or if anyone ever learned where he hid. Many of the old timers figured he'd built himself a dugout."

"His last name was Shaw?"

"Yes. That's all I was able to learn. Supposedly he was a young man."

"What's a dugout?" Colleen asked.

"Well, they're also called pit-houses or mud-huts," Cecil explained. "You've heard of the soddy's, with earthen walls and roofs that people lived in on the prairies?"

"Yes."

"Well, in this part of the country, because the land's not so flat, people sometimes dug a temporary shelter out of the side of a hill. Usually nothing more than a lean-to, with three mud walls and a grass roof, but sometimes more elaborate."

"But you have no idea where it might be?" Daniel asked.

Cecil shook his head. "No. Though Clarence used to say that our father built the cabin over it. That's probably why you heard about it at school." He smiled wryly. "Clarence had no more idea where it was than anybody else. My father also said it was untrue."

Daniel stood and walked to the river. He heard Colleen ask Cecil another question but his mind was elsewhere.

If he couldn't find the hideout, the only other lead they had was Terry. Cecil thought that he might have taken Pauly and could be staying at the cabin. They needed to take a look. If Terry wasn't there, they needed to go to Clarence's and contact the police, to tell them what they'd learned. Either way, there was no time to waste. Daniel walked back to the fire.

"Cecil, you were heading to the cabin. It's only a ten-minute walk. We need to check it out."

46

The River

Terry lowered the ladder into the hole and climbed down. He kept his pistol in his hand and circled behind Pauly, mindful to stay outside his reach. There was no need. Pauly's hands and feet were still securely bound.

When he'd put him in the hole, he'd carried him down over his shoulder, wrapped in the tarp. Pauly had been unconscious then. There was no way he was carrying him out. The little bugger was heavier than he looked. Plus, Terry wasn't sure that if Pauly fought back, that he'd be able to handle him. The kid was incredibly strong. Terry resisted the urge to climb back up and leave.

"I'm going to cut the tape from your ankles so you can walk," he said. "Then I'm going to tape your hands in front of you so you can hold onto the ladder." He pulled a jack knife from his pocket and flicked it open. "If you try to fight me, I'll shoot you." Terry knelt and freed Pauly's hands. "I'm going around front now, to do the same to your feet." He stepped back, circled in front, knelt and cut the tape. "Now, put your hands together in the air, in front of you."

Pauly tried to roll his shoulders and move his arms to his side. He grunted and moaned. They barely moved.

"I'm warning you," Terry shouted. "And I'm only going to say it once more. Raise your hands in front of you."

Pauly grunted and tried again. His arms moved to his sides and he lifted his hands into his lap.

Terry raised his pistol and stepped forward.

Pauly's arms shook as he raised them. Terry pulled a roll of tape from his back pocket, wrapped it twice around his wrists then cut it.

"Now stand up."

Pauly leaned to the side and placed his hands on the ground. He grunted as he tried to lift. Terry realized it was impossible.

"Oh, for crying out loud." He grabbed Pauly under his arms and helped him to his feet. Pauly swayed. "Hold onto the ladder." Pauly grabbed a rung and leaned against it. His legs shook. "Now climb."

Pauly lifted a foot but not high enough. Terry bent and placed it on the lowest rung then lifted his other next to it. Slowly he helped him work his way up. When Pauly was above the opening, he climbed under him and with his shoulder pushed him onto the floor. Then he climbed out and took his lantern from a hook.

"Come on, we're not done yet. We've still got a long ways to go."

Terry helped Pauly to his feet, into a smaller room, shut the door and led him outside. He grabbed the spade that he'd left leaning against the side of the cabin.

"Get going," he said, pointing ahead. "Down that path, into the trees."

Pauly mumbled something, his eyes were wide and excited. He raised his head and sniffed.

Terry looked at him. "What?"

Pauly mumbled again.

Terry debated with himself then shook his head. "If I pull the corner of the tape off and you start yelling, I'm going to hit you over the head and bury you right here. Understand?"

Pauly nodded. Terry pulled one end free.

"I can smell the flowers," Pauly said. "I can smell the flowers."

"What the heck are you talking about?" Terry sneered, pressing the tape back in place. "Dang dummy." He grabbed Pauly's shoulder and spun him around. "Get going."

Pauly stumbled and nearly fell. Terry cursed, stuck his pistol in his back pocket and grabbed beneath Pauly's arm. "Come on," he said, half dragging him across the lane and into the woods. "If I was smart, I'd shoot you right here, throw you in the tarp and drag you out. It'd be a heck of lot quicker."

Ten minutes later, they reached the river. On the edge of the trail was the spot where he planned to dig. He sat Pauly on the trunk of a tree that had blown over and was now lying along the water's edge.

"Don't move."

Terry hung his lantern on a tree. With his foot, he pushed the shovel into the earth, lifted the dirt and threw it to the side. He pushed it in again and began to laugh.

"Yep. When I was your age, my daddy used to toss me in that same hole you were just in. First, he'd beat me until I could hardly stand and then he'd say boy, ain't nothing going to make you a man quicker and toughen you up better than spending a few days down there doing nothing but thinking." Terry snorted. "Tonight, I'm going to give you a chance to think about all the trouble and money you cost me. And maybe, just maybe, if I remember where I put you, I'll come back in a couple of days and look you up."

47

The Outlaw's Hideout

Gus followed behind Colleen, Danny and Jack, his mind awhirl. He'd always considered himself a practical man. Liked to believe in things he could see or prove. To say he was confounded and bewildered by the events of the evening, would be an understatement. For crying out loud, he still hadn't come up with a reasonable explanation for how Jack knew the yellow Frisbee was leaning against the chimney.

Gus looked up ahead at his father, marching alongside Cecil, his lantern held shoulder high. Gus envied him. Daniel always kept such an open mind. Gus wondered how much of that was due to the events of his early life, or was simply the result of his natural optimism. His father never seemed to find a challenge too large to overcome, or a phenomenon too unbelievable to consider. Gus had to admit, it had served him well. Many times, he'd seen his father reach the bottom of a situation that stymied many others. Like this one.

How the heck had Jack dreamed of his grandfather's accident? Or of the people who'd rescued him? Gus was afraid for his son and mad at himself for letting things get this far. He'd allowed Jack to put too much belief in his dreams. Now if things didn't work out the way he wanted, he'd likely blame himself. A big part of Gus wanted to pick Jack up, take Colleen and Danny by the hand and lead them from the Misery. Dang, he shook his head - it would have been easier to explain to Jack that his dreams were the result of his addiction and withdrawal from the damn drug.

Daniel turned right onto the lane that led past the cabin. Gus looked down the other arm. It was the way they'd come in the previous day on the tractor. In truth, Daniel had little need for his lantern. The light provided by the moon seemed to be piercing straight down, granting little shadow. And just the slightest breeze whispered about, carrying the scent of the wildflowers from the clearing. Gus couldn't help himself. He smiled as he marvelled at the devotion his parents had for one another. He looked at Colleen. Maybe that was the lesson he should be taking from tonight? Perhaps he should be out front right now, walking beside his father, towards the unknown, as he knew his mother would have. Gus always had been the one with the habit of worrying about everything that might lie ahead.

Coming up on the left was the opening for the cabin. His father stopped and motioned to him.

"What's up, Dad? Did you see something?"

"No," Daniel said. "I just figure before we knock, we should formulate a plan. We don't know if Terry's inside, or if he took Pauly."

"How about I go?" Cecil said. "Maybe Gus can come with me. We'll see if Terry's inside, while you stay with Colleen and the boys. It's been a number of years since I've seen him. I don't know if he's the same person." He looked at Gus. "That would make me feel a lot better."

"Sounds sensible," Gus said. He turned to his father. "Let me have your lantern. I'll let you know when it's safe to come up."

Daniel nodded.

"Be careful," Colleen said.

"We will. Let's go, Cecil."

The cabin was small. Maybe fifteen feet by fifteen feet. It had been built tight against a natural rise that ran along the right, perhaps the bank of an ancient river. The berm ran out of sight behind the cabin. Out front it continued on the other side of the path, likely all the way down to the river, which couldn't be far away. The front door was in the middle. There was a small window to the left. At the berm end, another door opened to a small tool or supply room.

Cecil knocked. There was no noise from within so he rapped again.

"No one's here," he whispered. "Let's look around back."

The fire pit was cold and the beer bottles that Gus had seen the previous day were still on the ground. He couldn't be sure but it looked like there might be a couple more. They came back out front and Gus waved to his father. Daniel, Colleen and the boys came up.

"No one here?" Daniel asked.

Gus shook his head. "No. What do you think we should do?"

"I'd like to take a look inside," Cecil said. "To see if he's been here." He turned the handle, opened the door and was about to step in when Gus stopped him and handed him the light.

"Thanks," Cecil said, before he disappeared inside.

"We'll have to walk back and get Rosie," Daniel said. "This lane ends at Hagerty Road. To the left, about nine miles down, is where Clarence's farm is. We'll drive back the way we came in, then run over and talk with him."

"Dad, aren't those fresh tire tracks?" Gus asked. He pointed to a pair of dark stripes that led around the side of the cabin. In the moonlight, they stood out in sharp contrast.

"They are," Daniel agreed.

Cecil came to the door of the cabin. "There's clothes inside. Someone's been here and they're likely coming back."

"Cecil, bring the lantern," Daniel said. "Gus found tire tracks." He led the way behind the cabin. "They run into those trees." Daniel walked into them and then stopped. "There's a truck."

Cecil walked to the rear and lifted a tarp that covered the box then opened the passenger door. He shook his head. "My things are inside. It has to be Terry's. The keys are in the ignition. He must be nearby. Gus, we need to take another look."

"Boys, stay with Grandpa and your mother," Gus said.

They checked out back again and found nothing. Something tugged at Gus's memory. It was the spade. The other day there had been one leaning against the back wall but now it was gone.

"Let's take another look inside, Cecil. Then I want to check out that tool room."

There was nothing in the cabin to indicate that Pauly had been there.

Gus went to the door on the end.

"That room's pretty small, Gus. We never kept much in it."

"I'd still like to check it out."

Gus opened the door. Inside it was about four feet deep and the same across. Empty shelves lined the back and left wall. The spade wasn't inside, although there appeared to be muddy footprints on the floor.

"Cecil, hand me the light."

Cecil handed it to him and Gus bent down.

Someone had been inside recently. The footprints were wet. A couple seemed to be half prints, cut off against the right wall. Gus pulled on a wooden slat that ran across it. It seemed solid. He kicked it and it shook. A metal clasp, shaped like an upside-down hook, rattled in the corner. Gus pulled on it, there was a click and a section of the wall swung outward. It was a door. This wasn't an outer wall after all. There was another room behind it that was over twice the size of the one they were in. It had been dug out of the berm. Old heavy beams and grey planks covered the walls. Gus raised the lantern. A piece of the wooden floor in the middle was standing. He ducked and stepped inside. Cecil followed him, their footsteps echoed beneath them.

"What the heck," Cecil said. "I never knew this was here."

They went to the opening in the floor and looked down. A wooden ladder was leaning against it.

"Hold the light, Cecil. I'm going to take a look." Gus's heart began to pound in his chest.

At the bottom, he found pieces of duct tape, balled up and tossed against the wall. The floor was wet as though water had been spilled recently and it smelled like decay. On a hook hanging by the opening, was an old ball cap. He took it and climbed out.

"What did you find?"

Gus showed him the tape. "Someone's been down there. I also found this old hat."

Cecil took it. It was moldy and it smelled. "I remember this. When Terry was a boy, you couldn't get him to take it off. What's it doing down there?"

Gus's chest felt as though a belt were being tightened around it. He strode outside and breathed deeply with his hands on his knees. Cecil followed him.

"Gus, are you okay?"

"I think Pauly was down there, Cecil. He can't be far away. We've got to get the police out here."

When they reached the corner of the cabin, Cecil swung the lantern. Daniel, Colleen and the boys came from the trees.

"Did you find anything?" Colleen asked.

"Gus found a room, dug into the hill. There's a hole beneath the floor. He thinks Pauly was held inside."

"Oh, my Lord," Daniel whispered. "The hideout."

At that moment, a gunshot echoed through the trees.

Everyone except Daniel jumped and looked wildly about. He pointed across the lane. "It came from down by the river."

Gus took off running. "Get help," he shouted over his shoulder as he disappeared into the trees.

Behind him he heard Jack scream. "Pauly!"

48

Nightmare

Pauly was feeling better. His clothes were almost dry and the pain in his joints had eased, although the muscles across the tops of his shoulders still ached. He was also feeling hopeful, despite the man digging in front of him. His spirits had received a boost when he'd smelled the wildflowers from the clearing. At least that's what Pauly hoped the smell was. It sure seemed the same, but he wasn't sure what that meant. He'd only been in a forest once before and didn't know if they all smelled alike.

Pauly watched the man work. He couldn't believe that he was expected to lie in the hole when it was finished and allow himself to be covered. Pauly wasn't stupid. He knew the longer he stayed on top of the dirt, the better his chances of getting away. So, he decided that from now on, he wasn't doing what the man said. It was that simple. He was going to have to make him.

Pauly wondered why the man was so afraid of him. He'd seen the way he'd jumped and shook after he'd slapped him, and how fearful he'd been to climb down the ladder. He couldn't even look Pauly in the eye. He reminded Pauly of the neighborhood bullies who used to tease and call him names. They'd been scared of him too, which was why he'd never understood them picking on him in the first place. And one of the reasons why he felt so bad when they'd cried after he'd made them stop.

Pauly looked around, trying to figure a way to escape. Unfortunately running was never an option. And in this case, closing his ears and pretending not to hear wasn't going to help. The way he figured it, that left him with one choice - he was going to have to fight. But even if he were able to wrestle the man to the ground, Pauly knew he'd lose. He couldn't hold onto him forever. And he doubted the man would cry and run away. Especially once he realized Pauly had no desire to harm him. Pauly closed his eyes and wondered what Fatboy or his father would tell him to do?

The shovel struck something solid. The man cursed, bent and picked up a boulder. He carried it to the edge, set it down, then turned and smiled at Pauly.

"Wouldn't want you having to lie on top of that." He picked up his shovel. "Another few minutes and I'll be ready. You got any apologies or last words you'd like to say, before we part company?"

Pauly looked at him and the man laughed.

"I forgot. Your mouth is taped." He filled his shovel with dirt, threw it on the pile then leaned against it. "I got an idea. How about we pretend that you said you're sorry? That way neither of us will be left with any hard feelings. Sound good to you? Eh?"

Pauly looked at the ground and shook his head. And the bullies had said he was stupid and called him names.

"Don't be shaking your head at me, you little bugger. All you're going to do is make things worse for yourself." The man started digging again, muttering to himself. "It's all your own dang fault. You got nobody else to blame. You wouldn't even be here if you hadn't accused me of taking things and wanting to hurt Sweetpea."

Pauly looked up.

The man stopped and smiled at him. "Hey, I almost forgot about Sweetpea." He laughed. "Yes sir. That's what I'm going to do after I finish with you. I'm going back to get Sweetpea. Me and him are going to have us some fun. A whole lot of fun."

Something shook inside Pauly. For the first time in his life, he felt anger boil within him. And fear. There was no way he was letting his best friend get hurt. It didn't matter anymore what happened to him. The next time the man came near, he was grabbing him. He had to be stopped.

The man tossed his shovel from the hole. "It's ready," he said. "I dug it extra deep, so you won't get cold." He climbed out, picked up his shovel and leaned it against a tree. "Now, I want you to sit on the ground with your legs in front of you, so I can tape them."

Pauly didn't move. He stared into the man's face.

"Did you hear me?"

Pauly tried not to blink.

"Dang you're a hard-headed little bugger." The man reached into his pocket and pulled out his pistol. "I'm not going to tell you again. Either sit down or I'm going to shoot you." He pointed the gun at Pauly's chest.

The strangest thing happened. Pauly's muscles all relaxed as though the decision to fight had lifted a weight from him. He couldn't help himself, he smiled.

"What the heck? You want me to shoot you? Is that what you're trying to make me do?" The man stamped his feet and spun in a circle. "You know dang well I can't. People would hear it a mile away."

Before Pauly could react, he stepped forward and whipped the barrel across his face. Pauly almost fell. He turned his head and the man struck him again. He raised his arms to protect himself and slid to the ground.

"And there you go. Now you're doing exactly what I told you to do in the first place. But now you got yourself hurt again. And whose fault is that? Huh? You gonna blame me?" He kicked Pauly's feet together, wrapped tape around them then stepped back.

Pauly raised his hands to his face. Blood was pouring from his cheek. He looked at his fingers then directly into the man's eyes.

"Oh no, not that again. Not this time you don't." He kicked him. "Get on your feet. It's time to get in the hole."

Pauly didn't move. The man knelt and stuck the pistol under his chin. With his other hand, he grabbed Pauly's shirt front and pulled him up. The moment he let go, Pauly grabbed the pistol.

"What the… Let go."

Pauly leaned against him and held on as tight as he could. The gun raised into the sky. The man kicked him. Pauly grunted and squeezed tighter. The man was too strong. The gun began to lower.

"Let go or I'm going to shoot!" the man yelled.

Pauly didn't let go. He twisted the gun to the side and tried to push it away. The man turned it towards him and fired.

Pain ripped through Pauly's right side. His fingers opened. He fell back over the tree that he'd been sitting on and saw the man fall backwards too. Then Pauly's feet appeared above his head and he landed on his back before tumbling head over heels down the bank into the river.

It was his nightmare come true. He landed face down in the water with his arms extended in front of him. His fingers could barely touch bottom. His legs churned beneath him. He couldn't lift himself high enough to pull them under his body and he couldn't raise his head above the surface to breathe. Pauly sank to the bottom then pushed up as hard as he could. His face broke clear and he gulped air. In front of him, the branches from the fallen tree were hanging above the water. He reached up and grabbed them. When he began to pull himself forward, they broke and he slipped beneath the surface again.

This time he couldn't find bottom. Pauly rolled and twisted, trying to figure which way was up. His chest began to convulse and despite himself he sucked in a mouthful of water. He was drowning. A minute later Pauly quit fighting and floated beneath the surface. His eyes were closed. He was flying. Thousands of shooting stars filled his vision. They swooped down, creating a ball of light around him. Pauly smiled as strong hands cradled and lifted him, as though he were a child...

49

Great Honor

Two weeks after Pauly got shot, his mom and dad asked if we'd take them to the clearing in Skunk's Misery. They wanted to see where everything had taken place. It was decided that we'd meet them there after church. They said they'd drive up with Cecil and pick up Grandpa. I begged Mom not to make me go.

Since the night in the Misery, I didn't feel like doing anything. I'd barely left my bedroom and hadn't touched my new bike, though my legs were feeling a lot better. And I hadn't been able to sleep - my hallucinations had returned more frequent and terrifying than ever. But the worse part was - I couldn't fly anymore. Despite everything that Danny and I tried, I'd lost the ability to escape my nightmares. I missed Tika so much. All I could think about was how much I wanted to sit on top of the church with her, hold her hand and tell her about Pauly. The last thing I needed was to go back to where everything had happened. Mom cried with me and promised we'd stay only for a while, and that we could leave whenever I wanted. Then she wiped her eyes on my shirt sleeve and called me Honey. You can't tell me that girls don't know how to get what they want.

Dad parked at the bend along the river and we hiked in. He and Danny carried our cooler while Mom and I followed with the lawn chairs. It was still warm with the sun beaming down, but I could sense a change in the weather. Mom said that soon the leaves would all be changing and she hoped that some of the wildflowers might still be in bloom. Personally, I'd never heard the forest so noisy. It seemed as if every bird, bug, and frog wanted to make sure that we knew they were still there.

When we got to the clearing Mom stopped. It was as colorful as ever. Though many of the flowers that had been in bloom before now weren't, hundreds of new ones were. Mom smiled and said that Grandma sure knew what she'd been doing. She'd planted a variety of spring, summer, and fall flowers, to keep the opening as bright and fragrant as long as possible.

There was a picnic table next to the river. Dad said Grandpa must have brought it out with his tractor so we'd have a place to sit and eat. Mom thought that was a great idea. She spread a cover over it and began taking things from the cooler. I sat on the bank while Danny waded along shore, looking for snakes and frogs.

"Would you like something to drink, Sweetpea?"

I shook my head. Mom had been trying so hard to make sure that I knew she was thinking of me. I doubted I'd receive this much attention as a baby. I wished I felt better, so she wouldn't have to worry about me so much.

I lay with my head in the grass and closed my eyes, listening to the sounds of the forest. The next thing I knew, I must have fallen asleep, because when I opened my eyes Mom was sitting next to me with her arms wrapped around her knees, laughing at Dad. I sat up. He'd fallen in the water while having a splash fight with Danny. I smiled inside. I'd never seen him act like a kid before. Mom punched me in the arm then looked up the bank, toward the tree with the scar on its trunk.

She pointed. "Sweetpea, look."

I didn't want to, but noticed that Danny and Dad had stopped and turned, so I did too.

Walking down the lane towards us was Pastor Reg and Ida, Cecil, Grandpa, and Mrs. Cook. Out front, Mr. Cook was pushing a wheelchair with Pauly in it. I couldn't help myself, I started to bawl. Danny and Dad climbed the bank but I didn't move. I crossed my arms on my knees, lowered my head inside them and cried even harder. Mom put her arm around my shoulders.

"Come on," she said. "Let's go see him."

I shook my head and leaned against her. It wasn't that I didn't want to. I honestly didn't have the strength. Every ounce of my energy was being converted into crying power. We'd visited Pauly every day in the hospital since he'd been hurt and I hadn't cried once. In fact, I hadn't spoke to him. I was so ashamed that he'd been hurt because of me. Seeing him covered in tubes and bandages, I'd been terrified that I might say or do something new to hurt him.

Mom hugged me and then helped me to my feet. Dad and Danny had stopped by the tree and were waiting for us. We started towards them and then I took off running. I threw my arms around Pauly's head, careful not to touch the bandages and the sling around his right arm.

"I'm so sorry," I cried.

At least that's what I hoped it sounded like. Somehow, Pauly understood me, I don't know how. My throat had become so tight and my tongue so confused.

"Hey, Sweetpea," he said. He put his good arm around me and gave me a squeeze. Then he began to hiccup like he always did whenever he was trying not to cry. He patted my back. "You're my best friend. I couldn't let the badman hurt you." We stayed that way for a couple of minutes before he lifted his head. "Hey Fatboy."

Dad knelt and wrapped us both in his arms.

"Hey, Wolly."

Everybody laughed. I held Pauly's hand while his dad pushed him into the clearing. He parked him in the shade next to the table and set the brakes. For the first time in days, I felt myself beginning to feel happy.

"How come you're using a wheelchair?" I asked.

Mrs. Cook smiled at me. "Pauly's coming home today, Jack. The doctors don't want him to walk, not until his shoulder heals." She rubbed the top of Pauly's head. "We're going to keep the wheelchair at home from now on. Pauly will be able to use it whenever he wants. Sometimes his legs get sore and this will make it a lot easier for him to get around."

I was happy about that. I hated seeing Pauly fall.

"Come on everybody, lunch is ready," Mom said.

There were salads and meat and bread, devilled eggs and paper plates on the table.

"Reg, could you say grace? We've got a lot to be thankful for."

It was the best picnic ever. After lunch, everyone except Pauly and me went for a walk. We sat by the river and tossed pebbles into it. Pauly told me everything that had happened after Terry caught him and about the bright lights that had picked him out of the water and lay him on the bank.

Danny told me later that they'd walked to where the cabin had been. He said there was nothing left. Cecil had knocked it down with a tractor, filled in the hole and burnt all the wood. He told them that his brother, Terry's father, had passed away on the same day that Terry was taken from the hospital to jail. Cecil said that Terry's head was still all bandaged up, from where he hit it on the boulder and been knocked out after he fell when he'd been fighting with Pauly. Cecil said Terry was going to be locked up in jail for a long time.

When we left to go home, Mom and Dad let me ride with Pauly and his parents in their station wagon. Grandpa came too. When we stopped at his farm to let him out, I asked if I could talk with him for a minute. There was still something I was supposed to tell him from Sunkwa. The Cook's waited in their car, while we sat on the steps of his porch.

"Grandpa, there was one more thing Sunkwa wanted me to tell you."

Grandpa leaned forward with his elbows on his knees.

"Sunkwa told me that after you got shot, you spent a lot of time trying to find him and Tika's grandmother."

Grandpa's chin stopped flapping.

"He said you learned a lot about native people, and you and Grandma bought a lot of land in the forest, so that the trees wouldn't be chopped down and turned into farms. Sunkwa also said that you own the place where the flowers are, and the forest where Chief Tecumseh was killed. He said you wanted to make sure people remember him." I paused, trying to remember exactly what I was supposed to say next.

"Sunkwa said this next part, I'm supposed to tell you exactly as he told me."

Grandpa nodded and waited.

I closed my eyes. I could hear Sunkwa's voice.

"Grandpa, Sunkwa said you are a great man and you have the spirit of a warrior. He told me to tell you that the next time he sees you, great honor will be waiting for you."

Grandpa closed his eye and sat quiet. When he opened it, I could see it was wet. He stood, went down the steps and knelt in front of me.

"Come here," he said. He hugged me really hard and whispered. "The next time you see Sunkwa, you tell him I said thank you. That's the best gift I've ever been given."

"I will, Grandpa."

"You better get going," he whispered, after kissing my forehead. "They're waiting for you."

I ran down the steps and got in the car. When I looked back, Grandpa was waving.

On the way home, Mr. Cook kept looking at the clock in the dash. He said if we wanted, we had time to drive to Sombra and follow the St. Clair River home. Pauly and I said yes. We loved looking at the water and watching all the boats and lake freighters going by.

Just before we arrived home, after we rounded the curve at Baldoon School where the trading post is, and the cable ferry runs to Walpole Island, I noticed a lot of traffic ahead. I leaned over the seat and looked out the front window. Cars and trucks were parking along both sides of the highway and had already filled the parking lot at the Big Chief restaurant. People were walking across the road and standing in a crowd in our front yard and in the Cook's.

Pauly's mom turned and smiled at me. "Why don't you tell Pauly, Jack?"

For a moment, I didn't understand what she meant, then I smiled. This whole day was turning into one wonderful surprise after another. I looked at Pauly. His eyes were as big as saucers.

"Your dream has come true," I said.

"What?"

"Your true dream. When you were in the hospital, the people from Wallaceburg built ramps at the front and back of your house so you don't have to climb the steps anymore. They also made all the doors extra wide and the cupboards lower. And guess what?"

Pauly looked at me with his big goofy grin.

"They put handles on all of the walls so you won't fall down."

We pulled into their driveway. Mom and Dad and Danny were waiting at the end. Mr. Cook got out and helped Pauly from the back seat.

As soon as everyone saw Pauly, they started whistling, clapping and cheering. You see, every day for the past two weeks, the headline in the newspaper had been about *The Hero of Skunk's Misery.* Pauly was the hero they were talking about.

After Constable Goodall told the reporters how Pauly had been taken after confronting a thief in the neighborhood, who'd also been planning to abduct his best friend, Pauly was all that everyone talked about. He was the biggest thing that had ever happened in our area. While he was in the hospital, recovering after being shot, people started making donations for changes to be made to the Cook's home. They wanted Pauly's return to be made as comfortable as possible. Men and women showed up every day to help with the work. In no time at all, they'd finished everything then decided to hold a welcome home party for him. They never told me about that part. I guess they figured I'd blab.

Barbecue's were set up in the Cook's front yard and Mr. Benson also began cooking food at the Big Chief. Grandpa showed up in Rosie. He honked the horn loud and long before pulling into our driveway. Everyone laughed and then we had a great meal and afterwards people played music in the Cook's front yard. It was dark before everyone went home. I told Pauly that I'd be over first thing in the morning, then me and Danny went to bed right away so we wouldn't have long to wait.

I rolled over and looked at Danny. He was lying on his back, staring at the ceiling. I had a rhyme saved up that I knew he'd like.

"Fatty and Skinny went to a party. Skinny let a stinker and Fatty let a farty."

Danny laughed. I knew he liked it best when one of my Fatty and Skinny rhymes included the word fart.

"You're a lot happier," he said, after he'd stopped laughing and caught his breath.

He was right. I was feeling a lot better.

"Jack," he said. "I think you should try to have another flying dream."

I shook my head. I didn't want to be disappointed again. "No, I don't want to, Danny. It doesn't work anymore."

"Well, what if I had something that might help?" He smiled, slid out of bed and left the room.

I wondered what he was up to. I kept my eye on the door and waited for him to return. A couple of minutes later he came back, holding a plain cardboard box that was taped shut. He handed it to me. I sat up and opened it. Inside was a brand-new leather gun belt with pearl handled six-shooters in the holsters.

"On our way home, we stopped at the Met and I bought them for you," he said. "Stand up. We have to do this the same way as before."

Danny helped me buckle them on. "Remember, when you start to fall asleep, keep thinking about flying and pretend you're doing it, and I'll keep talking to you about it the whole time."

The last thing I remember hearing was Danny's voice.

"Fly, Jack."

The next thing I knew I was soaring through the sky. Thousands of shooting stars were crisscrossing above and below me, their long tails twinkling behind them. I lowered my nose and shot forward in a brilliant ball of light, towards the church with the cross set high upon it's steeple.

Standing at its base, waiting for me, with her smile so wide and beautiful, was Tika.

THANK YOU!

I'd like to thank you for reading, The Kid Who Couldn't Leave The Yard. I hope you enjoyed reading it as much as I enjoyed writing it.

This is my first novel containing the characters Tika, Jack, Pauly and Grandpa. If you would like to receive an email when my follow-up novel about their continuing adventures becomes available, please email me at lee.stanlick@gmail.com or visit me on Facebook at The Kid Who Couldn't Leave The Yard.

AUTHOR'S NOTE

The idea for this book has been brewing in my mind for over a decade. I don't know why but one afternoon I wondered - what would happen if two people shared a dream about each other, at the same time? It just grew from there. Now I'm wondering - would it be possible for them to meet? What adventures might take place if they try? Perhaps that will be included in my next story about Tika, Jack, Pauly and Grandpa.

Hyperactivity also has always interested me. More specifically, the common practice in North America of medicating children. I wonder what the long-term effects might be? What will we learn about the powerful drugs they are being given today that we are currently unaware of? The information I provided in this book about phenobarbital is accurate... And why in North America have almost 15% of children been diagnosed as *hyperactive,* while in Europe that number drops to less than 2%? What's in play here? I have my suspicions and enjoy hearing other people's points of view and personal experiences.

ABOUT THE AUTHOR

Lee Stanlick was born in Wallaceburg, Ontario. He married his high school sweetheart and they recently celebrated their 38th anniversary. They have four children and now live in Airdrie, Alberta to be closer to their three granddaughters. The Kid Who Couldn't Leave The Yard, is his first novel. His second, starring Tika, Jack, Pauly and Grandpa will be available soon.

72403400R00190

Made in the USA
Columbia, SC
20 June 2017